DANGEROUS SECRETS

DANGEROUS SECRETS

Pamela Oldfield

This first world edition published in Great Britain 2003 by
SEVERN HOUSE PUBLISHERS LTD of
9–15 High Street, Sutton, Surrey SM1 1DF.
This first world edition published in the USA 2004 by
SEVERN HOUSE PUBLISHERS INC of
595 Madison Avenue, New York, N.Y. 10022.

British Library Cataloguing in Publication Data

Oldfield, Pamela.
    Dangerous secrets
    1.   Betrothal - Fiction
    2.   Deception - Fiction
    I.   Title
    823.9'14 [F]

ISBN 0-7278-6041-0

Typeset by Palimpsest Book Production Ltd.,
Polmont, Stirlingshire, Scotland.
Printed and bound in Great Britain by
MPG Books Ltd., Bodmin, Cornwall.

One

Harriet opened the front door, her thoughts concerned with the pleasant things she had just been reading in her fiancé's letter. Impatiently she held the precious pages behind her back as she stared at the caller, taking a moment or two to recognize the woman who waited on the doorstep.

'Mrs Fenner, is it?' Harriet asked.

The woman nodded. She was short and shapeless and her clothes were dated but her black straw hat boasted a bunch of tired blue ribbons. A small defiance in the face of a drab existence, Harriet thought. 'Not Daisy Pritty again?' she said with a trace of exasperation.

'I'm afraid so, Miss Burnett.'

Harriet smothered a groan. Her mother, Agnes, would not be pleased by the news. 'Come in, please.' Hoping her resentment was not too obvious, she held open the door. 'Mama is not here at present but she may be back shortly. If not, I can give her a message if you wish.'

She led the way into the parlour – a room full of heavy dark furniture and heavy draped curtains. The walls were covered with photographs and framed needlework and the mantel-piece and tabletops supported potted plants and a variety of vases, small decorated boxes and porcelain figurines. Agnes Burnett was very proud of their parlour but Harriet found the room cluttered and claustrophobic. Today, however, she hardly noticed the oppressive atmosphere because she was wondering what exactly the awful Daisy Pritty had done.

Mrs Fenner was the matron at the nearby workhouse, which had been built two decades earlier at great public expense as a last refuge for the destitute and dying, whose corpses would otherwise clutter the streets of respectable

1

Maybourne. Residents of the up-and-coming town on the Kentish coast, however, had never quite reconciled themselves to the presence of the institution and the people who inhabited it. Prosperous people despised them, working-class people pitied them and the poor resented the money that was being spent on them, but all were daily reminded of the uncomfortable fact that with an unkind twist of fate any one of them might be unfortunate enough to end their days within the same grim walls.

Harriet had learned from her mother that Daisy Pritty was one of the unfortunate inmates who should appreciate the security of a roof over her head and three meals a day. Instead, at seventeen she was already a difficult girl with a reputation for causing trouble.

Harriet tried to look concerned but she was in fact annoyed that Mrs Fenner had called while her mother and Izzie, the maid, were out shopping because that meant Harriet had been forced to open the door to her. She preferred *not* to become involved with the business of the workhouse which took up so much of her mother's time and energy.

When they were both seated, Mrs Fenner said, 'Daisy Pritty's run off again, miss, and the Master's worried.' She leaned forward confidingly. 'More than worried, if the truth be told. Very red in the face, he was, with anger. Poor Mr Crane. He looked likely to throw a fit at any moment! He found her this job with the Dickinsons at the end of Mill Lane and now she throws the job in his face and does a runner. I feel sorry for the family. They took a big risk giving the girl a chance and now look! You may know them, miss. He's a cousin of Mr Harbreeds. George Harbreeds who a few years ago was expected to be made Mayor but it came to nothing.'

'Dickinson?' Harriet shook her head and managed to slip Marcus's letter into her pocket. 'The name's not familiar.'

'It should have been a fresh start for Daisy but oh no! The wretched girl steals a gold locket and some clothes and disappears. Pawned by now, I shouldn't wonder, and the locket was a family heirloom, so I'm told.' As she spoke, she glanced with interest around the room and Harriet realized that she had never been invited into it before. 'The constable's keeping an eye out for her but she could be anywhere and the Master said to let the Board know as how he's done everything in his power to rein her in and she'll be the death of him before she's through!'

'How very tiresome! The girl is incorrigible from what I hear.' Harriet's attention wandered as she remembered the letter she had been reading before the interruption. Marcus had hinted at a surprise he was planning for her birthday. Now she regretted asking Mrs Fenner inside. She did not want to hear about Daisy Pritty or anyone else from the workhouse. Her mother, full of righteous concern, spoke of little else and Daisy seemed to be a favourite of hers.

'The poor child could be so much better,' was her mother's constant complaint. 'Born into the workhouse – what chance does she have?'

Harriet, secretly rather jealous of the girl, pretended to find the whole subject horribly boring.

She now smiled briskly. 'I'll tell my mother what has happened as soon as she returns. Please tell Mr Crane that she will be in touch.'

Rising quickly and ignoring Mrs Fenner's obvious surprise, Harriet led the way back to the front door. If the woman's stay was extended, Harriet knew she would have to offer refreshment and she wanted to avoid that.

Following her dutifully, Mrs Fenner said, 'She'll be getting into mischief, I'll be bound.'

'Daisy? No doubt she will. Probably enjoying the money from the pawn shop.'

'The Master's fearful of *real* mischief, if you know what I mean, miss.' She gave Harriet a sly glance. 'Come back to us in the family way most like and land us with another workhouse brat to feed!'

'Do you think so?' Harriet was genuinely surprised. 'Mama gave me the impression that she she was quite young.'

'She's old enough, miss.' Mrs Fenner tapped the side of her nose. 'Girls like Daisy grow up very fast, if you take my meaning. "Precocious" is the word I'd use for that young madam! She may be a great trial to us but to the young blades in the town she'll be just another bonny young woman – a plum ripe for the picking, if you get my drift.'

Harriet, opening the door, chose not to answer this gloomy prophesy but deep down she wondered rather enviously what it was like to be a ripe plum among young blades. It sounded rather exciting in a dangerous way. Harriet had known for years that *she* would become Mrs Marcus Wellbury in due course. Her parents had chosen him as eminently suitable and she *did* like him a great deal (although he was older than she was) and Harriet knew that he adored her. But for the first time she suddenly regretted the loss of her freedom to choose for herself. Sighing, she reflected that she would certainly never have the chance to get into *any* kind of mischief, even if she wanted to. Not that she did, she reminded herself hurriedly.

As Mrs Fenner hesitated on the step, Harriet asked, 'Is she bonny then, this Daisy?'

'She would be if she took a bit of pride in herself but the workhouse uniform does her no favours, of course, and the horrible shoes don't help her none. But her hair's not bad if she'd keep it nice. Very fair with a bit of a wave in it but she scrapes it back and ties it with an old bootlace. That's when she's with us, of course. Out on the town I daresay she smartens herself up.' Sighing, she shook her head. 'I hate to agree with the Master but this time he's right. She's an ungrateful creature. No two ways about it!'

A moment later Mrs Fenner was on her way back to the workhouse and Harriet closed the door thoughtfully behind her.

'Why do you bother, Mama?' she muttered. 'They don't appreciate you.'

Jasper, the cat, ensconced on the third stair, yawned and stretched, then padded down to Harriet, who picked him up and petted him.

'You appreciate me, don't you my sweet.' She regarded herself in the small mirror which was part of the dark oak hallstand. Twenty-year-old Harriet had auburn curls and grey eyes in a sweet round face. But did she fall into the ripe plum category? And what exactly was a 'young blade' compared with any other young man? How would Daisy tell them apart? Her mother had kept her sadly ignorant, Harriet concluded and with Jasper in her arms and a vexed expression on her face she made her way into the large kitchen at the rear of the house. It was Tuesday but yesterday's washing still blew on the line in the yard outside the backdoor because May had been a rainy month but today the sun shone and a light wind was blowing. Cook, large and flustered, was at the sink peeling potatoes and she frowned when Harriet entered. 'Get that animal out of my kitchen, Miss Harriet. You know I can't abide cat hairs. They get everywhere.'

Harriet crossed to the open door, pushed Jasper out into the yard and asked, 'What's for supper?'

'A meat pasty, as well you know.'

Of course she knew. Cook was excellent with pastry and could also make a suet pudding that melted in the mouth but she was not very imaginative. Sunday was always roasted meat, Monday was a cottage pie and Tuesday was a pasty that used up the last of Sunday's roast. After Tuesday the menu varied but Friday was always fish, and usually pickled herrings or mackerel. Harriet complained occasionally, but her mother was not interested in food and found the unrelenting menu perfectly acceptable.

Feeling perverse, Harriet said, 'We never have coq au vin.'

Cook tossed her head. 'Coq au vin? I should think not indeed! I couldn't be doing with that French rubbish.' She cut up the potatoes, put them in a pan and covered them with water. 'Who was that at the door?'

'Mrs Fenner from the workhouse. More trouble.'

'Your poor mama! She's a saint, that woman!'

Harriet rolled her eyes. If only her father spent more time at home, her mother would be forced to share her time with her husband and daughter, but he was a sea captain on a small merchant ship that berthed regularly in Maybourne harbour and he was at sea for most of the year. Agnes Burnett was easily bored and had been co-opted on to the Board of Guardians of Maybourne Workhouse many years ago. Harriet couldn't remember a time when she could rely

5

on her mother's company. Sam, her much younger brother, was away at boarding school in Winchester and wouldn't be back until the term ended in July. She often complained of being lonely but her mother had no sympathy for her. 'You don't know how fortunate you are to have a comfortable home and a loving family,' was her usual tart response. 'Spare a thought for the unfortunates in the workhouse, Harriet. They need me more than you do.'

Cook smiled as she reached into the basket for the vegetables. 'We'll soon be getting the early peas. I do look forward to that. There's something about shucking peas. Very restful, somehow. Soothing, if you like. Specially on a summer's day when I can sit out in the yard.'

Harriet helped herself to a few currants from the jar on the table and drifted towards the back door. What was Daisy Pritty doing, she wondered, frowning. Had she found anyone to keep her company? A young blade? She imagined a lithe and handsome young man with bold blue eyes, a quick wit and winning ways and was aware of a growing disquiet. Her own husband-to-be was what her father called 'a steady, reliable man with proper ideas and a comfortable income'. In a way she envied Daisy Pritty, who could snatch at the passing moment however unwisely. So . . . was the ripe plum being picked? She felt herself blush. Fine for Cook to talk. She was approaching fifty and had once had a husband and three children. She knew what it was all about. Harriet did not.

Idly eating the currants, she wandered out into the back yard and watched Jasper stalking a sparrow, but when he finally pounced and caught it Harriet gave a scream of distress and fled back into the house and up the stairs to her bedroom where she reread her letter from Marcus. And found it wanting.

Less than two miles away, Albert Hawke was polishing the lid of a coffin in his workshop in an alley off Weapes Lane. A tall thin man, he had a long thin nose to match and sad brown eyes set a little too close together. Hardly handsome, yet he had a cheerful disposition and his smile went a long

6

way to compensate for his unlovely features and his soft voice had soothed hundreds of the bereaved who all recalled him with affection. Albert wore a large apron made from an old sack to protect his moleskin trousers and thick cotton shirt, the sleeves of which were rolled up above the elbow. The outfit was grimy with years of accumulated wood dust and hundreds of odd smears of polish and splashes of wood stain. His boots were caked with yesterday's mud and he presented a sad spectacle but he had never had a wife to point out his deficiencies, so didn't miss the feminine touch which might have been beneficial to him.

Albert was happy in his own way. He worked when he liked, ate when he liked and considered no one else in the whole world. Except Snapper, his mongrel dog, who kept down the rats and who had been known on rare occasions to wag his stumpy tail.

'That's coming up a treat!' Albert muttered, straightening up to admire his handiwork.

The dog, sprawled on the floor beneath the trestle on which the coffin rested, flicked an ear in response and settled his head more securely on his front paws.

'The poor old dear will go out in style!'

Not that Mrs Touche was poor in the monetary sense, Albert reflected. They had money and the funeral would be as lavish as the family would wish. A splendid death and an impressive funeral was the desire of all Queen Victoria's more wealthy subjects. Money was no object when a loved one was being laid to rest and Albert had found it easy to persuade the old lady's son that nothing but oak or mahogany would do for the coffin. This had been made to measure and designed with the fashionable sloping shoulders and the edges were decorated with a design in brasswork with handles to match. The Touche family were wealthy and this coffin would not go into the earth but be placed in their private vault alongside seven of the earlier Touches. That pleased Albert. He was also pleased that he had recently laid out a number of guineas to buy a simple funeral carriage in which to convey the coffin to the church. Second hand, certainly, but it was a fine-looking vehicle now that he had repainted it in gloss black paint and had had new glass put into the windows. And he knew where he could find two black horses to pull it along.

At that moment a tall, bluff-looking man appeared in the doorway. He carried a slim stick and he touched it to the brim of his hat in a confident flourish as he boomed a greeting. Snapper growled softly and Albert turned from his work. It was Mr Touche.

Albert smiled and laid down his cloth. 'Good day to you too, sir. I do like a bit of sunshine.'

Mr Touche nodded. 'How's it going then, Mr Hawke? My wife is anxious that it might not be ready in time.'

Albert smiled at his esteemed customer. 'Now, have I ever let the family down?' he asked reproachfully, stepping back to allow a better view of the coffin.

'Indeed you have not, Mr Hawke. My father went to his rest in a blaze of glory, thanks to you. A blaze of glory! That's how my wife described it and it gladdened my mother's heart.'

'And now it's your poor mother's turn to meet her maker, God rest her soul. You won't be disappointed. I've some new fancy handles come straight from London that will gladden your heart, sir. But as to the oak, you must take a look for yourself.'

'Ah! That's very fine, Mr Hawke. Very fine indeed.'

'Run your hand over it, sir, do.'

'May I?' He did so, nodding with approval. 'And the lining? White silk, wasn't it?'

'It was indeed and that will go in later today, crimped into pleats and held with brass tacks. It will be ready, sir, and you will find no fault with it. Rest assured on that count.'

Five minutes later, when he was once more alone, Albert sat down on a stack of planks from where he could watch his yard through the open door, and took out a clay pipe. He filled it with small, unhurried movements and was soon smoking contentedly as he stared in the direction of his new funeral carriage, which was discreetly hidden under a layer of blankets and waterproof cloth. He had heard it was for sale, second hand, from Needham's Discreet Funerals (a much larger firm), and had successfully negotiated a reasonable price for it in close competition with a rival firm of undertakers. Having less money than the other firm, Albert had cunningly offered a deal promising to hire candlesticks, black plumes and gold-trimmed black drapes only from Needham's in the future.

Puffing at his pipe, he was at peace with the world when a sudden sound startled him. From his vantage point in the workshop doorway he saw a slim figure climb from his new vehicle and he gave a shout of surprise and anger.

'Oi! You! What d'you think you're doing there, eh?' He rushed out, followed by Snapper, who was barking furiously. Flinging the pipe aside, Albert grabbed the now fleeing figure while Snapper paused long enough to investigate the broken pipe and the scattered shreds of burning tobacco. Scorching his nose, he gave a sharp cry, jumped back and then rushed forward to take out his anger on one of the alien ankles.

'Ouch! Damn you, dog!'

Albert blinked. A young slip of a girl in the uniform of the workhouse was wriggling fiercely in his hands and doing her best to punch him in the face. Fair hair straggled from beneath a cheap straw hat and their was a wild look in her deep blue eyes. She kicked out at the dog. 'That animal's dangerous . . .*Ouch!*' she screeched. 'It's got my ankle! Call it off me, you miserable old sod!'

Albert said, 'Leave it, Snapper! *Leave it!*' and the dog obeyed, springing back immediately but with a mean look in his eye that spoke longingly of a second chance at the intruder.

Albert shook her. 'What's your game, then, eh? What you doing in my new carriage? You could have damaged those windows.' Still grasping her by the wrist, he moved so that he could glance into the carriage and reassure himself that all was well.

'Damn your windows! What about my ankle? It hurts like hell!'

'They're special glass, those windows. Engraved with a pattern of ivy leaves and—'

'I never *touched* your bloomin' windows.' She glared at

9

him. 'Just sleeping, that's all. What time is it?' She squinted up at the sun. 'It never is!'

'Nigh on midday,' he agreed. 'Workhouse, are you?'

'None of your business!'

'Got a name, have you?'

'Daisy Pritty but what's it to you?'

She twisted to examine her injured ankle. There was a hole in the thick brown stocking and blood trickled feebly from a small wound. 'Look what your dog's done. Mangy cur!'

'Whose fault's that then? Snapper's a watchdog. You shouldn't have been trespassing.'

She turned to stare at the carriage. 'Oh Gawd! It's not a blooming funeral cart is it? I slept in that? Ugh!'

Her shudder was exaggerated and Albert bridled. 'Cart? *Cart?* That's a funeral carriage, I'll have you know. There's nothing wrong with that vehicle. Good as new, that is.'

'I could've had nightmares in the bloody thing.'

'No one asked you to sleep in it – and mind your language.'

'Couldn't see in the dark, could I? Could have been a baker's cart for all I knowed.' She stared round and caught sight of a couple of cheap coffins which were propped against the wall. Nearby was a broken tombstone. She crossed herself hurriedly and then, with a final twist, she was free of his restraining hand and quick as a flash was running toward the high wooden gates that opened out on to the street beyond. Albert ran after her but purely from curiosity because he knew the gates were locked. Seeing a second chance, the dog made another dash for the intriguing ankles but the girl was too quick. She leaped upwards and somehow scrambled up and over the gate. There was a thump as she fell on the other side and Albert heard a cry of pain followed by more curses. Snapper went mad, leaping and howling to be allowed out after her but they heard her retreating footsteps as she limped away and then all was quiet again.

'Well, that was fun!' Albert felt strangely bereft. It was a long time since he'd chatted with a young woman. He patted the dog, who was panting with a mixture of exertion and frustration. 'You shouldn't have bitten her, Snapper. Poor kid. Not much of a life in that place. God save me from the workhouse!'

Ignoring his shattered pipe, he resumed his seat on the planks and thought about the encounter. He had rather enjoyed the excitement and even a bleeding ankle glimpsed through a torn stocking was better than nothing. He could still see the ugly shoes scrabbling their way up the gates.

'A real wild thing!' he muttered with grudging admiration for her courage.

Under her plain bonnet he'd seen a few tangled curls the colour of butter which reminded him of his two sisters who had died in infancy. Everyone had admired their bright curls while his own hair was disappointing – a mousy peppery colour that did him no favours. Not that you could tell nowadays for the amount of wood dust that was in his hair for most of the week. But never for the funerals. He smiled. Sometimes Albert earned a bit extra by acting as one of the mutes in a black suit and top hat. Albert had a naturally mournful expression with a turned-down mouth and large sad eyes. The loved ones of the dearly departed really appreciated that. When called upon, he washed himself carefully all over in the tin bath in the privacy of his outhouse and when he walked alongside the coffin, his hair, which was still thick and springy, shone from below the black hat.

Dismay set in as he recalled the girl's disconcerting bursts of conversation. 'A sod I may be, but *old* – at twenty-six?' He shook his head. 'Not only wild but saucy with it!'

On Thursday Harriet set out to walk the three miles to Havely House with a little more enthusiasm than usual. Her father's uncle, Robert Burnett, was now eighty-seven and was top of her mother's list of people who should be visited. Not for his money, because he obviously had none. Nor for his charm because that was also lacking – but as 'a family courtesy'.

'He's *family*,' she had told Harriet. 'Kith and kin. Blood thicker than water. Understand?'

Harriet had complained, bitterly demanding that Sam should go instead of her.

'Your great-uncle asks for *you*,' Agnes insisted. 'Sam is

11

hardly ever home whereas you *are* and you have all the time in the world. Don't be so selfish, Harriet. Think of others less fortunate than yourself. Uncle Robert is a lonely man and you should look on it as a duty to visit him.'

'But he's so strange – even his housekeeper says he is. And I never know what to say to him. If he's lonely he should have married. Why didn't he?'

Her mother shrugged. 'No doubt he has his reasons. It's not for us to pry. Everyone has secrets.'

'I don't have any!'

'You're not old enough, that's why!' She glared at Harriet. 'God willing you will one day be eighty-seven and *you* will want to be visited.'

Harriet felt she had lost that particular argument.

Now, two days after Mrs Fenner's visit, Daisy Pritty had still not been found and Harriet was tired of hearing about her. In a way she was glad to be out of the house, away from her mother's constant worrying. She was also happy to be seen by passers-by, for she was wearing a new navy-blue jacket (nipped in round her tiny waist) over a blue and white striped skirt and knew that she would provoke a few whistles of approval from the men – which she would pretend to ignore. Perhaps, in her finery, she would remind them of ripe plums! The women, too, would admire her and heads would turn. One way and another Harriet felt somehow compensated for the time she would have to spend with Great-Uncle Robert.

Arriving at Havely House, she was as usual depressed by its gloomy exterior. The house had been in the family for more than a hundred years and was a large timber-framed building with white weatherboarding which had been seriously neglected and was crusted with an unsightly green mould. It had seven bedrooms, four of which were never used. As a child visiting with her mother, Harriet had found it a wonderful place to explore and had raced to and fro along the echoing passages but as she grew older and visited on her own, she found it less enjoyable. The housekeeper, Doris Lester, slept in one of the smaller rooms and when her son was in England, he slept in another. Robert Burnett occupied the large master bedroom in the main part of the house.

12

Outside, a vast lawn was deeply shadowed by huge oaks and chestnut trees and bordered by thickly clustered rhododendrons. In contrast to the house the garden was kept in immaculate condition by a gardener and the tennis court at the side of the house was maintained by a firm from Faversham although to Harriet's knowledge, no one ever played on it.

When she arrived, Doris Lester opened the door to her with a shriek of delight and a deep curtsey. As a girl of twelve, Doris had once had occasion to curtsey as Queen Victoria and Prince Albert had passed by their cottage in their carriage and Doris, having studied the curtsey, now seized any excuse to use it.

'Miss Harriet! Come in, come in! Your great-uncle will be so pleased to see you. He's shut himself away in the library to write one of his articles on the philosophy of life – whatever that is! He's a great one for writing. Yesterday it was a letter to Queen Victoria, though I don't know if she'll ever get to read it. All I know is I have to post the blessed things!' She laughed breathlessly, one hand on her heart. 'I'll tell him you're here and he'll come down eventually and in the meantime you must have a cup of tea and a biscuit. Is your family well? Your dear mother? I well remember how she walked through all that snow last winter to bring me some calf's-foot jelly because of my indisposition.' She took another quick breath. 'Old Mr Burnett was only talking about you all the other day. He'd come to visit you but you know the way he is, poor tortured soul.'

Harriet nodded. Over the past nine or ten years the old man had developed a deep fear of open spaces and hadn't set foot outside the house. Not that he would go far if he had *no* fear because he was now very frail – a tall, gaunt figure with a gruff voice that Harriet had hated as a young child.

Harriet said, 'It's very sad.'

'Sad? Perhaps . . . but he's happy in his own way. We're all God's creatures, Harriet, even your great-uncle Robert. He simply suffers a disabling malady and has learned to deal with it. One day, no doubt, the doctors will find a name for it and maybe a cure.'

'How near is it, do you think? The cure, I mean.'

'Lord knows! I don't know what he'd do without me though I do wish I could leave him and go back to my poor mother in Dorset. Her sight's so bad I'm afraid she won't be able to look after herself much longer.'

'But will he take to anyone else?'

Doris Lester shrugged. 'The way I look at it, he's got family. Your father would have to make some kind of arrangement. Find another housekeeper. I mean if I pop off he'd have to, wouldn't he, and if push comes to shove I can't abandon my own mother in favour of a stranger.'

Minutes later, Harriet sat alone in a large but sparsely furnished reception room nibbling an almond biscuit and sipping tea. The large house was too much for Mrs Lester to manage but the old man refused to have any other help. Robert had a deep mistrust of strangers coupled with a reluctance to have any of the outside doors opened more than was necessary. A visit from the doctor was always very traumatic for him and without Mrs Lester, whom he trusted, Harriet suspected his life would be impossible.

The door opened and Harriet glanced up, expecting to see Mrs Lester but instead a young man stood smiling in the doorway.

'I'm Godfrey, Mrs Lester's son,' he said. 'Please don't get up. Mother has sent me in to keep you company while she tries to persuade the old man to see you. May I join you?'

'Most certainly. Please sit down.'

Harriet was agreeably surprised. Doris Lester had spoken often about her son who was travelling in Europe in preparation for his future employment as a translator. Godfrey Lester, she knew, was a graduate in languages and had studied at Oxford University with the financial help of a distant relative who was without a family. Harriet had always found this true-life story terribly romantic and now – here was Godfrey in person.

'Your mother has spoken often to me about you,' she told him a trifle nervously. In fact she was impressed by him. He was sturdily built with smooth auburn hair, grey eyes and pleasant features that were almost handsome. A smile lit up his face as he crossed the room to sit opposite her.

14

He said, 'Mr Burnett has spoken about you many times. He really looks forward to your visits although I imagine for you it is more in the way of an ordeal.'

Startled, Harriet stammered, 'In a way yes but . . .' and not wishing to tell a lie, trailed into an awkward silence.

'He is a difficult man in many ways but Mother is convinced that he has a heart of gold hidden below that gruff exterior. She should know if anybody does.'

Harriet was trying not to stare at him. He had returned to England with traces of foreign fashion evident in his clothes. A fancy waistcoat was worn over a white lawn shirt and there was something about his highly polished shoes that struck her as Italian. Harriet felt ridiculously pleased that she had worn her new outfit and could see from his expression that he found her attractive. She wondered how old he was.

She said, 'Does my great-uncle know you are here? He is usually very wary of strangers.'

He shrugged. 'Mother has told him I was coming home but he merely grunted.' He laughed. 'There was some talk of me translating some papers for him before I return to London. It seems he, too, travelled extensively when he was a young man. Some kind of explorer, I believe, searching for mineral deposits in far-flung corners. A rather lonely existence, I understand.'

'Mama says he is lonely. Perhaps he doesn't care for the company of others.' She took a quick breath and said casually, 'Will you stay on for a while?' She uttered a silent prayer that the answer would be in the affirmative.

'I should be happy to spend a few weeks here if he is serious. I'd also love to play some tennis but I have no one to play with. Mother thought that you might –'

'Oh yes! I would – except that I don't know how.' Harriet found it impossible to look away from him. Was this how Daisy felt about the young blades of her acquaintance? The slightly dizzy feeling was new to Harriet.

Godfrey laughed. 'Then I'll teach you if you'll allow it. But what about you? Have you travelled much? With your mother perhaps?'

Reluctantly Harriet shook her head. 'Mama has a fear of

the sea, which I think is a result of Papa's job. I remember as a child that there was always tension in the house when Papa's ship was late into harbour. I heard her tell a friend that one member of the family was quite enough to venture on to deep waters! She is also very busy with her charity work. She's on the Board of Guardians to Maybourne Workhouse, about which she is quite passionate. The poor are a great source of concern for her.'

'And for you, I suspect?'

Harriet struggled with her conscience. 'I'm afraid I do not share her interest. Isn't that a dreadful thing to say?'

He smiled. 'I don't think so. You are still very young. Sadly, as I travelled round Europe I realized that the poor are everywhere. It's a problem that has no boundaries and will probably never be solved. In Italy there are children begging on every corner. In France the streets of Paris are rife with young criminals.' He shrugged. 'But I had my wallet stolen by a pickpocket in Jermyn Street in London and the constable showed little interest in catching the young thief.'

Harriet shrugged. 'Mama says there are the unfortunates and the undeserving but both end up in the workhouse.' Harriet regarded him earnestly, wishing she had paid more attention to her mother's accounts of the various inmates. 'She has little sympathy for those who are idle or shirk work but much for the others who are sick or have been thrown out of their homes without just cause . . . There is one young woman who is nothing but trouble. Utterly ungrateful and to my mind undeserving. She lies, steals . . . And yet Mama is sure she can be saved from herself!'

'Your mother is an optimist!'

Harriet was aware of a sudden longing to confide in him. 'She spends more time worrying about the inmates than she does about me!'

Her words hung in the air and she immediately felt ashamed.

Godfrey said, 'Perhaps she feels that you have very few problems compared with those luckless creatures.' After a moment he added gently, 'I'm sure it is not through any lack of love, Miss Harriet.'

Harriet swallowed. She wanted to answer but no words came and at that moment the door opened and Mrs Lester beckoned to Harriet. 'I've told Mr Burnett you're here but he won't leave the library. We'll have to go up.' To her son she said, 'You'd best set about unpacking since you may be here for a few weeks. The same room – the second bedroom on the left at the top of the stairs.'

Outside the library door they stopped and Mrs Lester knocked loudly. 'Mr Burnett! I have Miss Harriet with me.' She tried the handle but the door was locked.

'Who is it?' the voice quavered anxiously.

'It's Miss Harriet. Your great-niece. She's come to see you. You wrote to ask for her.'

'Miss Harriet? Did I?'

The housekeeper turned apologetically to Harriet. 'He's very forgetful about the present but ask him about his past life or when he was a boy and he remembers as though it was yesterday. She rattled the door handle. 'Open the door, Mr Burnett. Please.'

Behind them, Godfrey was climbing the stairs with his luggage – a small bamboo trunk and a bulging carpetbag. He caught Harriet's eye and winked and she smiled back, her heart thumping erratically. She was annoyed that he was having this effect on her for she could see that he appeared entirely unruffled by *her* appearance in *his* life. He travelled light, she thought and envied him his freedom to explore the world. For a moment she allowed herself a flight of imagination and saw the two of them tramping across desert sands, the sun beating down, a camel or two in the hazy distance . . . or wandering through Paris beside the Seine hand in hand . . . Abruptly she frowned. *Hand in hand?* Whatever had happened to her beloved Marcus? Her guilt was interrupted as the door to the library opened suddenly, but only about six inches. 'Who's there?'

'It's me. Harriet.'

'Ah, so it is!' He opened the door just wide enough for her to enter, then locked it again.

From outside the door, Mrs Lester said loudly, 'Stamp on the floor if he won't let you out again. He means no harm.'

Great-Uncle Robert shuffled back to his wing-backed chair and sat down. Harriet pulled up a chair. She had never been in the library before and was somewhat overwhelmed by the sombre tone of the room with its dark leather furniture and dark velvet curtains which half covered the windows. Fascinated, she glanced around. The library was in an incredible muddle. There were piles of magazines stacked on the floor around the desk, boxes overflowing with papers and dozens of books that tumbled across every available surface.

Harriet tried to think of something to say but the polite phrases she had planned on the walk over to Havely House had vanished from her mind and all she could think of was Godfrey Lester.

'You'd better start,' her great-uncle said at last. 'I'm no good with conversation these days. I've nothing to say, you see. Never see anyone . . . but I write letters. Lots and lots of letters. I have friends, you see. Friends and acquaintances. But they can't come here so we correspond.' He sat back as though exhausted. 'Ask me something and I'll answer you. That's the way to do it, I think.'

The only question Harriet could think of was, 'How can you live like this?' but instead she searched for something to say that would lighten the mood. 'Your garden is looking very neat.'

'That'll be the gardener. He's comes and goes. Odd chap. Can never recall his name. Begins with M . . . or is it N?'

Harriet could smell mildew and candlegrease and something else that might be soot that had fallen into the grate. There were no flowers to brighten the gloom.

He frowned. 'Cummings! That's his name. Yes, he potters about out there but nary a word!'

Harriet's thoughts wandered and she wondered if Godfrey Lester had ever had a woman in his life. Surely he had not wandered around Europe without meeting any attractive women. The thought jolted her composure and she forced herself to concentrate on her conversation. 'It will be a picture when the rest of the rhododendrons are in bloom.'

'The what?'

'Rhododendrons. The shrubs.' Perhaps she could find a

way to ask Mrs Lester. Not directly, of course. It would never do to let her suspect that she was interested.

'I never go into the garden,' Robert confided. 'You can never tell . . .'

'Yes.' She smiled. 'I mean, no you can't . . . Mama sends her kind regards for your health.'

'Does she?'

'Yes.'

Thus prompted, Robert asked after Harriet's health and that of her mother and even enquired after Sam's welfare. Harriet relaxed slightly and decided not to stay long. Her mother would never know.

'Sam is fine. I'm looking forward to his school holidays,' she confessed. 'He is such fun.'

He leaned forward and lowered his voice. 'Who was that young man I spotted earlier on the stairs? Did you see him?'

Harriet explained and his face cleared.

'Ah! That's him, is it. Mrs Lester's boy . . . You can't be too careful you see. Can't let just anyone roam about. It's a big house.'

He lapsed into a long silence and Harriet took advantage of it. She imagined herself and Godfrey playing tennis together. Did he know that she was already betrothed? Well, not exactly betrothed *yet* but there *was* a firm understanding between them. And she must do nothing to endanger her future.

At that moment the clock struck twelve and, seizing her chance, she jumped to her feet. 'Oh dear! Is that the time? I shall have to be going, I'm afraid. Mama will worry about me if I don't get back.' She stood up, glancing nervously towards the locked door.

He nodded. 'I'll be writing to you in due course.'

'I shall look forward to your letter.' She smiled. 'Shall I let myself out? There's no need for you to disturb yourself.'

Staring up at her, he made no answer. Taking silence for an affirmative, Harriet leaned forward and touched his hand, then hurried towards the door. She unlocked it and stepped outside and within seconds she heard the lock being turned again. For a moment she remained outside the door, guiltily

19

aware that she had not given him enough time or attention but she consoled herself with the thought that perhaps he found the visits tiring. Maybe to him, too, they were a necessary chore. Finally exonerating herself from blame, she hurried downstairs but to her intense disappointment there was no sign of Godfrey. Making her way to the kitchen, Harriet said goodbye to the housekeeper, who walked with her to the front door.

'Thank you for coming to see your great-uncle, Miss Harriet. He doesn't say much but he'll probably remember that you came. He's a poor old thing but we all do what we can. Shall I tell him you'll call again?'

'Oh yes!' said Harriet with a new enthusiasm that had much to do with Godfrey. 'I . . . I was so pleased to meet your son. Will he be staying here at Havely House?'

'For the time being. Mr Burnett has agreed he should have one of the bedrooms and his keep in return for some clerical work.'

'He's a very . . . That is, you must be very proud of him. Does he . . . Is he . . . Is there a special woman in his life?' She felt her cheeks burn with embarrassment but there was no way she could leave Havely House without knowing.

'I don't think so. Not at the moment. There was one a year or so back. An Italian woman. Amelia. I think that was her name. He wrote about her in glowing terms but then it came to nothing. I don't know what happened.' She leaned forward and lowered her voice. 'I suspected at the time that she was already married! Not that I've dared to ask and he didn't tell me anything. Young men! They have to sow their wild oats. You wait till that brother of yours is a few years older. He's going to turn a few heads, bless him!' Laughing, she shook her head fondly.

'Sam?' Harriet thought about it and realized that her brother *was* good-looking.

Mrs Lester laughed. 'Godfrey fell in love for the first time when he was seven! Brought her home from school and said he was going to marry her. Ginger hair, she had. I remember that. And her poor mother waiting at the school gates and wondering where she was. I had to rush back to the school with her. Lucy, that was her name. Oh yes! Proper devil for the girls, was Godfrey! Takes after his father, God rest his soul!'

So there was nobody in Godfrey's life. Harriet's smile was heartfelt.

She made her farewells and walked home in a haze of excitement. Perhaps Daisy Pritty wasn't going to have all the fun!

The following day, the last Friday in May, was a day Harriet would never forget. Or so she told herself when it was over. It was the first time she had allowed herself to be persuaded by her mother to attend one of the weekly meetings at Maybourne Workhouse and her acceptance had been prompted purely by her recent conversation with Godfrey Lester. Harriet had felt, on later reflection, that he had expected more compassion from her and might have been disappointed in her lack of interest, so she had decided to find out for herself the conditions in the workhouse. When Godfrey next spoke with her she would be able to impress him with her knowledge and understanding.

Agnes, hiding her surprise at this unexpected change of heart, said, 'Certainly you may come with me, Harriet, but do wear something less fine. A plain skirt and jacket, perhaps. We don't want to draw attention to the contrast between the inmates' drab clothes and what they might see as our finery. And hurry. It starts at ten o'clock and I make a point of always arriving fifteen minutes early. I like to think it keeps the staff on their toes and inspires the other Board members to be punctual.'

Promptly at quarter to ten, Harriet and Agnes arrived at the door of the workhouse and Harriet experienced a brief moment of inexplicable panic as the large red-brick building loomed up before her. Why had they chosen such a grim design, Harriet wondered, not for the first time. It reminded her of a prison. Grim and faceless. If the look of it was meant to act as a deterrent, then it served its purpose. No one in their right mind would want to set foot inside such a forbidding place.

Agnes took one look at her daughter's face and grasped her arm. 'Too late, Harriet,' she murmured, reaching for the bell pull with her free hand. 'We are going in. High time you learned about life on the other side of the fence. It's not all roses round the door!'

Harriet closed her eyes as the jangling of the bell echoed inside the building and footsteps sounded on the other side of the door. An old woman admitted them. She was small and bent and smelled of camphor. After an involuntary shudder, the smell of the place was the first thing that Harriet noticed. It reminded her of the local hospital – a strong smell of carbolic and stale food – but there was something else. Something undefinable which she would later identify as an atmosphere of hopelessness.

Mrs Fenner appeared from a small office. She smiled at Agnes and gave Harriet a surprised look. 'Welcome to Maybourne Workhouse,' she said, her smile faintly mocking. To Agnes she said, 'That wretched Daisy is still missing. Do go through.' She opened a door and Agnes preceded her into the room where the meetings were held.

Hanging back, Harriet glanced at the high ceiling of the passage, the stone-flagged floor, the dark-green painted walls. There were no pictures, no furniture, no carpets, no flowers. Nothing, in fact, to lighten the initial forbidding impression. From somewhere to Harriet's right, steep stone stairs led to the first floor and from here she could hear strident voices followed by a slap. Ahead of her, at the end of the passage, an old man in a pair of crumpled trousers slopped water over the floor from a leather bucket and swished it to and fro with a mop. He gave no sign that he registered Harriet's presence.

'Harriet!'

With a sense of relief, Harriet rejoined her mother and was welcomed by the other Board members. James Wellbury she already knew as Marcus's father and they exchanged the usual courtesies. A large man, James Wellbury had money and was well known to the residents of Maybourne as a man with a finger in many pies, many of them charitable. On his left Miss Boothby was an imposing figure with steel-grey hair and a permanently stern expression but Agnes spoke well of her, so Harriet reserved judgement. Miss Boothby gave Agnes a polite if distant nod and smiled briefly at Harriet. They all sat down at the table except Harriet, who, not being a member, sat against the wall a few yards away from them.

Without preliminaries, the meeting began. Mrs Fenner explained that two members were absent. Mr Touche had a death in the family and a Thomas Phillerby had taken to his sickbed troubled with gout and might be absent for some weeks according to his doctor.

Harriet glanced curiously about her. This room was well furnished with solid wooden cupboards, a large jute mat, and two framed pictures – one of grazing sheep and one of a mossy lock gate surrounded by banks of willowherb.

The Workhouse Master, Herbert Crane, then arrived. Harriet now had a chance to consider the man whose name was familiar to her from her mother's work over the years and a number of indiscreet comments she had made during moments of extreme exasperation. Harriet recalled that he had been appointed seven years ago and that her mother had mixed feelings about him. He could be harsh, she had confided, but it was difficult to criticize him because the previous master had been too lenient, so that the workhouse regulations were regularly flouted and financial records were chaotic. Herbert Crane had previously worked in accountancy and had resolved all the muddles but he had little patience with his staff. Nor, Agnes had alleged, did he have any patience with or sympathy for the inmates *and* he had clashed with the Board of Guardians on several occasions. Herbert Crane was a florid-faced man, stout with a bored expression and a weary way of moving as though his weight was too much for his legs. Harriet decided that on balance she didn't like him either.

There were one or two matters on the agenda, the first concerning the casual ward and the second being the quality of the mutton that was being delivered by the new butcher. Harriet listened with interest as it was decided that Mrs Fenner should not be expected to administer the casual ward on her own as it was not unusual for unruly incidents to occur among the men. Harriet wondered exactly what these incidents amounted to and decided to ask her mother after the meeting. The butcher was to be given a warning that the workhouse money was as good as anybody else's and Mrs Fenner should warn him that poor-quality meat was not good enough. After these issues had been dealt with, Herbert Crane turned to Mrs Fenner. 'Any new applicants?'

'Two, Mr Crane.' She handed him two papers that Harriet assumed were forms of application. 'One for indoor relief – Jake Tummer – and one—'

'Jake Tummer? Again?' Mr Wellbury snorted indignantly. 'I don't know how he dare show his face here after the trouble he caused last time we had him in.'

Agnes leaned forward. 'Is that the man who broke the window?'

Mrs Fenner nodded. 'Said he was sick. Got the doctor in under false pretences. Picked a quarrel with him and threw a chair through the dining hall window! Proper firebrand he is!'

James Wellbury said, 'Then I for one think we should refuse permission even to *apply* for relief!'

'Can we do that?' Agnes looked worried. She tapped her pencil on the table unhappily. 'He's a poor misbegotten creature. Only one eye. How can he hold down a job of work?'

Crane turned to her. 'He can do labouring. You don't need two eyes to sweep the streets or trim the hedgerows. But he never turns up for work. Claims sickness or a pain in his head. Tummer's just bone idle. Doesn't deserve any help. Request turned down. We don't want his sort here.'

Mrs Fenner said, 'He'd be taking a bed that some poor soul might *properly* deserve.'

Miss Boothby said, 'I reluctantly agree with Mr Wellbury.'

Heads nodded in agreement. Harriet looked curiously at Miss Boothby. Harriet knew that she was a wealthy spinster. It was Miss Boothby who had paid the entire cost of the installation of a drinking fountain in a corner of the workhouse yard. Agnes had been overwhelmed by her generosity and wouldn't hear a word against her.

'Who else?' asked Crane, picking at his fingernails.

24

Mrs Fenner consulted her notebook. 'Mrs Bly, mother and child. Husband was a carpenter but has recently died. She's been thrown out of her lodgings.'

'Family?'

Mrs Fenner read from her notes. 'Only a father in London. The dead husband comes from these parts. Margate to be precise. She was most insistent that she didn't want indoor relief. Insisted she wasn't destitute and would take in washing if she could lay her hands on a mangle and had a roof over her head and a bit of a yard in which to put the washing to blow.' She glanced round the table. 'She said she'd rather die than come into the house.'

Crane snorted. 'Plenty of people think like that and they end up in the gutter, dead as mutton! All down to stupid pride!'

James Wellbury shook his head. 'Self-respect, Mr Crane, not pride. There's a big difference. I know what I'd choose in her position.'

Crane's eyes narrowed as he doodled on the page in front of him but Harriet was too far away to see what he was drawing.

Crane said, 'We could find her rent for a week or two but not the mangle. That's it then. She has to come in.'

'No! We must help her!' Agnes's voice shook. 'She should have outdoor relief. If she can find a ground-floor room we could find her a mangle.'

Harriet looked at her in surprise.

Crane frowned. 'Much simpler to bring her in.'

Mrs Fenner looked at him nervously and Harriet could see that she was torn. She was an employee and didn't want to oppose Herbert Crane but her sympathies were probably with the applicant.

Agnes, whitefaced, said, 'We mustn't do this to her because we all know what will happen. With no way to earn a living she'll stay a dependent for the rest of her life.'

Mrs Fenner looked from one to the other. 'But they'll have a roof over their head and regular meals.'

Agnes said, 'But her child will be a workhouse child and . . .' Her expression was agonized as she searched for

25

a way to convince him. 'If either of them get ill there'll be more expense for the workhouse! But if she's given outdoor relief . . . If she's given a chance to make a fresh start . . .' Her voice broke and she tried to turn it into a cough.

Harriet could sense her mother's growing agitation and suddenly found herself on her feet. 'Mama, have you forgotten? We have an old mangle in the shed in the yard. Mrs Bly could have that.' It was a blatant lie but she hoped her mother would see her intention.

'Have we?' For a moment Agnes hesitated. She turned towards her daughter.

Harriet said, 'We were going to give it away last year but then . . . then it wasn't necessary and . . . and—' She looked desperately at her mother.

'Oh yes! Certainly! Now I remember it.' Agnes turned quickly to Mr Crane who was looking unconvinced by their performance.

Miss Boothby said, 'That's settled then.'

As one, the Board looked at the Workhouse Master and he knew when he was beaten.

'Two weeks' rent,' he agreed reluctantly, 'but only if you provide a mangle.'

Mrs Fenner wrote in the book before he could change his mind. Two shillings a week was granted for the next two weeks and a room would be found for the unfortunate Mrs Bly.

Harriet, however, had decided to slip away. She had learned enough, she felt, to convince Godfrey of her good intentions towards the poor and she desperately wanted time on her own to think about him. With a whispered excuse she left the room and stood outside, breathing deeply. She at once became aware of a man standing further along the passage, his hands thrust deep into his pockets, a sullen expression on his face. After a moment he was called into the room and Harriet realized that this was the notorious Jake Tummer about to be told that his application for relief had been refused. He came out almost immediately, grumbling and cursing. He stormed out of the building almost knocking over a woman who carried a young child in her arms. This must be Mrs Bly.

Harriet smiled at her, intrigued inspite of herself, but received only a frightened nod in return.

Mrs Fenner came to the door and said, 'Mrs Bly!'

The woman drew herself up and pushed stray strands of hair up inside her bonnet. She knocked on the door and went in. Harriet went outside and lingered in the vicinity of the door. Moments later the woman reappeared. She took a few steps before bursting into tears of relief as she clutched the child to her in a fierce hug and hurried away. As Harriet turned towards home she was surprised to find her own eyes full of unshed tears.

Two

It was the twenty-eighth of May and the good weather had brought the people of Maybourne out on to the streets in search of exercise, fresh air or entertainment. The Pot & Kettle was always busy but Fridays were particularly so because large numbers of working men were celebrating the end of the week by spending some of their hard-earned wages before going home to their long-suffering wives. The public house was situated in an alley near the centre of Maybourne and was a rowdy, raucous place where men met to laugh and boast of their conquests and women met with their friends to gossip and dream of romance. The public bar was full and spilling its customers on to the street – sailors, tailors, butchers and bakers mingled with costermongers, dockers and various day labourers. Flower girls gossiped with dairymaids while orange sellers joked with nursemaids.

On the floor, largely ignored, half a dozen mongrel dogs lay in the sawdust jealously guarding their masters' feet. Young women perched on men's knees; old men smoked pipes and coughed. Old women, their heads together, regaled each other with dirty jokes and shrieked with lewd laughter. The potmen drew pint after pint and the barmaids threaded their way through the crowd with two or three mugs in each hand. A tuneless piano was being thumped by a young dandy who had already had too much to drink and was singing music-hall songs off key while a rival sing-song had started at the far end of the bar.

Daisy Pritty sipped her gin, eyes darting over the men in search of one she could fancy. She was sitting on the lap of a fat, balding man who had bought her the drink but his podgy hands were all over her and she was hoping to make a better catch before the evening was over. She might be lucky and find a young chap with a room of his own where she could spend the night but if not, she would have to spend a second night in the undertaker's cart – a prospect which frightened her more than she cared to admit. She was wearing a new straw hat which she had bought and a lacy blouse she had stolen from a market stall but she had enough money left from the pawned locket to stay free of the workhouse for another two days. Unless her luck changed . . .

The door swung open and three young men stumbled in. Two she dismissed but the third interested her. He was thin and as wiry as a weasel with a gaunt face and eyes like dark stones. His mouth was a thin line and there was an air of quiet confidence about him. He wore a brown serge suit with a collarless shirt and a crushed felt hat rested at an angle on his dark curls. As soon as he stepped inside the door he caught sight of Daisy and she returned his gaze with a provocative flutter of her eyelashes. Slipping from the fat man's lap with a murmured excuse about the needs of nature, she mingled with the crowd and eventually made her way to the bar. The three young men arrived at the same time and someone pinched her bottom.

She turned, pretending indignation, and glared at the weasel. 'You keep your poxy hands to yourself!'

He grinned and she saw that his teeth were good. None missing, one broken. Had he been fighting? He said, 'Couldn't resist a pretty Polly like you!'

He offered to buy her a drink and Daisy accepted with alacrity. She could no longer see her fat man, so presumed he couldn't see her. No doubt he'd find himself another woman, she told herself. Someone his own age or size! She put him out of her mind.

Minutes later she had joined the weasel (whose name was Digger) and his two friends. One, the red-haired man, had a squint and the other's face was badly scarred from smallpox. Mentally Daisy labelled them Squinty and Scar. Soon all four of them were squeezed companionably together on a wooden bench under the watchful eye of a bad-tempered mastiff who was slumped nearby.

Daisy regarded it balefully. 'I hate dogs. They're all the same. Nasty vicious creatures. Look what one done to my ankle this morning.' She hoisted up her skirt to reveal the torn stocking and the newly formed scab where the coffin-maker's dog had bitten her.

'Oh, that's very nice!' Digger poked a finger into the hole and tickled her ankle. 'The brute did me a favour!' he laughed.

Squinty said, 'Ooh! Nice little ankle. Show us a bit more. Go on!'

Daisy promptly drew down her skirt. 'Cheeky devil! What d'you think I am? A penny peepshow?'

'How'd it happen?' Digger looked concerned.

Daisy hesitated. Better not tell them about the funeral cart. Barely faltering, she at once invented a story about a crazy dog that leaped out on her from beneath a parked hansom cab as she was innocently passing by.

'Minding my own business,' she said earnestly, 'with a basket on my arms and a list of shopping from my mistress. Never even saw the brute but out he come in a flash and his teeth were clamped into my ankle. Bit right through to the bone, he did, and I was yelling and this nice young toff was tugging at the dog to get him off me!'

'A toff.' They looked impressed.

Digger said, 'You a scullerymaid or something, then?'

She raised her eyebrows. '*Housemaid*, you mean! Blooming sauce!' She gave him a light punch on the shoulder and thus encouraged, he slipped his arm around her waist.

'So you're not stepping out then?' he asked. 'Not spoken for?'

'Not allowed, am I.' Daisy shrugged. 'House rules. No followers – but I don't take no notice of their rules. Made to be broken, rules are.'

Squinty leaned across and whispered, 'I had you down for workhouse!' He tapped the side of his nose. 'Can smell it a mile off! 'Cos I've been there, see. Long time ago but you never forget. Me gran died there, poor old duck. I can see her now, all blubbery.' He screwed up his face at the memory.

Daisy frowned. 'How *blubbery*, exactly?'

30

'Dropsy. 'Orrible!' He grinned slyly. 'But you can't fool me, Daisy Chain! You're no housemaid.'

Crushed, Daisy swallowed hard, hoping that her expression didn't give her away. He sat back with a look of triumph on his face and Daisy's mind raced.

She opened her eyes wide as she looked at him. Then – 'You filthy little devil!' she cried suddenly. 'You keep your mind off my titties and your hands off my leg!' She turned to Digger. 'I'm not staying here with the likes of him!'

Confused by her totally unwarranted attack, Squinty watched open mouthed as she jumped to her feet and began to push her way through the crowd.

'What?' he stammered. 'I never even *thought* about her titties! And I never touched her leg! All I said—'

But Digger had risen also and he swung a punch that connected with his friend's nose and brought a spurt of blood and a feeble wail of protest.

As he reeled back from the blow, Digger leaned over him and said, 'Fine friend you are!'

Scar said, 'What happened? What did he say to her?'

But Digger was not going to let Daisy out of his sight. 'Daisy! Wait!' He elbowed his way towards the door, where Daisy was arguing with a balding, fat man. She threw Digger an appealing look and he immediately faced up to her tormentor with his fists up.

'You want these?' he demanded. 'Come and get 'em!'

The fat man retreated hastily saying, 'Keep the silly bitch!'

'What's that you called her?'

'Nothing! My mistake.' In his haste he tripped over one of the mongrels and fell backwards and at once there was uproar. It was the moment the dogs had been waiting for and they all joined the mêlée, urged on by their excited owners. They rushed for the fallen man, who fought them off with kicks and curses, and the onlookers cheered them all on with whoops of merriment.

Digger grabbed Daisy's arm. 'You're with me. Come on!'

Daisy felt her heart swell with gratitude and she allowed

31

him to steer her out of the door and into the gloom of the gas-lit street. Arm in arm, they made their way between the groups of merrymakers who collected under every street light. These flickering gas jets sent harsh shadows across their faces and gave them a sinister appearance, but Daisy felt wonderfully protected as they crossed the road and headed . . . where?

'Where we going?' she asked, tightening her grip on his arm. 'Back to your doss?'

He stopped suddenly. 'Good question. Better get you back to your place of work before they suss that you're out.'

She thought quickly. 'No need. They won't never know long as I'm back before six tomorrow. I leave the window open a crack and climb back in.'

'You never!'

'God's truth I do!'

He eyed her admiringly. 'You're a cool one, you are.'

'So if you've got a bed big enough for two . . . ?' She giggled. Crossing her fingers, she waited.

'It's not much. An attic in March Row. I bunk with a mate.'

'Will he be there?'

'Might be. You coming or not?'

Seconds passed as Daisy wavered. Two men?

Digger said, 'He'll most likely be dead to the world. Drunk. Snoring like a pig!'

So he'd be no trouble. Daisy made up her mind. 'I'm coming.'

Three days later, a Monday, Harriet awoke just after six thirty and couldn't get back to sleep. Outside, she could hear the town coming to life. Carts rattled past, horses' hooves clattered on the cobbles and an early rag-and-bone man shouted wearily for customers.

'Ra-a-g-a-bo-o-ne! Any rags, bottles or bo-o-nes?'

Harriet listened distractedly. Downstairs, she heard the ashes being scraped out from the kitchen range as Izzie prepared to relight the fire.

Irritably Harriet slid further under the bedclothes in an attempt to shut out the noise. She wanted to think. Marcus had sent a note to say he would call on them at eleven o'clock with some exciting news and she was full of curiosity. His father, James, had said nothing when they met at the workhouse the previous week and now she wondered uneasily if the news would affect the date of their marriage which still remained undecided.

After tossing and turning for some time, Harriet climbed out of bed and pulled back the curtains. The window was at the rear of the house and she looked out over the rooftops towards the centre of the town and on in the direction of Canterbury. Today the tiles shone with recent rain although the clouds were breaking up and the sun was almost through.

Pulling on her robe, Harriet returned to sit on her bed with her knees drawn up – a favourite position, which enabled her to think seriously. She could not remember a time when she had not been promised to Marcus Wellbury. Even as a child of eleven her father had spoken of Marcus and of his parents' approval of the match. Marcus had seemed positively elderly to Harriet, being twelve years older than her but he, too, seemed willing to wait for the marriage. How was it, she now wondered, that he had not already found himself a young woman? Men as young as eighteen had been known to fall desperately in love – it happened in many of the books she read when her mother was safely out of the way on one of her missions of mercy.

'Are you ever going to propose to me?' she whispered to the absent Marcus. Would he ever go down on one knee or did he take it for granted that she would say, 'Yes'? Was he ever going to kiss her or look at her in 'that certain way'? More importantly, would he ever make her feel as excited as she had been with Godfrey Lester? If not then she was very disappointed. Where was the *passion* in her relationship with Marcus? Did she still *want* Marcus to want to marry her? It was so confusing.

Sighing heavily, she reached for her diary and crossed to the small writing table. Seated there, she wrote busily for some minutes, trying to clear her mind. Sometimes it helped to see the problem spelled out on the page but this morning the magic didn't work for her. She laid down the pen and crossed again to the window.

She whispered, 'Marcus!' Nothing happened. Then she said, 'Godfrey!' and closed her eyes. There was no doubt about it. The thought of Mrs Lester's son was infinitely more thrilling than that of Marcus, who was going to be her husband and the father of her children. But how would it be if Marcus did *not* want to wed her? If he *refused* to wed her? Suppose he had met a young woman who excited him more than Harriet did. What would he do? Would he admit it or keep it to himself?

'The latter!' she murmured. Marcus was nothing if not a gentleman.

Restlessly, Harriet turned towards the door. She would creep downstairs and into the kitchen and heat a cup of milk. With her hand halfway to the door handle, she stopped and tutted irritably. It was Monday and Mrs Parkin might already be busy with the copper, preparing for the day's wash. Piles of sheets and pillowslips and towels, underclothes, blouses, petticoats and stockings. The kitchen would be no kind of sanctuary today.

Throwing herself back on to the bed, she tried to take her mind off the subject of men, marriage and duty and thought instead about Daisy Pritty who was still missing. Nobody seemed very worried about her but surely there was a small possibility that she had come to some harm. Her body might be lying in a gutter somewhere or she may have been captured by Orientals who would transport her to China and sell her to the highest bidder! *Or* she might have been abducted by a young blade who would fall madly in love with her and propose on one knee . . .

'*Daisy!*' she muttered.

It was all so unfair.

By five to eleven Harriet was dressed in her best spring suit of crushed lilac silk. Her hair had been coiled into long ringlets and her cheeks pinched to bring some colour into them. The maid had lit a small fire in the parlour to take the chill from the room and Harriet, struggling with a guilty

34

conscience, waited for Marcus with a piece of embroidery in her hands. Marcus arrived promptly and was shown into the parlour. She put aside the embroidery and rose to greet him with a smile on her face and he clasped both her hands and kissed them. The maid took his coat, offered him refreshment and bustled away to fetch tea and biscuits.

'So, my dear Harriet, do I find you well?'

'Indeed. And you?'

Marcus threw open his arms and said, 'As you see – in the pink, as they say!'

For the first time in her life, Harriet really looked at him. He was a good-looking man, sturdy with well-shaped hands which she had always admired. His eyes were blue and his fair hair curled slightly as it rested on the nape of his neck. The Wellburys were landowners on the outskirts of Maybourne and had farmed the Maybourne estate for four generations. Occasionally they grew a little grain, at other times they raised a few cattle but mostly it was sheep. On his father's death, Marcus, the only heir, would take over and Harriet's future prosperity would never be in doubt.

Noticing her scrutiny, he smiled good-naturedly. 'It's me – Marcus!' he teased. 'Have I grown horns or something?'

Harriet's laugh came a little too swiftly. 'Not at all, dearest. I didn't realize I was staring at you.'

She sat and he followed suit, sinking on to the chair with the confidence of long familiarity. 'And what have you being doing, Harriet, since I last saw you? I see you're busy with your needlework.'

She nodded and held out the pillowslip on which she was embroidering their initials in silver silk thread.

'Beautiful, Harriet. What a clever wife I shall have!'

Harriet laid it aside and turned to give him her full attention. 'What have I been doing? Let me see . . . Ah yes! I visited Great-Uncle Robert and I accompanied Mama to the workhouse meeting.'

'So I was told. My father was very pleased to see you taking such an interest. But Great-Uncle Robert! My poor darling Harriet! Rather a trial for you, as usual, I imagine.'

'It was,' she agreed. 'I fear he is getting worse from one

visit to the next. Now he feels under threat from anyone who calls at the house. After I joined him in the library he locked us in! I have to admit it was rather worrying.'

'Locked you in? How very extraordinary!'

Harriet opened her mouth to say that the housekeeper's son had arrived home. She was longing to talk about him but fearful that her excitement would become obvious. Instead she said, 'So what is your exciting news?'

He waited until the maid had brought in the tray and poured the tea. Then he began.

'I have been offered some work with my father's cousin. He wants a manager for his printing business. He produces stationery, special leaflets, funeral cards, business cards – anything, in fact. Only the highest quality. His manager was due to return after a short absence to attend a funeral but collapsed last week with breathing problems. They fear his lungs are diseased, poor fellow.' He shook his head. 'Consumption, of course. The doctor says he will never work again and my uncle thought at once of me, Harriet.'

Harriet was staring at him, trying to disguise her agitation. 'Not the cousin in London?'

He seemed unaware of her concern. 'That's the one. John Scotts. I've heard a lot about him but can't remember when we last—'

'You are going away *to London*?'

'Certainly. It's the most wonderful opportunity for us.' Finally, it seemed, he became aware of her expression. 'London isn't far, dearest. You see, while my father is hale and hearty there is really no opening for me on the farm. This work as my uncle's manager would be wonderful business experience and I've said I will seriously consider the offer. I wanted to talk to you about it first because it means, my dearest, that we shall be separated by seventy or eighty miles.'

Harriet wasn't sure whether to be pleased or not. Surely Marcus's enthusiasm to be so far away from her was not a good sign but it *did* mean that she would see him less and *that* meant she might have more opportunities to spend time at Havely House. Feeling treacherous, she nodded cautiously.

'Harriet, please don't look so unhappy. There is always

the railway, so we should still be able to meet from time to time. I would come home whenever possible and you could come up with your mother for a whole weekend. I would find you a room in a good hotel.' He smiled. 'And I would be earning good money and could save up for a rather special honeymoon!'

He was looking at her with such affection that Harriet was overcome with remorse. Marcus cared so much for her that he had waited for her approval for this new opportunity and she mustn't spoil it for him.

She said, 'Of course you must accept the position. I would never stand in your way.'

He smiled broadly. 'I was hoping you'd say that. You see, Harriet, that I would be in a position to ask for your hand once I was established with an income of my own. Instead of moving into Maybourne Manor to share the house with my parents, we could rent a little house in London!' He put down his cup and stood up and held out his arms. 'Come here, my love. You still don't understand. This changes everything!'

Harriet rose and threw her arms around him. It certainly was more exciting than anything that had happened between them to date. Their own home! It had a wonderful ring to it. But London! The idea was rather unnerving but she would die rather than say so.

'Then write to – to this cousin, Marcus, and accept the offer. What did you say his name was?'

'John Scotts of Scotts, Barling & Co!' Marcus lifted her from the ground and swung her round so that her feet left the floor. 'Barling is dead, poor chap, but they kept the name because his widow still has shares in the business. Sit with me on the sofa and I'll tell you all about it.'

Harriet listened but her thoughts raced. How was this going to affect her future? She wasn't sure that she was ready for such a sudden and dramatic change in her life. She wasn't sure if she wanted to move to London with Marcus. Meeting Godfrey Lester had changed everything. She needed time to discover where her affections truly lay. Now Marcus was rushing her into a decision. She watched him as he explained the details of his intended move and saw the exhilaration in his face. A face she thought she had grown to love over the years. But was that wishful thinking? Was it a dutiful love, an acceptance of a relationship planned for her by her parents?

Godfrey had appeared in her life like a breath of fresh air and had offered excitement and a secret romance but she was so naïve in matters of the heart and for that she now blamed her mother and father who had never given her the chance to experience the thrill of sudden attraction.

Ten minutes later, when Marcus had talked himself to a standstill, Harriet took a deep breath. 'I have to ask you this, Marcus,' she began, 'because it's begun to trouble me.'

'Oh dear! That sounds ominous.'

'Not at all. But Marcus, can you remember exactly when you first knew you wanted to marry me?'

He looked bewildered. 'When I first knew? But I've always known! We've both always known . . . haven't we? Dearest Harriet, where on earth is this leading?'

'I've just been wondering – did we ever fall in love?' Her voice was suddenly anguished. 'Or did our parents make us believe . . . Did they want the marriage so much that . . . I mean, Marcus, was it really our decision?' She closed her eyes, reluctant to ask the next question but sure that it needed an answer. 'Is this a *romance*, Marcus. Do you really *love* me?'

She watched the confusion sweep through him, leaving fear and doubt in its wake, and knew how much her questions had shocked him.

'Most assuredly I love you,' he stammered. 'I didn't need my parents to *tell* me. I just *knew*! Wasn't it the same for you? Oh darling, don't tell me . . . I couldn't bear it!'

Harriet cursed herself. Her question had hurt him. She said quickly, 'It *was* for me also, Marcus. I love you. Indeed I do. I was so afraid they had not given us the chance to discover it for ourselves. I wanted to be sure this was what you wanted.'

He put his arms around her and hugged her so tightly that she could hardly draw breath and his relief was overwhelming. 'Dear God! You frightened me, Harriet! For a moment I thought – that is, I doubted. Oh my love, how can I convince you?'

Harriet discovered there were tears in her eyes. 'I am convinced, Marcus,' she told him shakily.

But he was not satisfied. Falling to one knee, he looked up at her and clasped her hands in his. 'Dearest Harriet, I adore you and I always have. Please say you love me and will be my wife.'

So this *is* romance, thought Harriet, fighting down disappointment as she bent to kiss him. No woman in her right mind should ask for more.

It was six o'clock that same evening. Agnes had taken advantage of the improving weather to walk round to Miss Boothby's house to discuss workhouse matters. The members of the Board of Guardians frequently met out of business hours to plot against the authorities. The present matter was a scheme to find ways to improve the heating at the workhouse during the winter. The coal allowance, on paper, should be sufficient if not exactly generous but in effect it was not. Agnes had noticed that during January and February, when snow was common, the inmates shivered but the office was always cosy. She suspected also that some of the coal was being diverted upstairs to the private quarters where Herbert Crane lived with his wife and the last of their seven children – a boy with a malformed foot.

Harriet was in her room writing to Great-Uncle Robert when Izzie shouted up the stairs that there was a Mrs Bly at the door. Harriet frowned, unable to recall the name, and with a sigh of exasperation she went downstairs to where Izzie waited in the hallway.

'Where is Mrs Bly?' Harriet asked.

'I left her on the doostep, Miss Harriet. I-I didn't know if you'd want her in the house.'

'Why not?'

Izzie lowered her voice. 'She looks a little undesirable.'

Harriet nodded. 'Go back to your work,' she said. 'I'll see to it.'

Opening the door, Harriet was confronted by a woman holding a young child and at once recognized her from the workhouse. 'Mrs Bly! From the –' She stopped quickly as the woman's expression changed.

'I'm *not* from the workhouse!' she said, her tone sharp with objection. 'I pray God I never shall be. Two weeks' rent was all I was given but I'm thankful for that.'

'No. My mistake. Do forgive me.' Harriet was thankful her mother wasn't able to hear this conversation.

'I got *out*door relief,' Mrs Bly persisted, her cheeks now flushed with indignation. 'There's no way I'd go into that place! Never! Nor my son. I'd die of shame . . . I need to speak to Mrs Burnett about the mangle.'

'Please come in.' Harriet thought quickly. The household only boasted one mangle and that was used every Monday by the woman who did the rough work – the laundry and scrubbing the floors.

As she showed Mrs Bly into the parlour, she saw how thin she was. Her face was drawn into lines of worry and the corners of her mouth drooped with misery. Her clothes had once been decent enough but were now crumpled and stained and Harriet wondered if they had slept rough the previous night. The child was hardly visible under the threadbare blanket and occasionally whimpered feebly.

The woman perched nervously on the edge of the sofa and patted the child.

'I was promised a mangle,' she said firmly. 'I've found myself a room and I need it to start work right away so . . . The landlady's going to give me some sheets and whatnot of hers to do each week as part of the rent and she'll recommend me to her friends. I can use her washing line in the backyard.' Her face softened as she spoke and Harriet saw the anger drain away as she described her hopeful prospects. 'I've an iron too and will buy another so that one's always heating at the fire.' The child wailed and she stopped to rock it.

Harriet smiled. 'You've worked fast, Mrs Bly. I'm very impressed. I'm sorry about your husband. You must miss him very much.'

The woman swallowed. 'I do and I don't. He was a good man once and a good carpenter but seems over the last year or two the drink's got to him. He got careless at work. I should have realized what was happening when he got sacked from one job and wouldn't tell me why. Said they'd no more work but I didn't really believe him.'

'But people always need carpenters.'

She shrugged. 'He soon got another job but it ended in disaster. Too much ale with his dinner then he's up in the rafters of the house repairing the rotten beams. And he's larking about. The foreman told me.' She rolled despairing eyes. 'Somehow he misses his footing, falls and breaks his neck! Leaves us alone in this pickle. He must be turning in his grave, the stupid—' She bit back the unkind word. 'I never took charity in my whole life nor has anyone else in our family – and it's come to this! I daren't write to my father. He'd be horrified.'

'Wouldn't he help you?'

'He'll never get the chance.' She tossed her head. 'He's a hard man and I'm not asking for his pity nor anyone else's but Mrs Burnett offered me a mangle. *Offered* it!'

Harriet came to a decision. The mangle would have to go and they must buy another one. Her mother had promised and Mrs Bly had come to collect. 'It's heavy,' she said. 'I'll find a couple of lads to carry it round for you but we'd best go with them in case they have other ideas.' She had visions of the mangle being spirited away and sold for a quick shilling.

'I can't pay them!'

'*I'll* see to that. You wait here while I organize every-thing.'

Telling Izzie to provide cake and tea for Mrs Bly and milk for the little boy, Harriet threw on a shawl and went outside. She made her way towards a nearby cluster of houses and there she collected Tom and Luke, two hulking lads on whom her mother called from time to time when strong arms were needed. Back at the house, she explained briefly to Cook what was happening and ignoring her scandalized expression, led Mrs Bly, child and lads into the yard. The mangle was produced from the outhouse and they set off for Mrs Bly's lodgings, which proved to be a converted but substantial lean-to, built against the wall of a red-brick house which stood alone in a quarter acre of land.

41

The landlady came out to see the mangle installed in a corner of the yard where it was duly admired. The lads were each given a sixpence and ran off cheerfully to spend the money. Harriet lingered for a few moments before deciding she was no longer needed. She wished Mrs Bly well and walked home deep in thought.

The next few days passed quietly. A new mangle was purchased but Agnes made no complaint. She had offered it and was happy that Harriet had honoured the promise. Harriet spent a great deal of time talking with her mother about her forthcoming marriage, trying to decide upon a suitable date. Harriet also spent time thinking about Godfrey Lester and volunteered to visit Great-Uncle Robert again.

'So soon?' Agnes stared at her. 'I thought you hated going to Havely House.'

'I do – but I feel perhaps it is my duty.' The word 'hypocrite' sprang to mind but Harriet tried to ignore it. 'Great-Uncle Robert is very frail and if he takes pleasure in my company—'

'Which you always insist he doesn't!' Agnes narrowed her eyes. 'Do I detect an ulterior motive here? A certain young man by the name of Lester?'

'How did you know he was home?' Harriet felt a twinge of conscience for what she *hadn't* told her mother about the previous visit.

'Your great-uncle writes to me also, remember!' Agnes narrowed her eyes. 'Is he personable, this Godfrey?'

Harriet decided to brazen it out and shrugged. 'Pleasant enough, I daresay, Mama. And very amusing company. His presence certainly made the visit more tolerable.'

Her mother nodded. 'That may be so but just you remember that Marcus is the man you will wed. I trust you to behave with proper decorum, Harriet.'

'His mother is always there, Mama.'

'Let us hope so!' There was a steely look in her eye which Harriet noted. Not that she had any intention of misbehaving but just being with an admiring member of the opposite sex was something to be appreciated.

*   *   *

42

Sunday came round and Agnes was unwell with a sick stomach and confined to her bed. Harriet went to church on her own. As she made her way to the family pew she caught sight of Mrs Bly sitting in the space at the rear of the church which was reserved for the poor. The little boy was on her lap. If Mrs Bly saw Harriet, she gave no sign.

The service was long and tedious but Harriet, wrapped up in her own thoughts, scarcely noticed the passage of time. She was thinking about Godfrey and the fact that she was thinking unlawful thoughts while sitting in church made her feel sinful and that felt delightfully dangerous. Not that the thoughts were actually *sinful*, she assured herself, but she should have been praying to God about Marcus and their future life together.

As they knelt to pray she substituted her own prayer. *Dear God, please let me see him again. I promise I will do all that Mama asks of me and will write more often to Great-Uncle Robert and remember him in my nightly prayers and I will take an interest in the workhouse and its inmates and prepare my household linen for my approaching marriage and complete my book of recipes – if only I may spend a few more hours in Godfrey's company before it is too late. I promise I will allow no undue familiarity and will not provoke his interest other than in a friendly way nor say anything to him that Marcus might object to. Amen.*

As she raised her head she felt that the eye of the Lord was undoubtedly upon her and was surprised that she felt so little remorse.

Later she was crossing the town square when she became aware of a scuffle at the far side where a small crowd was gathering. Quickening her steps, she found that a brawl was in progress. This was hardly unusual but Harriet was normally accompanied by her mother and was hurried away from such a distasteful scene. Today, thankful that her mother was at home in bed, Harriet pushed nearer to the front of the crowd to see what was happening. From the other side of the square two constables were converging, blowing their whistles and shouting to the crowd to 'Stand back in the name of the law!' Everyone ignored this order as the fight had abruptly taken a dramatic turn. Two men were fighting, one dark haired, the other a red head. Red faced with anger, they pummelled each other, urged on by the cheers and jeers of the onlookers.

'Talk about pat-a-cake!'

'*Give* him one!'

'Lordy! Call that a punch?'

'Punch him! An uppercut! *Uppercut*, I said, not a poxy pat on the head! Gawd love us!'

Harriet watched, entranced, using her elbows to repel those nearest her who were also trying to get a better view.

'Land him one, you mimsy devil! Don't play with the bogger!'

'I could do better than that with one hand!'

Enthralled, her heart racing, Harriet watched open mouthed as a young woman suddenly darted forward and tried to insinuate herself between the two men – doing her best to separate them but without effect. She was flung aside like a rag doll but returned mouthing obscenities, scratching and clawing at the red-haired youth. Grunting with effort and rage, the two young men lashed out again and again, sometimes grappling with each other, sometimes losing their balance and tumbling together to the ground but always staggering up again to renew the fight. The young woman was flung to the ground but willing hands lifted her to her feet again, urging her to 'Have another go, doll!'

A woman shouted, 'You sort 'em out, lovey!'

It was a street spectacle they could all enjoy but from the corner of her eye Harriet saw respectable citizens keeping their distance, hurrying past or watching with grim glances of disapproval as they waited for action from the police who were now forcing a way through the crowd. Regretfully, Harriet decided she ought to withdraw in case she should be called as a witness. If her mother found out that would certainly put the cat among the pigeons. As she turned to go, a knife flashed and there was a loud groan from the spectators as the girl, stepping between the men, was stabbed through the shoulder and fell screaming to the cobbles.

At once the crowd drew back, falling over each other in their haste to avoid a similar fate or to be held responsible in any way for the crime. Without warning, Harriet was pushed over by the swaying crowd and went down with a scream of panic. She was trodden on and tripped over before she finally found her feet again and stumbled to a safe distance to recover her breath and fight down her growing panic. Turning back, she saw that the man with the knife was in handcuffs, the dark-haired youth was holding the girl in his arms and his shirt and jacket was red with her blood while around them the erstwhile eager crowd was melting away.

Sickened by the sight, Harriet tried to tidy herself before going home. She also tried to steady her nerves which had been jangled by the dangerous turn of events. She stayed long enough to see the red-haired man led away by the constable and watched from a safe distance as a stretcher arrived from the hospital. The girl was laid on it and wheeled away while the dark-haired youth seized his chance and disappeared.

A little the worse for wear, Harriet walked slowly home. Now that the drama was safely at an end she felt vaguely heroic and wondered whether she dare confide in Godfrey. There was no way she could tell her mother but she longed to share the adventure with someone. In her mind's eye she kept seeing the same image, the young 'blade', his head thrown back, his expression anguished, holding in his arms the limp body of the girl who had risked her life to save him. Terrible, true, but undeniably romantic and wonderfully passionate!

Unable to keep the tale entirely to herself, Harriet confided a modified version of the affair to her mother but made light of the danger to herself, pretending that she had seen it from a distance but that while watching she had tripped and fallen which explained her dishevelled appearance. To her relief Agnes showed no real concern except to enquire after the girl. It was only later, just before nine o'clock that evening, that Miss Boothby called in to say Daisy Pritt was back in the workhouse infirmary – recovering from a stab wound in her shoulder.

Three

D aisy woke early next morning and tried to roll over but found the exercise painful and her joints stiff and unco-operative.

'Ouch! Gawd love us!' Memories flooded back. She remembered the fear and pain as the knife plunged into her, slicing easily through the thin stuff of her shawl and ruining the front of her new blouse. 'That bogger!'

Opening her eyes, she saw that she was in the workhouse infirmary and groaned. So her short-lived freedom was at an end. She put a hand to her shoulder and felt a thickness. A quick peep revealed bandaging and she cursed Squinty.

'You didn't last long out there!'

A wheezy laugh accompanied the remark and Daisy turned to glare at the old man in the next bed.

He said, 'I'm Daniel Stubbs.'

'I bet I lasted longer than you'd last, Mr Stubbs!' she snapped.

He went on as though she hadn't spoken. 'They weren't half narked when you went missing with that locket! Old Crane was going on at Fenner like it was *her* fault. Didn't you like the job?'

'Too much like hard work. The missus was a miserable cow and her husband was a nasty-minded pig!'

'Sounds more like a farm!'

Stubbs, fifty-three years old give or take a year, was bald headed, his face grey with stubble. He'd been wandering in the town square two Christmases ago, wearing only a nightshirt and slippers. Frail both in mind and body, he didn't know who he was or where he lived. They never did find out, so they gave him a name and he'd been in

46

Maybourne Workhouse ever since, too weak to work for his keep and confined to the infirmary on doctor's orders.

Daisy regarded him wearily. 'Squinty stabbed me. He was trying to kill Digger.'

The old man propped himself on his elbow and straightened the cotton night cap which kept his bald head warm at night. 'I heard they arrested him. Caught him red-handed.'

She frowned. 'I don't remember coming back here.'

'You were out for the count, as you might say. White as a sheet. We thought you were a gonner.'

Cautiously, Daisy explored her various aches and pains. Her arms were black and blue and there was dried blood in her hair. 'What happened to Digger?'

He shrugged. 'Who knows? *You'll* most likely be arrested next. Stole that locket, didn't you!'

Daisy swore under her breath but she was more concerned about Digger. Would he still be keen on her when she got out again? Was he angry that she got herself stabbed and did he blame her for the fact that Squinty was in prison? She stared round the infirmary – a high-ceilinged room with windows high up in the wall like a school house. Not much chance of escaping through one of those, she reflected. The dark-green walls made the room darker than it need be and the only decoration was a large wooden sign supported on chains from the ceiling: 'GOD IS THY SAVIOUR'.

Daisy snorted. 'He didn't save me!'

At one end a large cupboard held the laundry and there was a table for the nurse's notebooks, an inkwell and a couple of pens. A small cupboard held the cutlery and crockery for the patients' meals. There were twelve beds, six down each side of the room, but at present only five were occupied.

Apart from herself and Daniel, there was a twelve-year-old boy who suffered from convulsions. Recently he had fallen on to the stone floor, struck his head and gone into a coma. He hadn't spoken since and wasn't expected to survive. Daisy didn't even know his name. Connie was a middle-aged consumptive who somehow still survived six months after they'd ordered her coffin – a cheap affair of wooden planking which was now propped in one corner, waiting for her to

47

die. Daisy wondered suddenly whether Albert Hawke had supplied it. Then there was Ben Finch – a layabout, cheat and thorough scoundrel who'd recently managed to contract a mysterious illness (brought on, it was rumoured, by sucking bars of soap) and thus avoided his share of stone-breaking by which the men earned their daily keep.

Ben Finch now sat up. He always reminded Daisy of a scarecrow with his tufty hair that refused to lie flat. 'Oh! You're still alive then, Daisy,' he said cheerfully. 'More's the pity!'

'Go and suck soap!' she snapped, making a rude gesture with her fingers.

'Your fancy lad stabbed you, did he? Can't say I blame him.'

'No, he did not! It was his friend who done it.' She slid out of bed, wincing as the movement pulled at the stitches in her shoulder, and padded the length of the room to reach the curtains which hid the piss pots. She could hear the ward coming to life. Connie's thin voice asking for water – a voice which grew weaker day by day.

Daisy called out, 'Give her a drink, someone, for Pete's sake!'

An argument was developing between Daniel and Ben about a recent dog fight which Ben insisted had been rigged with the result that he had lost his wager. Nothing unusual there, thought Daisy. Then she heard the clipped sound of the nurse's shoes and wondered if Doctor Chisom would be in today.

The elderly doctor was on call for the workhouse emergencies but was also a local doctor. It was rumoured that he would shortly be giving up as he was becoming forgetful and his sight was failing but his stepson, also a medical man, was planning to take over the practice when the time came.

Daisy walked carefully back to her bed, wondering if the doctor would decide she needed a better diet to help her recover but it seemed doubtful. He would probably say she had brought her injuries on herself, so didn't qualify as genuinely needy. Sighing, she climbed back into bed and watched the nurse checking on Daniel. The nurse had once been a lady's companion and had some nursing experience but Daisy guessed she had never dealt with a stab wound before. The nurse's regulation dress was dark blue and she wore a bonnet to match but the large coarse apron needed a wash. Catching sight of Daisy, she called, 'You had to have stitches. They called the doctor in. Don't you go pulling them loose now.'

'It hurts!' She flopped back on the pillow.

'What d'you expect? Serves you right for brawling in the street. On the Sabbath, too!'

'When's the doctor coming to see me?' Daisy was looking forward to the attention.

'He's not. He died late last night.' All eyes were suddenly on the nurse. 'He went to supper with friends and collapsed as he was about to go home. He was climbing into a hansom when he staggered, fell under the horse's feet and got himself kicked to death!'

For a moment Daisy was both shocked and thrilled but then she felt annoyed because she realized the doctor's dramatic end would overshadow her own injuries. She had been in the limelight for such a short time. Why did Fate play such mean tricks on her? she thought resentfully, and was unable to say anything nice about the old doctor.

Ben said, 'Lucky old blighter! I wouldn't mind dying after a big meal and a few jars of ale!'

Daniel laughed wheezily then began to cough. 'He was a very decent man, was Doctor Chisom, and a good doctor. No one had a bad word to say about him.'

Connie whispered, 'Poor man. I always liked him.'

The nurse wrote something on Daniel's chart. 'We'll have to see what his son's like. His name's Phineas.'

'Ooh! Hoity toity!' Daisy snorted. 'He probably won't bother with the likes of us.'

'Why not? His father did.'

'He's not his father, though, is he. He's his *step*father. Phineas might think we're the lowest of the low.'

'We are,' said Ben.

'*You* are, yes!' Daisy stuck out her tongue.

49

The nurse helped Connie to her feet. 'We should give the new doctor a chance,' she said. He might be a good man.'

Daisy scowled. 'And he might not!'

Harriet arrived at the workhouse just after three o'clock and was directed up the stairs to the infirmary.

'. . . then turn right and follow the groans!' Mrs Fenner laughed. 'They know you're coming, so they'll overact. They love to get into the infirmary because the food's better. We had a man once shot himself in the foot!'

Harriet frowned. 'He brought a pistol into the workhouse?'

'No. Got a friend to smuggle it in then shot himself and chucked it out the window. Thought we wouldn't rumble him but we did. They think they're so smart, some of them. Think because we work here we can't get anything better.'

'And?' Harriet raised her eyebrows.

Mrs Fenner shrugged. 'It suits me well enough. I can walk to work in less than fifteen minutes and it's not exactly demanding. But go on up.' She peered into the basket. 'Looks like you've brought a picnic!'

'Mama insisted.'

Harriet's footsteps echoed on the stone stairs. From somewhere outside she could hear the rumble and crash of stones being struck with heavy hammers. So the men were stone-breaking. According to her mother, the women picked oakum, whatever that was, and the men broke up stones. Harriet had never bothered to ask, but now she was curious.

As she stepped through the doors into the infirmary, she braced herself against the unpleasant smell of disinfectant, stale food and sickness and glanced up at the windows, which were all closed. A coffin propped in one corner startled her but she moved quickly on. Proceeding down the ward self-consciously, she forced a smile. The basket she carried made her feel like Little Red Riding Hood and her smart clothes made her feel like Lady Bountiful but her mother was still indisposed and had been adamant that someone must visit Daisy and take her some nourishing food.

Harriet had been told by Mrs Fenner that the invalid was in the end bed on the left but Harriet gave a cheerful nod to

50

the other patients as she passed. A boy who seemed to be asleep, a middle-aged woman who was coughing too much to respond, an elderly man who waved shyly and a younger man who seemed to be frothing at the mouth and from whom she quickly averted her gaze. Thankfully, Harriet reached Daisy Pritty, who, as predicted, was groaning softly, her eyes closed, her face twisted in agony.

'Miss Pritty? My mother has sent me to . . .'

Daisy sat up slowly, clutching the bandaged shoulder. Her expression was agonized. 'They said you was most likely coming.' She eyed the basket.

From the corner of her eye, Harriet noticed the frothing man sitting up and wiping his mouth. A sudden recovery, she thought, puzzled.

'Food?' Daisy said eagerly.

Harriet nodded and began to unpack the contents of the basket. The frothing man joined them. Harriet wondered whether he should be out of his bed but Daisy seemed unperturbed. 'There's a jar of honey,' Harriet explained, 'from a friend's hive, four eggs, goat's cheese . . . and a cherry cake. My mother—'

Interrupting her, Daisy told the young man to fetch a knife from the cupboard and within minutes the cake had been divided into five large chunks and she was gobbling her own share down with exclamations of delight. Harriet watched her surreptitiously. She really was quite pretty

'None for the boy?' asked Harriet.

Daisy explained, spluttering cake crumbs over the bed. ''Cos he's not with us,' she tapped her head meaningfully, 'and is never going to wake up. One bit's for the nurse when she comes back. She's off to the apothecary for more medicaments. Have to keep on the right side of Nursie!'

'So are you feeling better?' Harriet smiled at her. 'My mother sends her good wishes for a speedy recovery. It must have been painful. I was – I was passing and saw the fight – from a distance, of course. You must have been very frightened.'

'Wasn't time to be frightened, tell you the truth. I was that angry. Squinty called me a workhouse slut! I saw red, I tell

51

you! So did Digger – he's my young man . . . Or was . . . Anyway, Digger goes for him then, 'cos I pretended to be a housemaid but Squinty told him to look at my hands.' She held them out and for the first time Harriet noticed the dark stains in each crease of her flesh and the broken stained nails. 'Bit of a giveaway.'

'How do you mean, exactly?'

'It's the tar from the oakum. Can't get rid of it, not without creams and suchlike and where am I going to get them?' She shrugged. 'I said I'd been gardening but I doubt he believed it. Still, let's hope, eh?'

'And that's why he stabbed you?'

'No! He was trying to stab Digger and I got it by mistake. Doctor Chisom says I'll survive so no harm done. Probably the last thing the old boy said 'cos he dropped under a hansom cab last night and he's dead now.'

Harriet stared at her, startled. 'Doctor Chisom is *dead*?'

'As a doornail! Seems he—' She broke off as the doors opened and a man stalked into the room.

Almost stout with dark-brown hair already thinning at the temples, he was wearing a black suit and a stern expression. Seeing that he had everyone's attention he said loudly, 'My name is Phineas Chisom. Doctor Phineas Chisom. I think you know that my stepfather is dead. His death was very sudden, very unexpected, and we are deeply shocked but I thought you'd be reassured to know that I will also attend Maybourne Workhouse.'

There was a whispered comment which provoked smothered laughter but he ignored it.

'I shall make a professional visit after the funeral, when I've finished reading through my stepfather's records. Be assured that I shall root out slackers and malingerers.' He glared at each patient in turn. 'Only the seriously sick will occupy these beds when I am in charge. I'm not prepared to help waste honest men's taxes.'

He looked at Daisy. 'I understand my father stitched you back together yesterday. A knife wound, I believe. Tell the nurse to change the dressing daily.'

'She's off to the apothe—'

'I know where she is, thank you.' He gave Harriet a haughty look. 'And you are?'

'Harriet Burnett. I'm visiting Miss Pritty. My mother is—'

'On the Board. Ye-es. I know the name.' He turned sharply on his heel and walked out of the room.

Ignoring the interruption, Daisy said, 'I'll share the honey but keep the eggs. Thank your ma from me.'

'I will.' Harriet lowered her voice. 'Why is that coffin here?'

'That? That's for Connie when she goes. They brought it one night but then she rallied and they've never taken it back. Connie's getting quite fond of it. Not that there'll be much of a funeral but who cares about folk like us?' She looked at Ben. 'Find us some spoons before Nursie gets back and we'll get rid of the honey.'

Harriet was beginning to feel superfluous. 'I'll be on my way then.'

Nobody tried to dissuade her, so she left them to it and made her way down stairs. Halfway down she decided to try to see a little more of the place and when she reached the ground floor she turned right instead of left. If challenged, she thought, she would pretend she was lost but at the moment there was no one in sight. Walking swiftly, she came to a door on the right which was already ajar and edged it a little wider. A murmur of voices came from within and she saw about a dozen women crouched on benches in a rough circle. Beside each woman there was a basket and in the middle, shared by all, was a pile of tarry rope ends. These were being picked into separate strands which were dropped into the baskets. The women seemed resigned to the work but Harriet could see by the way they wrestled the strands that it was sticky, unpleasant work. Now she understood Squinty's remark to Daisy about her stained hands. Without stopping to think, she stepped into the room and abruptly the murmur stopped and all faces turned in her direction.

Someone muttered, 'Ooh look! It's Lady Muck!' and they all tittered.

With her face burning, Harriet stammered a quick apology and retreated. A burst of laughter followed her and she stood

53

in some confusion, blaming herself for her tactless curiosity. She had made them feel like animals in a zoo. Interesting specimens! She hoped her mother would never hear of her stupidity. Agnes was always talking about the inmates' right to some privacy, away from curious eyes.

Mortified, she set out to walk home but gradually the sunshine and the normal world smoothed her ruffled feelings and before she was halfway home she was thinking about Godfrey and the miseries of the workhouse were forgotten.

> *Dear Uncle Robert,*
> *Thank you for your letter which arrived this morning. I am pleased to hear that you enjoyed my daughter's visit. Harriet was delighted to find you in such good spirits . . .*

Agnes looked at her careful handwriting and wondered how many times she had written those words to her husband's uncle. But George was a Godfearing man and he believed in duty and the sanctity of the family. She had promised to write regularly to his uncle while he was away and she tried to do so with a good heart. The problem was that news was scarce and two letters a week strained her imagination.

> *Harriet's husband-to-be has been offered an excellent job in London and they are talking about renting a house after they are married. I wonder how I shall feel when she leaves me. No doubt I will be lonely but there are the grandchildren to look forward to . . .*

Would Harriet make a good mother? Agnes tried to imagine her daughter carrying a baby with another older child running alongside, holding on to her skirts. The thought amused her but then she realized that they would probably be able to afford a nanny. She continued her letter.

> *I am entirely satisfied that Marcus Wellbury is the right choice for Harriet. Not only that but he loves her*

deeply. With Marcus I am sure she will be respectably settled. That is all I have ever asked for – that and her happiness, of course. For reasons I need not explain I have always feared for her but God has been good to us and her future is now secure . . .

She paused, uncertain, and reread the last few lines. Had she said too much? It was such a temptation to confide in someone who never could or would be tempted to betray her. Dipping her pen into the ink, she continued.

George will be home soon. I have heard from the harbour master that the Saint Augustine has been reported and should make land within a few days. It will be wonderful to see George again. Our time together is so short, it is always precious. He and I will visit you. He is always keen to reassure himself of your welfare . . .

She laid down her pen. A red admiral butterfly had drifted in through the open window and Agnes paused to catch it in her cupped hands and toss it outside. As she leaned out, she caught the scent of lilac and smiled.

My work on behalf of the Maybourne Workhouse still takes up a great amount of each day but it is time I give willingly. The unfortunate inmates are desperately short of goodwill and are mainly looked upon as undeserving which in nine cases out of ten is unmerited. They are more often the unfortunate victims of adverse circumstances and detest the need to throw themselves on the mercy of the state. Sadly, the spectre of the workhouse casts a shadow over people's lives. On a brighter note, however, I am glad to say that Harriet is at last showing an interest in our workhouse and consequently thinking a little less about herself.

She finished the letter and signed it then added a postscript to tell Robert that the family doctor had died.

*   *   *

Agnes and Harriet awoke on Saturday morning, washed and dressed and paid extra attention to their appearance. George Burnett's ship was due. When Harriet set out to walk to the quayside she went alone because her mother preferred to wait for her husband at home. As Harriet neared the harbour her spirits rose as she imagined the scene that awaited her. The quayside would be full of children waiting for the first glimpse of the *Saint Augustine*. Each child wanted to be the first to catch sight of the sails on the horizon. It was a matter of pride whenever a ship docked. From around nine o'clock, children bowled iron hoops, threw balls or whipped tops or simply sat on the wall, staring out to sea in eager anticipation.

It was exactly as she had thought and Harriet waited quietly to one side. When the ship finally appeared as a smudge on the distant horizon it was greeted with cheers and caps were thrown into the air. The ship's outline grew rapidly, nearer and nearer until the sails were discernible, until finally the shrill cries of the assembled children alerted the wives and sweethearts, mothers and sisters, who came hurrying from their homes to shout at the more adventurous children who cavorted too near to the edge of the quay. When the *Saint Augustine* finally docked, there were tears of relief in Harriet's eyes. Her father was home again.

She waited until she saw her father come up on deck and then she hurried home with the news. It would be hours before George was free to leave the ship and in the meantime the entire household prepared for his return. Mats were shaken, beds were changed, furniture was polished and fresh flowers were purchased. Food was prepared. Jasper, the cat, chased from one chair to another, retired to the yard in disgust, his tail rigid with indignation.

Agnes stroked him. 'Poor cat. You don't understand, do you? The master's coming home so you'd best keep out of the bedroom. He abhors cats on the bed!' Leaning down, she whispered, 'Take my advice and stay outside out of the way!'

She sighed. Her husband's return always sent her into a spin of nervousness. After months without him she felt like a young bride again, eager for love and companionship but apprehensive. Would he still love her? Had his feelings changed towards her? Had he met another woman in those far-off ports? Infidelity was not an uncommon occurrence among the ratings but rarer, though not unheard of, among senior men. It was Agnes's nightmare. It seemed unlikely, for George Burnett was a quiet, contained man but Agnes knew this hid a steely core as many an unruly seaman had found out to his cost.

Somehow the hours passed. Soon after eight o'clock that evening there was a knock on the door and Izzie flew down the hallway to open it. George stepped inside and they exchanged a few words as the housemaid hung up his coat, by which time Agnes had appeared, arms outstretched, and as she flew into her husband's arms, her eyes brimmed with the familiar tears. For Agnes alone knew that she didn't deserve his love.

Harriet, lingering on the upstairs landing, allowed her parents their greeting. 'Please, *please*, Papa!' she whispered. Her fingers were crossed behind her back as she waited in an agony of mind for her father's first words but on this occasion she was disappointed once again.

'So how's that boy of mine, Agnes?!' he demanded. 'You must tell me all about him.'

Slowly, Harriet came down the stairs, struggling with her emotions, telling herself yet again that this was perfectly natural. The natural bond between father and son. Only to be expected.

'You and I have a bond between us, Harriet,' Agnes had insisted all those years ago when Harriet was young enough to ask questions without wondering if she would like the answer. 'Mother and daughter. Your father loves you very much. Never doubt it, dear.'

'I shall ask him then,' Harriet had argued, her voice quivering.

Her mother's expression had changed. 'Please don't, dear. You will only irritate him by silly questions. Trust me, Harriet. Your father loves you but he is not a demonstrative man. Some men cannot easily show affection.'

'But he ruffles Sam's hair! He never ruffles mine.'

'I should think not, Harriet. Girls have curls and want to look pretty. They take care over their looks. You would hate it if Papa mussed up your hair. Do you see your father ruffling my hair?'

'Maybe he doesn't love you either.'

Suddenly, to Harriet's horror, her mother had burst into tears. 'Oh you wicked girl! Why do you torment me this way! If you only knew . . .'

Harriet had watched with a pounding heart as her mother fled upstairs and locked herself in her bedroom and she had never dared raise the subject again. The scene, however, had left questions in her mind. She imagined a variety of scenarios which might explain her father's lack of interest in his daughter and of these her favourite was that she was another man's child. He would, of course, be a wealthy gentleman and one day he would seek her out and carry her away to a life of luxury. Naturally, this real father would adore her. Sadly Harriet could not entirely believe this because she could not imagine her mother being unfaithful to her husband. It was utterly impossible.

Today, following her parents into the parlour, Harriet smiled. 'Welcome home, Papa.'

He turned at once and held out his arms. 'Mr dear girl, let me look at you! I do declare you are a woman already.' He held her close and kissed her.

Harriet tried to imagine that his arms were firmer around her and the kiss was more fervent. She stepped back from his embrace in order to see his expression. 'I've missed you, Papa. We all have.'

He looked older. His dark-brown hair was greying at the temples and there were worry lines that she didn't recall. Perhaps he had had a troublesome voyage. Her eyes narrowed. Did she detect the smell of whisky on his breath? Surely not.

Agnes gave a little laugh. 'We have so much to tell you, George. We'll talk over a pot of tea. Harriet was at Havely House last week visiting your uncle.'

George settled himself in the large wingback chair that was traditionally his although Agnes used it in his absence. He asked after his uncle and listened courteously as Harriet described her visit but then her father turned back to Agnes and enquired after Sam.

'How is he doing there? It was a fine school when I was there. Strict, I grant you, but fair. How is he at mathematics? I remember that was my best subject. I loved figures. Still do.'

After dealing with all his questions about Sam, Agnes turned the conversation to her own efforts at the workhouse and he listened attentively as he sipped his tea which the maid had brought in the best china tea set, which was only brought from storage in the boxroom when George was at home.

Harriet made her excuses and returned to her room. Jasper, ignoring Agnes's advice, was curled up on the bed but when Harriet threw herself down beside him, he awoke in a fright and fled from the room. For a while she sat hunched in self-pity but then scenes from the workhouse infirmary slipped back into her consciousness and she felt ashamed. Daisy Pritty would no doubt love to be in her shoes, she reminded herself, with or without a doting father.

'And I'll be married soon and gone away to London.' Harriet tossed her head. 'So what do I care about Papa . . . and his beastly mathematics!'

In defiant mood she fetched pen and paper and began a letter to Marcus, asking that their wedding be celebrated as soon as possible but her heart wasn't in it and in a fit of dejection, she eventually tore it into shreds and hurled it around the room.

Four

The desk was stuffed with papers, files and ledgers and Phineas stared at them with ill-concealed dismay before sitting down in front of them once again.

'God what a mess!' he muttered. 'How did he ever find anything? He should have been struck off for mismanagement!' Tentatively he reached into the top drawer and extracted a sheaf of forms. Copies of ancient prescriptions. He tried the second drawer and discovered letters written to his stepfather in a multitude of different styles, mostly clumsy and misspelled. Glancing briefly at a few of them, he rolled his eyes in despair. *Deer Doctor . . . Dewtifuly . . . graitfully yours . . .*

'All this money spent on schooling,' he grumbled, '– and the lower classes are as dull as ditchwater! Dunderheads! How on earth are we managing to build an empire?'

He began to drop the papers into the waste-paper basket which stood to the right of the desk. He found Christmas cards and letters – and even saucy postcards from Bognor. He went out into the kitchen, where his mother was preparing supper and held up the postcard.

'Who did Father know in Bognor?' He picked up a slice of raw carrot and crunched it noisily.

She glanced at it and smiled. 'That would be the Barkers, our old neighbours. They spend a week there every summer and always send a card.'

'But why on earth keep a postcard from Bognor?!'

She smiled. 'You know what a hoarder he was, Phin. Did you find what you were looking for?'

'Hard to tell – it's such a mess.'

'If not then it's with the solicitor – or maybe the bank.'

Phineas returned to the small room adjoining the surgery

60

which his stepfather had used as an office. He had already searched the bureau without finding the will and his mood darkened. Who in his right mind kept his affairs in such a state? Not that he could entirely blame his stepfather since he had died from an accident but a professional man should manage his affairs in a professional way and should have made preparation in case of an early demise.

Sitting down again, he pulled open the bottom drawer and yet more papers met his appalled gaze. He withdrew a handful and leafed through them, idly at first but with increasing agitation. Butcher's bills, coal bills, a reminder from his mother's dressmaker, a last warning from the tiler who had repaired the roof, a sharply worded note from a moneylender . . . Phineas closed his eyes and groaned. Unpaid bills! It was the last thing he expected to find.

He reread the note, gathered up a handful of bills then took them out to the kitchen. He tossed the bills on to the kitchen table and said, 'Listen to this, Mother! *"Dear Mr Chisom, The interest on your loan is now outstanding and I see from our records that it is now nine weeks since you have made payment of any kind. It is my reluctant duty to remind you that we will take action through the courts to recover this debt unless you make a considerable payment within one calendar week."* We're in debt, Mother. Did you know about this?'

They stared at one another in horror. Slowly his mother put down the glass dish she was holding and picked up one or two of the outstanding bills. Then she sat down on the nearest chair. 'In debt? No! I – I don't believe it.'

Phineas glanced at the date. 'This was sent eighteen months ago.'

'So what did he do?' she stammered.

'Probably borrowed from someone else to repay it?'

'But what was the money for, Phin?'

'Don't ask me, Mother. I was abroad eighteen months ago. Did you have any major expenses?'

'Not that I know of but he was very generous. Always willing to help an unfortunate. People used to write to him. He sent his aunt two shillings on her birthday without fail.'

'Very generous, I'm sure!'

'Oh Phin, don't talk that way. He was very good to me, too. And you, Phin. He sent you to Italy to study medicine, didn't he, *and* he adopted you when we married, remember. He meant to see that you were well provided for.'

'He left me his debts by the look of it!' Phineas knew he was being unkind but he felt deeply aggrieved. The chances for his future prosperity were dwindling rapidly and he was fighting down a deep fear. Without money he would never make a decent marriage and without connections his prospects were less than rosy.

His mother wasn't listening. 'He bought me those pearls and we had that holiday at Deauville . . . *Deauville!*' Her eyes widened as a thought occurred to her. 'But no! That's nonsense.'

'What is?' He looked at her sharply.

'We went to the races at Deauville.' She faltered. 'Your father did sometimes have a little flutter on the horses – but he *always* won!'

'Nobody *always* wins! They lose most of the time.'

'Oh no, dear. He would have told me.'

'For heaven's sake, Mother! I'm telling you. Nobody always wins. You cannot be so naïve.'

She regarded him earnestly. 'I mean it, Phin. He was very good at it. He said he had an eye for a good runner.' Her face crumpled. 'Oh dear! You don't think . . .'

He sat down heavily. 'I'm afraid I *do*! He didn't tell you when he lost, Mother, and so he got into debt. God! This is a nightmare!'

The silence lengthened until she said, 'But he may have settled them all. How do we know he still owes money?'

'We shall soon find out because now that he's dead the creditors will write to us demanding settlement. The stark truth is that he spent more than he earned and we are going to suffer for his extravagances. Doctors do not earn large sums of money,' he said wearily. 'You don't think he would have been involved with the workhouse unless he needed the extra money.'

His mother shook her head at this. 'Oh no, dear! He did it

from a sense of duty. They pay a pittance, you know, and it is hardly a prestigious appointment! Doctor Grantney wouldn't touch it with a barge pole but his wife has family money!'

'And we don't.' Restless, he stood up again. 'All the more important to find his will – if he made one.'

'Oh, I'm sure he did make a will, Phin. He was very sensible like that.'

'Very sensible? Of course he wasn't sensible! He was stupid. You should never have married him. I told you at the time but you wouldn't listen.'

'But that was twelve years ago. You were only a boy, Phin.'

'I was sixteen and more worldly than you'll ever be!'

Her eyes filled with tears. 'But what was I to do, Phin? I was a young widow with failing health and a son to bring up. Your dear father, God rest his soul, was young when he died. He loved us dearly but he left me with nothing but a three-year-old son. I was penniless, Phin. Should we have ended up in the workhouse? I doubt you would have liked that. I *had* to remarry.'

'We could have gone back to your family.'

She hesitated then said quietly, 'My parents wouldn't have us. They disapproved of your father.'

Angrily he crossed to the door then paused. 'Then you should have made a better choice of a second husband. It looks as though he has squandered what money there was and has left us in a Goddamned mess!'

'Oh, Phin dear! *Don't* speak ill of the dead.' Tears sprang into her eyes and trickled down her plump cheeks. 'He always meant well by us.'

He was fighting back angry words but his mood was unforgiving. 'Meant well? *Meant well!* It's not enough!' he snapped and the sound of her sobs followed him as he returned reluctantly to his self-imposed task in the office.

He opened a few letters at random. Begging letters from friends and acquaintances.

Dear Mr Chisom, You will recall that you were kind enough to lend me half a guinea when I was out of

63

work with my stomach. A similar sum at the present
time would tide me over as I am forced to stay at home
and nurse my wife who is dying of consumption . . .

He crumpled the sheet into a ball and tossed it into the
waste-paper basket. Where was the will? Maybe there were
some shares – anything of value. He felt perspiration on
his forehead and wiped it away angrily. He was sorry he
had spoken harshly to his mother but he was gripped by a
growing sense of desperation. What were they going to do?
Phineas groaned aloud. Everything could be blamed on an
accident of birth. His father had been a young and handsome
actor and his mother an infatuated girl. Star-crossed lovers!
No wonder his grandparents had disapproved.

Half an hour later he had found no will nor anything to
raise his spirits. The he drew out a large folder tied with string
and read the faint copperplate inscription. His stepfather's old
medical records going back for years. Inside the pages were
browning with age and the writing faded but just readable.
He groaned as he began to skim through them.

On Friday morning Harriet set out with Izzie to do the
shopping because Agnes had decided to make one of her
unexpected visits to the workhouse to satisfy herself that all
was in order. The day was fine so far but there were clouds
in the south-west which threatened rain later. The two young
women dawdled, appreciating their freedom and enjoying the
sights and smells of the harbour as they passed. Maybourne,
on the southern coast, was not a large town but the colourful
harbour on the eastern side was a popular area with locals and
holidaymakers alike, serving the local fishing fleet as well as
being deep enough for medium-sized merchant ships. The
large quayside was well equipped and properly organized.
Barrels, crates of fruit, bales of cloth and stacks of timber
were familiar sights and the air was always scented with a
mixture of spices, fish and wood amid a bustle of activity
as the dockhands laboured to load or unload cargoes and
seagulls swooped and dived on the fishy entrails which were
tossed overboard around the fishing boats.

At the far end of a long promenade, well away from the commercial aspects of the port, a long sandy beach attracted a growing number of holidaymakers. This area was highlighted by the long row of gaudily painted bathing huts and the waiting horses which would be used to pull them into the shallow water so that bathers could enter the water discreetly away from lascivious or mocking eyes. By the middle of June, the holiday season was well under way and the town was thronged with strangers enjoying the bracing sea air and everything else that the seaside town had to offer.

Harriet and Izzie, each armed with a shopping basket, arrived at the beach. They slowed even further as they set foot on the promenade and prepared to enjoy a leisurely walk. When George Burnett was at home there was always an atmosphere of restraint about the house which was felt by family and servants alike. Now Izzie scurried along cheerfully beside Harriet, pleased that they could talk freely.

'So when's young Master Sammy coming home?' she asked, sidestepping to avoid a Bath chair being pushed by a young man in a boater and striped blazer. 'Cook wants to do baked apple 'specially for him, stuffed with dates and dried cherries the way he likes them.'

'A few more weeks from now,' Harriet told her. 'Sadly, Papa will be back at sea by then but he may arrange a school visit. He likes to see Sam whenever he can.'

'It's only natural, isn't it. Cook says he was so proud when young Master Sammy was born. The master was home, not like when you were born. Cook says he went away before they knew you were on the way and he came home to find you there. A bit of a shock, you see. But with young Master Sammy he was pacing up and down the parlour, waiting for his first cry! He went into the kitchen and said, "I have a son, thank the Lord!" and gave all the servants a glass of Madeira!'

'Did he!' It was not a question.

Harriet stopped and leaned on the railings that overlooked the beach. Immediately below her she saw three young men, each armed with a fly-swatter, lying full-length on the sands. So far they had not removed a single item of clothing but had tilted their hats over their eyes and appeared oblivious to the screaming children who ran to and fro and occasionally jumped over their legs. Small girls and boys paddled in the sea their clothes hitched up to avoid the waves. A woman walked among the crowds, selling toffee apples. The women sheltered beneath parasols and the men stared at the sea from beneath their hats, occasionally running a finger round their collars to loosen them.

Izzie joined Harriet and said, 'Do you ever take to the water, Miss Harriet?'

'Never. I cannot fancy it, somehow, and I know Mama would disapprove. But I have tried the warm spa bath and that was very pleasant. Mama says a nicer class of people use the spa baths.'

'My uncle works for a man that goes in the sea regular.' Izzie put up a hand to shade her eyes from the sun. 'Hires a bathing machine, nips down the steps into the water and Bob's your uncle, as they say! He can't swim, of course, but he splashes about. Reckons it does him good. Tones him up, whatever that means . . . Ooh, look! Here come the donkeys. I had a ride once when I was a littl'un. Sixpence, it was, and my grandpa give it to me. Lovely, it was. I can still smell that funny donkey smell! All warm and furry. And wobbling along, terrified of falling off!'

She laughed and Harriet managed a smile but Izzie's careless words earlier had spoiled her mood and she felt unreasonably depressed.

They had just resumed their walk in the direction of the market when Harriet felt a tap on her shoulder. Turning, she was astonished to see Godfrey Lester's smiling face.

'Mr Lester!' she gasped. 'What an amazing coincidence! What are you doing here?'

Izzie was gaping at him and he gave her a quick nod.

He said, 'I'm walking for my health – a habit I adopted recently. I needn't ask you where you are going for I see the shopping baskets.' He was looking at her with great intensity and Harriet could read the message in his eyes which she translated as, Please get rid of the maid!

'Izzie, perhaps you should hurry on ahead,' she suggested breathlessly. 'I think you have the list of vegetables required.

66

Don't buy the best potatoes because they are going to be mashed. You can meet me at the butcher's in twenty minutes.'

Izzie, startled, opened her mouth to protest that leaving her young mistress with a strange man was hardly right. Meeting Harriet's gaze, however, she changed her mind and said, 'Yes, miss!'

Disappointment rang in her voice but Harriet hardened her heart. A few moments alone with Godfrey on the seafront was quite an adventure and it would punish Izzie for her hurtful remarks about her father's excitement at Sam's birth.

As soon as they were alone Godfrey grinned. 'Forgive the lie,' he said. 'I'm not really taking a constitutional. I just wanted to see you again and thought you might be out shopping. It's . . . It's very good to see you again. Extremely good.'

'And to see you!' Harriet could hardly speak for excitement. Meeting a young man on the seafront was hardly decent especially when the young woman concerned was promised to another man. 'How is Great-Uncle Robert?'

'Does it matter?' He leaned closer and whispered. 'I didn't come after you to talk about your great-uncle.'

So he had 'come after her'! Harriet's pulse quickened alarmingly. 'I suppose not,' she whispered.

He slid an arm through hers. 'May I?'

She should have said, 'No,' but she didn't. Instead she nodded wordlessly and trembled at the warmth of his arm and the nearness of his body.

'Shall we walk towards the pier? Then at least you are going in the right direction. That was your maid, I take it.'

'Izzie. She's a good girl.'

'Will she say anything – about us?'

'Not if I bribe her to silence!' She laughed.

'I had to see you again, Harriet. Are you annoyed with me? Did I do wrong?'

'No . . . I wanted to see you again.'

Harriet felt as though she were floating, hardly aware that her feet touched the ground. She was with Godfrey and that was all that mattered.

He said, 'Will you be coming again to visit the old man?'

'I'll try but Mama is already suspicious.'

'We could meet here on the promenade one evening or afternoon – or is that too much to hope?'

Harriet was lost for words. Confusion robbed her of coherent speech as she wrestled with her conscience. This was quite definitely wrong. She was going to marry Marcus and she hadn't told Godfrey, which meant she was misleading Godfrey *and* betraying Marcus's trust. She stammered, 'Meet here? Why not?'

'We could go to the show on the pier. The Pierrots! I'd be honoured to buy you a ticket.'

'Oh Godfrey!' Going to the pier concert with him would be wonderful but out of the question. Mama would be horrified if she even suggested it and Papa would never allow it. Not that he cared, she thought bitterly. He was too concerned about Sammy, his longed-for son! Would he even notice what his daughter was doing? Perhaps she could sneak away from the house when her parents went to Winchester to visit Sammy. She would pretend sickness and then miraculously recover and hurry into the town to meet Godfrey, but that would have to be in the middle of the day . . . but she knew about matinee performances. Was it possible?

'I'd love to,' she told him, 'but it would have to be a secret between us. My parents would never approve. They . . . They think the pier rather vulgar.'

'I'm sure it is but—'

'I don't think it's vulgar.'

'You don't?'

She laughed tremulously. 'The truth is I have no idea. I've never been.'

'Born and bred in Maybourne and never been to the pier? Then we'll walk there right now.'

It seemed the matter had been settled. They talked about the how and when and made plans. Still Harriet said nothing about Marcus. The pier was a cheerful, noisy place but Harriet enjoyed every minute of her visit. When time was up and she had to go to meet Izzie, Godfrey was reluctant to let her go.

'Not without a kiss,' he whispered. 'I've been thinking of nothing else ever since I first set eyes on you!'

A kiss! 'Godfrey! No!' Instinctively she took a step backward, shocked by the speed of events. She thought suddenly of Daisy and her young blades. Was this how dire events started – carried away on a rush of enthusiasm? Giddy with excitement and longing?

At once he was all contrition. 'Oh Harriet! Please forgive me. That was crass. Of course I cannot ask such a thing. Don't be offended. I take it back unreservedly! Please say you forgive me.'

They stood in the middle of the pavement as the holidaymakers surged past them. A child on a scooter collided with Godfrey and a small elderly dog pottered between them as they stood staring at each other.

'I forgive you. Don't apologize.'

'But I must. Whatever must you think of me? I'm not usually so forward but . . . Harriet, the truth is I can't stop thinking about you. Imagining . . . 'He drew a deep breath and his expression left nothing undeclared. He leaned towards her.

Harriet knew she shouldn't allow him to kiss her but she found herself unable to resist.

That evening Agnes grumbled about Izzie. 'The silly creature bought the wrong potatoes and too many parsnips. You must remember to keep an eye on her, Harriet. She cannot be trusted to shop on her own.'

'Did she – did she say anything?'

'About what exactly?'

'Oh, nothing'

'We've been invited to the Wellbury's tomorrow. Now that your father is home they want to celebrate the betrothal. They are full of plans for the wedding and we must agree a date . . . Harriet, did you hear me?'

'Yes, Mama.' Harriet wondered what they had been talking about.

'So wear your spring lilac and if you wish, I will lend you my pearl earrings.'

'Thank you, Mama.'

Agnes gave her a sharp look. 'You don't sound very enthusiastic, Harriet. Is anything the matter?'

'Of course not. I have a slight headache, that's all.'

'You poor dear. It has been a rather close day. Maybe a storm is on the way. Your father and I are planning a visit to Winchester to visit Sam, and Papa thought you might like to come along. We may stay over at a hotel. Your father sails again three weeks from today.'

Harriet found it difficult to speak. Why was fate conspiring to help her in her wrongdoing? She said, 'I think I would come with you – unless I stand in for you at the workhouse. I'd like to become more involved.' She almost shivered with guilt and shame. Was she adding hypocrisy to her other sins?

Agnes hesitated but then she smiled. 'What a generous thought, Harriet. We'll talk about it nearer the time but meanwhile, why not go and lie down. A rest might ease your headache. Pull the curtains to darken the room.'

Obediently, Harriet escaped to her bedroom but she didn't lie down. Instead she took out her diary and wrote three and a half pages about Godfrey.

The Wellburys lived in a large, beautifully designed house, Maybourne Manor, which had been in the family since Sir Charles Wellbury sold a successful tea plantation in Ceylon and moved back to England with his family. The neglected house had been lovingly restored, the ground round it professionally landscaped and the rest developed as a farm with plenty of woodland left for the pheasants. The present occupiers were James and his wife, Cecile, and his son, Marcus. Their older child, a daughter, was married and lived elsewhere.

By eight thirty the Wellburys and the Burnetts were seated round the large refectory table beneath the chandelier and had finished the first course of their meal – a creamy leek soup – and were chatting animatedly while the maid removed the soup bowls and discreetly brushed crumbs from the table.

Harriet did her best to join in the conversation, terrified that someone would notice her distracted manner. She felt trapped by the situation. Her perception of her marriage to Marcus, which had always been a distant event, had been changed by the prospect of his new job and the prospect of a move to London. Marcus, delighted by the turn of events, was watching her from across the table and his obvious happiness was like a knife in her heart. He was a wonderful man and she had promised to become his wife, but Godfrey filled her thoughts from the time she awoke to the time she fell asleep at night. How could she tell Marcus? And if she did, what chance was there that her parents would approve a match with Godfrey, the son of a poor housekeeper?

She smiled at Marcus, then turned to the head of the table, where his father had risen to his feet.

'This evening is one of the happiest of my life,' he told the assembled diners. 'Another was the occasion when I announced the betrothal of my daughter, who sadly couldn't be here with us tonight. She does, however, send her best wishes to all of us and especially to Harriet and Marcus, who before too long will be husband and wife.'

Agnes glanced at Harriet, who, heart thumping, pretended not to notice and kept her gaze firmly on their host. Cecile was smiling at her son, who reached across the table and gave his mother's hand a reassuring squeeze.

James went on. 'Before the night is done, we hope our respective children will agree a suitable date for the wedding.'

George said, 'Hear hear! And about time!' and everyone laughed except Harriet who smiled at no one in particular.

James said, 'And now I believe my son wants to say something. Something important!' and sat down.

Harriet froze as Marcus rose to his feet. In his hand he held a small box that could only contain one thing. He walked round the table and stood before Harriet. 'My dearest Harriet, you have kindly consented to be my wife and to make me the happiest man on earth. I want you to have this ring to celebrate our betrothal on this happy occasion.'

Harriet tried to speak. Her mother was indicating that she should stand to accept it and she did so on trembling legs. This was the moment, Harriet told herself. Her last chance to do the decent thing and confess. It would ruin the evening and break Marcus's heart but at least she would be behaving honorably – although no one would see it in that light. She took a deep breath – but then she caught sight of her father's face and for the first time she saw real pride in his eyes as he looked at her and she recalled how thrilled he was with her approaching union. His daughter was marrying into one of the wealthiest families in Maybourne and his own standing in the community would rise accordingly. George came from less exalted stock and for him the transition was extraordinary. One day his daughter, Harriet, with her husband and children, would inherit Maybourne Manor. It was a glittering prospect in George's estimation. It seemed that at long last, by marrying Marcus, Harriet would at last meet with her father's wholehearted approval. George Burnett would finally appreciate his daughter and this was something she had always craved. Was she really going to throw it all away?

Desperate for guidance, Harriet closed her eyes and heard Cecile say, 'Oh, poor soul. She's quite overcome!'

'Harriet, dear, are you all right?' That was her mother, concern in her voice.

'It's a momentous moment!' That was James Wellbury.

George said, 'Harriet!' and there was no mistaking *his* tone.

Opening her eyes with an effort, Harriet looked into Marcus's face and saw nothing but love and hope. Finding a little courage she stammered, 'Marcus, I have to . . . Dearest Marcus I . . .' His expression changed. 'I need to talk . . .' she whispered but her father was watching her closely and she saw that a frown was gathering. He said brusquely, 'Give her the ring, man!'

Embarrassed, Agnes said, 'George!' and gave Harriet a look of deep pleading.

The Wellburys exchanged uneasy looks and Harriet's courage failed her.

Forcing a smile, she gathered her wits and with a trembling hand accepted the ring which Marcus was now offering. It was a broad gold band set with amethysts and seed pearls and with only the barest struggle she slipped it on to her finger to spontaneous applause. Marcus took her in his arms and kissed her. 'I love you!' he whispered. 'Everything will be fine!'

Blinking tears, Harriet bent to kiss her mother then straightened again. Somehow, she knew, she had to regain her composure, to dispel the hint of reluctance and impress the little gathering with her sincerity. Hopefully they would put her hesitation down to nerves and assume she was overwhelmed by the importance of the event. 'I will do my utmost to – to make Marcus as happy as he deserves to be,' she told them. 'And to be a credit to both families.'

James looked relieved and raised his glass. 'A toast to the happy couple! May their union be long and blessed with children.'

George, his face glowing, reached across the table and took Harriet's free hand in his and kissed it. The gesture almost undermined her but somehow she managed to return his smile.

As the evening continued with talk of venues and the lists to be made of guests, Harriet smiled and smiled and sipped her wine but it tasted bitter in her mouth. She found the delicious food hard to swallow and could not dispel the feeling that she was on the outside of this happy gathering looking on like a ghost at a feast. Continuing the pretence of happiness became an ever increasing strain and as the clock ticked on, Harriet began to think the evening would never end and was deeply thankful when it was time to go home.

Once there, she made her excuses and fled upstairs to her room, where she tugged off her clothes and tossed them aside and slipped into the comfort of a familiar nightdress. Throwing herself on top of the bed, she lay in a state of panic until the early hours of the next morning.

Harriet awoke on Sunday with a feverish headache and refused to get out of bed even to go to church. Sick and ashamed, she was miserably aware that, no matter what she did, she was in serious trouble. The date for the wedding had been agreed and on September the fourth she would become Mrs Marcus Wellbury. Telling Godfrey that she was betrothed meant they would no longer be able to meet away from Havely House. Not telling him meant that she would have to remove her engagement ring every time they met and that involved a deceit she could not even contemplate. She could not confide in her mother nor her father. How, she wondered wretchedly, had her life changed so dramatically? A few weeks earlier she had been happy and innocent. Now she was leading what the women's magazines described as a double life and she was full of doubts and fears. If only she had never met Godfrey! How simple her life would have been.

'But I did meet him,' she whispered, 'And I'm glad I did.' Whatever happened, she had tasted a few heady moments of the freedom she had craved – but what had it brought her! Days earlier she had been envying Daisy Pritty for her unchaperoned life on the streets and the chance to meet 'young blades' and be engaged in dangerous exploits. Now Harriet felt she would give anything to return to that placid life she had once led under the caring eyes of her mother.

The church clock struck half past eight but still she could not find the will to leave her bed. She was troubled by so many doubts. Did she really love Godfrey? She hardly knew him, so it *might* be merely infatuation. And what did he feel for her? Suppose she were to run away with Godfrey . . . Her parents might disown her! She might never see her mother or brother again and her father's wrath would be terrible.

There was a knock at the door and her mother came in. 'How are you feeling now, dear?'

'A little better, thank you, Mama.'

'It was too exciting for you.' Agnes sat on the bed and stroked Harriet's hair. 'Too sudden, although they meant well. They are very decent people. But I felt for you. I thought you were going to faint. Cecile Wellbury thinks very well of you. She told me she couldn't have chosen a better future daughter-in-law!'

'How very kind.'

'So you rest today and tomorrow we'll start making plans. The Wellburys have said we could use their garden for the wedding reception. They have two small nieces who you might like for bridesmaids.'

'I'm sure I will, Mama.'

'We must think about the guests and what you will wear and Harriet . . . Nearer to the wedding, you and I will talk about . . . about married life and what it means for a woman . . . to be dutiful, I mean. There really is nothing to fear, Harriet. I don't want worries to spoil the next few months. Getting married is the most exciting time for a young woman!' She smiled happily. 'Go back to sleep now, dear. I'll send up a light lunch around twelve o'clock.' She leaned over and kissed Harriet who suddenly clung to her.

'Mama . . . What does Papa say about . . . about the wedding? Is he truly pleased?'

'Pleased? What a funny question. Of course he is pleased.'

'He has never actually said so.'

Agnes gave a slight shrug. 'Your father is very undemonstrative, I'm afraid. But he is pleased, Harriet, and so very proud. Like a dog with two tails!'

Laughing, she left the room and Harriet was once again alone with her thoughts.

The following morning, while Harriet's fear and confusion continued, Daisy Pritty was back at work picking oakum with the other women. The wound in her shoulder throbbed but the new doctor had decided that it was hardly life-threatening and that she should resume work for two hours daily instead of three. Her fingers picked quickly at the tarred rope end and she tugged at it irritably when it resisted her efforts to separate the strands. She was thinking about Digger and now she said, 'He'll be back! He knows what's good for him.'

One of the women hooted with laughter. 'You? Good for him? You nearly got him killed!'

'I never did! They was arguing fit to bust. It was me saved his blooming life. He'll be back. You'll see.'

'Does it still hurt?'

'Course it hurts! Hurts like Hell! But I've got an idea.' Grinning, she tapped her forehead. 'I know how we can get some dosh!'

Wiping her fingers on her skirt, she reached for another strand and said sharply, 'You! Mave! D'you think you could go a bit slower! I been watching you.'

Mave, a new inmate, blushed as they all fixed her with accusing stares. 'I can't hurry. My hands are so sore.' Her eyes filled with tears. 'I've never done this kind of thing before.'

'You should have thought of that 'fore you come in here!'

At that moment an old man put his head round the door and hissed, 'There's a fella to see you, Daisy. He said to say "usual place"!'

She jumped to her feet and grinned triumphantly at the other women. 'Told you, didn't I! That'll be Digger.'

Making sure that the coast was clear, she hurried along the passage to the dining room which looked out on to the yard. Pushing up a window, she leaned out and there he was, as handsome as ever and twice as bold. Leaning out of the window Daisy gave him a resounding kiss.

'Miss me, did you?' she asked.

'What if I did? You all right now?'

'So-so! Some old duck sent her daughter along with eggs and honey and stuff. Nice cake, too. What's happened to Squinty?'

'They threw him in jail.'

'Damn his eyes!'

'He got three months. Good job you didn't croak on him. They'd have hanged him! About that house you was telling me . . . ?'

'Where I was working. Yeah. There's good pickings there if you can get in while they're out – or asleep. They keep a spare key under the flowerpot beneath the second window on the left. Or maybe the first window. Don't remember exactly. There's five in the family – mother, father and three little'uns plus a housekeeper and a couple of odd bods. Maybe a nurse for the kids . . . Maybe a handyman or a gardener. I'm not sure.'

'Not a lot of help then, is it, you doll-brain!'

'Oi!' She reached out and tugged playfully at his hair. 'Wasn't there long enough to find out, was I!'

He frowned. 'I'll try it tonight then. What have they got?'

'Ssh!' Hearing footsteps approaching, Daisy glanced quickly over her shoulder then relaxed. 'They went past. Right – what have they got? There's pewter on the sideboard that'll interest Sid Crow, silver cutlery in a big box, jewellery in the main bedroom, nice glassware . . . Good clothes in every wardrobe might be worth a bit to Old Mikey. There's money in a safe in the middle of—'

'In a safe! What d'you take me for?'

'Just telling you, that's all. Just do what you can and remember, it's fifty-fifty and no messing me around.' She leaned down and kissed him. 'Now hop it, Digger, before someone spots you or we'll both be in trouble again!'

She watched him, then closed the window and went back to her work with a smile on her face.

Five

A week later Izzie was handed a letter by the postman and took it in to Agnes, who was in the kitchen, helping Cook to pluck a pigeon.

'My hands are sticky from the feathers,' Agnes told the maid. 'Leave it on the dresser behind the big teapot. My husband will be down directly.'

'It's for you, ma'am. Not the Master.'

'For me? From Uncle Robert, I suppose.'

Izzie shook her head. 'Not his handwriting, Ma'am.'

'The Board then.'

Cook laughed. 'Sounds like a guessing game! What's the prize?'

Izzie stood her ground. ''Tis rather odd, ma'am, truth to tell. There's a red line round the edge and 'tis all in capitals. Higgledy piggledy like.'

Finally intrigued, Agnes abandoned her task and washed her hands at the sink. 'I'll take it upstairs,' she said.

As she picked up the letter she felt a frisson of unease. There certainly *was* something odd about it. Hurrying upstairs, she was about to go into her bedroom but then realized that George was still in there, dressing. Harriet's room, then. Her daughter was in the yard, brushing Jasper – but might finish at any moment and return to her room. Agnes hesitated, then went into the boxroom and closed the door quietly behind her. The small room was filled with boxes of every description – round leather hatboxes, tea chests, a bulging carpet bag, George's sea chest, wooden crates full of china left to Agnes by her mother, raffia baskets and a travelling trunk bound with copper. As her fingers fumbled with the envelope she assured herself that it was nothing to worry about. That silly girl had put fancy ideas into her head. What could she possibly have to fear from a letter? *Any* letter?

It was written on cheap paper, in a large spidery hand with occasional ink blots and something about the clumsy appearance of the capital letters made her think it was a disguised hand. Perhaps the writer, right-handed, had used his left hand. As she began to read, her own hand trembled and she drew in her breath fearfully. It was dated the twenty-seventh of June, the previous day.

> *Mrs Burnett,*
>   *Your secret is no longer safe. I know everything. Your son was your firstborn child. I suspect your husband would be surprised to know that. Perhaps you should confess all. Or should I be the one to tell him? On the other hand you may wish to buy my silence. You will need fifty guineas. Get it. You have seven days. I will write again . . .*
>   *A Well Wisher*

The letter fell from Agnes's fingers and she sank on to the sea chest. As though hypnotized, she stared at the fallen letter, reached for it, then drew back. A black mist seemed to surround her and there was a roaring sound in her ears.

'No!' she whispered. 'How could you . . . how could *anyone* know? *Who are you?*'

Her mind raced, heavy with dread. Somebody knew the truth. Suddenly, after all these years, the truth was out. It would do untold damage. George would be incandescent with rage if he even suspected . . . Poor Harriet would be ruined and even Sam would suffer. She, Agnes, would be in desperate trouble. The whole family would be destroyed unless she acted promptly.

'Fifty guineas!' she muttered. It was impossible.

Minutes passed as Agnes remained in shock, her body slumped, her thoughts as thick as treacle – she lost track of time. Eventually, however, one fact became clear in her mind. She alone could prevent the catastrophe. It was up to her to deal with the problem. That meant finding the money and paying it over to the blackmailer. Since she had no money of her own she would have to sell whatever she could as quickly and as quietly as possible. A sound outside the door made her glance up fearfully.

'Mama?' Harriet had entered the room and now stared down at her mother. 'I wondered where you were. Izzie said . . .' She took a closer look at Agnes's face and said, 'Is something wrong?'

'Nothing at all!' Agnes forced herself to her feet.

'Izzie said you had received a strange letter.'

Agnes shook her head and as she did so, stepped on to the letter to hide it from her daughter's eyes. 'Izzie is a very fanciful, silly girl. Now, let's go downstairs.'

'But the letter?'

'From the dressmaker about your wedding gown. She will be here at the beginning of next week.'

Shooing Harriet out of the room, Agnes closed the door behind them. She *must* return to collect the letter before anyone else could find it. As she went down the stairs, the shock was fading to be replaced by anger and a growing determination to save the family at all costs. There was some jewellery she could sell but she would have to go to another town where she was not known. Selling it locally would create comment and might arouse suspicion. There was also the china in the boxroom which should have gone to Harriet on her wedding day. But even that wouldn't be enough. Fifty guineas!

'Oh God!' she whispered. She had a very fine leather-bound bible tooled in gold which had been given to her by her godmother. What else? There must be more. The problem was that Agnes had no real knowledge of the value of these items and an unscrupulous person might try to cheat her. As they reached the bottom of the stairs, Harriet turned to speak to her and instinctively Agnes threw her arms around her.

'My dearest, *dearest* girl!' she cried in a voice choked with emotion. 'My darling Harriet!'

Harriet suffered the embrace then stepped back and regarded her mother anxiously. 'What is it, Mama?'

Agnes struggled to hold back tears. 'It's nothing. Nothing at all. You must think me a foolish woman but . . .'

'Mama, you have tears in your eyes!'

Desperately, Agnes cast about for an excuse for her behaviour. 'But you are soon to be married and I shall lose you!'

Harriet stared at her. 'But we shall only be in London, Mama – but if you wish, we could delay the wedding.'

Agnes was horrified. 'Delay it? Heaven's sake, Harriet! What on earth are you saying?'

'Nothing Mama'

'The wedding must go ahead as planned.'

'But I don't want you to be upset or unhappy.'

Cook appeared in the doorway holding aloft three plucked pigeons. 'They look a bit scrawny, ma'am. Should I add a bit of chopped bacon?'

'A good idea, Cook. Thank you.' Agnes turned as George came down the stairs and at the sight of him her self-control deserted her. The thought of all they had to lose closed in on her and swaying, she cried out.

He said, 'Agnes!'

And as the darkness closed in, she fell straight into his arms.

Albert Hawke had finished his mutton pie and was enjoying a smoke when he heard the bell ring in his office. Snapper immediately rushed into action, barking furiously, and Albert rearranged his features into a suitably sad expression. He brushed a little sawdust from the sleeves of his jacket, took off his apron and followed the dog through into the shop to greet his next customer.

'And how can I be of service, madam?' he asked.

He moved a chair so that the dumpy little woman could sit down and as he moved towards her, so his nose twitched. To his surprise she looked fairly cheerful and her eyes showed no sign of recent tears although her nose was pinkish.

'It's the boy,' she told him. 'Eleven or twelve years old and been unconscious for weeks. There's a name for it . . .' She sniffed hard. 'Pardon me. Got a cold from somewhere. So draughty that building . . . Yes, starved to death, I reckon, 'cos he couldn't eat or drink, poor lad. Just lay there, his eyes closed, like he was asleep but he wasn't. The new doctor was

81

amazed he'd lasted so long. Couldn't get over it!' She smiled. 'Tough little devil! That's what he called him.'

Albert was beginning to wonder if grief had affected her mind. 'Your son?' he asked gently.

'My son?' She blinked. 'Lord no! A workhouse brat.'

So that was the smell on her clothes, he thought.

She continued. 'I'm Mrs Fenner from the workhouse. I usually send the nurse down with details but she's off sick with a black eye. I think her husband knocks her about! It's a wicked world, Mr . . . ?'

'Hawke. Albert Hawke, Funeral Director and Coffin Maker. A wicked world indeed.' Albert reached for his book and a pen, feeling cheated. He was very good with grieving relatives and Mrs Fenner's attitude gave him no chance to offer his usual solicitous performance. The soft look, the lowered voice, the understanding words and the hint that he, too, had known grief and loss. Still, he had prepared coffins for Maybourne Workhouse before and would give the humble coffin as much attention as he could. The pay was poor but the work was easy. A few planks knocked together. He might even have a spare in stock. 'His name, please.'

She pursed her lips. 'I did know it . . . Frederick something . . . Can't remember. We always called him "the boy".'

'We shall need a name and date of birth if anyone knows it . . . So when shall I call round to take the measurements?'

'There's no need for that. He was about this long . . .' She held out her hands by way of demonstration. 'Only a boy. What d'you think? Five feet? Four and a half? Coma! That's the word! Very nasty. You don't want to catch that! That's what he had. It won't need to be very wide 'cos he's so thin. Like a rake. No flesh on his bones.'

'I'd prefer to measure for myself, Mrs Fenner. Even for the basic coffin. Please tell the Workhouse Master I'll call in tomorrow. Mr Crane, isn't it? I need to know if he wants a lining in the coffin. And we do now have a very suitable funeral carriage to transport the deceased to the—'

Mrs Fenner blew her nose noisily. 'A lining? Shouldn't think so and I expect some of the inmates'll carry the coffin

82

round to the church the same as usual. No fuss for paupers. I fear. Now me, I appreciate fuss. Specially at a funeral. Horses, black plumes on their heads. Jingling bells on their manes. A lovely sight, that is.' She gazed round the small office and Albert hoped she was admiring the sample headstone and the large photograph of an elaborate funeral involving a road full of black-draped carriages, plumed horses and at least twenty men in black accompanying the coffin.

'Who was that?' she asked.

'Our late departed mayor,' Albert told her proudly. 'Some years ago now. It was a lavish affair but I'm proud to say I was responsible for part of it. I myself made the coffin. Beautiful oak, French polished, lead-lined.' He wrote again, then straightened up. 'No headstone, I suppose.'

She frowned. 'I think the Master said something about a small iron cross.'

'Ah yes. Well, I'll call tomorrow morning at . . .' He consulted his diary. 'At eleven. Be assured of my best attention.'

They both stood.

'Good day to you, Mrs Fenner.'

On the way out she sneezed expansively and as soon as she had gone Albert propped the door open to rid the room of the workhouse smell.

Later that afternoon Albert examined the spare coffin shells and found one that would probably fit a boy of eleven to twelve years and he was dusting it out when he heard the shop door jangle. Fourth time in one day, he marvelled. Business was brisk.

'It's me again. Daisy Pritty.'

Albert felt ridiculously pleased to see her again. 'So I see! How's your ankle?'

'I'll live – no thanks to your poxy dog.'

'What's up with your shoulder?'

'Bit of an accident.'

He grinned. This was an unexpected pleasure. With any luck she might stay a bit longer this time. He said, 'Come to arrange your funeral?'

'Very funny!' She tossed her head then gave him a sly look. 'Like to see me laid out, would you, Mr Hawke?'

83

Albert reddened. He was shocked. Swallowing awkwardly, he cleared his throat. 'So what do you want, Miss Pritty?'

'It's about the boy. Mrs Fenner was here earlier.'

'*That* boy.'

She leaned closer. 'I want him to have a silk lining in his coffin. But don't tell no one. They'll want to know where the silk come from and I don't want to say. D'you understand?'

'Ah!' He looked at her curiously. 'And you're going to pay for this silk, are you?'

She shook her head. 'I'm going to give you the silk – but only if you swear to keep quiet about it. Unless you want to get me chucked into gaol.'

Oh dear. He might have known the young woman was trouble. 'You're going to steal it, are you?'

'No! You promise, then I'll fetch it.'

Rashly Albert promised. There was something about the girl that aroused his curiosity and it wasn't just the pretty ankle he had glimpsed on her earlier visit. There was an archness in her tone which he didn't care for although he found it exciting but there was something else – a refreshing honesty. What you see is what you get, he thought. Although honesty was probably not the right word, he reflected, if her comments about the silk were anything to go by. More than anything he wanted to prolong her stay.

He pulled out a handkerchief and pretended to mop his brow. 'Hot today. I was just going to pour myself a glass of ale. Want one?'

'Don't mind.'

'Come through into the yard. We can chat for a minute or two.'

'You haven't promised – about the silk.'

'I promise.'

'Right then!' To his surprise she bent forward and lifted up her skirts. Below the plain serge skirt she was wearing a beautiful blue silk petticoat decorated with white and gold embroidery. Even Albert, knowing little of women's clothes, could see that it was an expensive garment. So she had stolen it! He, Albert Hawke, was knowingly receiving stolen property! He smiled nervously, then his eyes widened as she slipped it down to her ankles, stepped out of it then gathered it up into a roll. She handed it to him, still warm from her body. 'Make it real good,' she instructed. 'I want pleats and things. Pad it out a bit. I want him to rest comfortable on it.'

'A friend of yours, was he?'

'Hardly. He was out for the count when they brought him in off the street. No mother. No father. Lord knows where he came from. We kept waiting for him to wake up.' She shrugged. 'Least I know I did have a mother 'cos I can remember how she smelled. Like soap. Nice soap. She died soon after we was taken in to the workhouse. I was only a littl'un. Didn't know any better. Played with the other kids . . .'

Albert wanted to comfort her but instead he said, 'Right, well, I'll make a very nice lining for your young friend's coffin. There'll be enough silk to pad out the lid and if you like I'll make a small pillow for his head. And I won't charge you because Snapper bit your ankle. How would that do?'

She beamed at him. 'You're a darling, you are!'

Then she threw her arms round his neck and kissed him.

Two days later, Wednesday, Harriet and her father sat opposite each other on the train as it rattled and swayed towards Winchester. George's visit to his son had been arranged for three o'clock, when Sam would be excused lessons and they would take him out to tea in a shop in the town. Agnes should have accompanied her husband but she had claimed sickness and nominated Harriet in her place. Harriet had been reluctant because she had been secretly planning a visit to Havely House but without revealing this, she had no reason not to go to Winchester. Sitting beside the window, watching the windswept scenery pass, she was reconciled to the idea. She missed her brother and sharing a pot of tea and cream cakes had a certain appeal.

Throughout the journey her father had said very little because the carriage was full and the noise made conversation difficult. A man with a restless boxer dog gave the animal a constant stream of commands which the dog ignored. A woman read from the Bible to a bored little girl and two young men discussed the state of the country in a way that was obviously meant to impress their fellow travellers. A woman with five unruly children sat nearby but Harriet, busy with her own thoughts, was able to block out all extraneous sounds. Suddenly, however, when the unruly family left the train, her father suddenly leaned forward.

'I'm rather worried about your mother, Harriet. She seems very confused these last few days. Do you know what I mean? Have you noticed a change in her?'

Harriet frowned. Had she? Had she noticed *anything* that was going on around her? 'I don't think so, Papa. Confused, you say?'

'Yes. There's a certain vagueness to her manner. It takes her a few seconds to answer a simple question as though she cannot properly grasp what is being said. Or perhaps her thoughts are elsewhere. Has she made any new acquaintances, for example. Or . . . or met someone from her past?'

'I don't think so.' Harriet stared at him uneasily. Where were these questions leading? she wondered. And was her father avoiding her gaze? He was leaning forward with his elbows on his knees with his chin resting on his hands. He did not once look up at her.

He went on. 'I'm sure I'm not imagining it. I wondered if there have been signs of this before, while I was at sea.'

Harriet hesitated. Perhaps her mother *had* been a little more distracted of late and somewhat unpredictable. What was it she had said not so long ago? 'You wicked girl! If you only knew!' Harriet had pushed that particular memory to the back of her mind but now she thought it very strange. But should she tell her father? Considering the little attention he paid her, Harriet decided against it. It would be a secret between herself and her mother. She said cautiously, 'Mama is always nervous when you're away. I daresay it takes a few days for her to adjust to your being home.'

'I thought she had been crying yesterday, but she denied it. Is her health satisfactory? Would she tell you if it were not so?'

Harriet regarded him guiltily. If her mother *was* distressed for some reason, then Harriet had been too selfishly wrapped up in her own affairs to notice.

'Perhaps it is the wedding, Papa.'

He shook his head. 'She never was one for confidences. Agnes is a very independent woman and usually very strong . . . Her mother, though, was something of a creaking gate.'

Harriet could not remember her grandmother but knew the old lady had been bedridden for years for no good reason and against the doctor's wishes. Her much younger husband had cared for her until he wore himself out and died at fifty. Then his wife had left her bed and resumed a normal life.

'Oh no!' cried Harriet. 'Mama is nothing like Grandmother in that way. She is too involved in the workhouse to even consider taking to her bed.'

The train was slowing down and, with a rush of steam and a screech of brakes, it slid into Winchester station and Harriet's conversation with her father came to an abrupt end.

An hour later the three of them sat in the Copper Kettle Tea Shop while the waitress brought a tray of tea and a large plate of cakes. Sam beamed at his sister. There were rock cakes, slices of currant cake, éclairs, jam tarts and iced buns.

George said, 'Your sister must choose first, Samuel.'

'Of course, Papa.' Sam pushed the plate towards Harriet, who, knowing his tastes, chose a jam tart. 'Papa?'

George took a slice of currant cake and cut it carefully into three equal pieces. Samuel took an éclair and bit into it with a contented sigh.

Ignoring his cake, George rested his clasped hands on the chintz tablecloth and smiled at his son. 'Your housemaster seems satisfied with your progress, Samuel, I'm happy to say.'

'Thank you, Papa.' Sam took another bite.

Harriet poured the tea.

'Your report is favourable also. An average mark for English grammar. Very good at mathematics. I was too, you know. Third in my class in fact.' He waited.

Harriet said, 'Well done, Papa!'

Her father continued. 'You are promising in Latin. A poor grasp of composition in art but that's of no consequence . . . "He shows an interest in botany." Not bad at all, Samuel.

You've obviously worked hard.' He frowned. 'Geography – fair. Don't gobble that éclair, Samuel. Grove Court feeds its pupils well enough, as I recall.'

'They don't, Papa!' Sam chewed quickly and swallowed. 'We never have second helpings – only the senior boys do – and when it's custard tart—'

Harriet gave him a warning look.

Sam caught her meaning but pressed on with his complaint. 'Well, it's jolly well not fair. We're still growing, Papa, and they—'

'Thank you, Samuel! We are talking about your progress, which is the purpose of this visit. Grove Court is an expensive school and you are there to receive an education. A *good* education. Second helpings of custard tart are not really relevant.'

Harriet was aware of the familiar pang of resentment. Her own education had been considered unimportant by comparison. She had attended a small private school locally where she had excelled at history, art and English composition but her father had never even enquired about her progress. At least not to her knowledge.

He straightened up and reached for his teacup. Harriet winked at her brother, who grinned.

Harriet said, 'Would you like another cake, Sam?'

'Yes, please!' His hand shot out and the deed was done before George could raise any objection.

Harriet said, 'I think I'll join you, Sam. They are delicious. Thank you, Papa, for this little treat.' She gave her brother a meaningful look.

'Yes,' Sam said quickly. 'Thank you very much, Papa.'

George made no answer but began at last to eat his currant cake, chewing each mouthful carefully. 'I spoke to your sports master, Mr Bragg, who was not particularly impressed. I was in the cricket team in my day but you, apparently, are too slow and show little aptitude for the game. That *is* rather disappointing.'

Sam smiled cheerfully, uncrushed by this criticism. 'I'm a good runner, though, Papa, and I enjoy the cross-country events.' He was nibbling carefully around the edges of an iced bun, saving the cherry until last.

While three cakes remained on the plate, their father declared the meal at an end and called for the bill.

Harriet whispered, 'Never mind, Sam. We brought you a chocolate cake which Cook made for you and I've handed it in to matron. You can collect it later today!'

They delivered him back to the school and found the hansom cab waiting to take them to the station. George was deep in thought and for once Harriet didn't resent his silence. Tomorrow she would go to visit Great-Uncle Robert and would see Marcus.

As soon as her husband and daughter had left for the station, Agnes rose from her bed, pulled on her summer coat and went downstairs. Izzie, polishing the dining-room table, looked up in surprise. 'Feeling better, ma'am?'

'Yes, thank you.' She was not prepared to bandy words with the servants. 'I do not want my husband or daughter to know that I went out. Is that clear?'

'Yes, ma'am!'

'Tell Cook. I have private business to attend to and . . . and it is no one's business but mine.'

If anyone betrayed her, Agnes vowed, it would be instant dismissal. Collecting a basket she had filled earlier, she hurried outside and made her way to the bus stop. When the bus arrived, the blinkered horse stood shaking its head, disturbed by the gusting wind, while a handful of passengers dismounted. As she found a seat, her heart was beating erratically and she actually felt as ill as she had pretended to be earlier. This trip must be the last. She could never go through these agonies of mind again. Closing her eyes, she prayed that no one would see her and that her blackmailer would be satisfied. She could never ask her husband for help.

Arriving at the next town, Agnes climbed carefully down the narrow stairs and stepped on to the pavement. This particular shop had quality antiques in the window and Agnes hoped she could interest them in her own items.

A middle-aged man greeted her. 'Madam?'

'I have some items I would like to sell.' She glanced nervously round the shop, fearful that by some unlucky

89

chance, she would be seen by a friend or acquaintance. She unwrapped a teapot with trembling hands and saw his eyes light up with interest.

'Spode!' He took it gently, turning it this way and that, watching it with narrowed but appreciative eyes. 'That's very nice. Do you have any more of the set?'

'A complete service. I also want to sell this bible – if I can get a good price for it . . .' She handed it to him and he took it reverently. Agnes had no way of knowing if she could trust this man but if he intended to resell the items he would know that *she* would know if the resale price exceeded the purchase by an indecent amount. The other risk was that he would underestimate the items through genuine ignorance.

'I also have a brooch.' This was gold in the shape of a rose and the flower itself was studded with rubies. He was still examining the bible.

'I see this has been in your family for many years. Are you sure you want to part with it? I ask because people do sometimes change their minds only to find they are too late and the treasured object has been sold.'

'Needs must,' she muttered, embarrassed by his kindness.

'I see. The bible is beautifully crafted. Exquisite lettering, an uncracked spine and first-class leather.' He put it down on his desk and took the brooch from her. For Agnes, the waiting seemed interminable.

'I suggest we go into my office with these items,' he said at last, 'and I will work out a price for each of them.'

Agnes followed him into a small cluttered room and was offered a chair. The man sent his assistant into the shop and seated himself behind the desk. He found a magnifying glass and studied the brooch. 'The rubies are not first class, I'm afraid, but the brooch in its entirety is very attractive . . . I might even say highly desirable. Now let me see.' He found a pencil and made a few jottings in his notebook. 'You have a whole set of the Spode? Nothing cracked or damaged in any way?'

'Twelve of everything,' Agnes agreed. 'And no damage. We have always been afraid to use it!'

'Very wise, if I may say so.'

90

He wrote again, then handed her the notebook. Agnes read:

One leather-bound bible (hand tooled) – £4
One rose-design brooch with rubies – £6
One tea service, Spode (57 pieces) – £32
Total £42
Collection of crockery if desired by arrangement at a
small cost

Agnes felt her throat dry with disappointment. The black-mailer had demanded fifty guineas for his silence. 'I'm sorry,' she stammered. 'I need more than that. I need fifty guineas. I'll have to try elsewhere.'

'You're looking for fifty?' He shook his head. 'I really can't improve on that offer. All I could say is that if you wanted to offer the brooch to a jeweller as opposed to an antique dealer, you might get a better price but I doubt if you would get another eight pounds.'

'I see. Thank you.' She didn't know what to do. It had taken all her energies to get this far. Another eight pounds. What else could she sell?

He went on. 'You might get slightly better prices in Maybourne. A bigger town attracts . . .'

'Maybourne? Oh no!'

He nodded slowly and she was mortified to see compassion in his eyes. Abruptly she held out her hand. 'Would my engagement ring make up the difference? I could say I'd lost it. They're good diamonds. It is insured against loss.'

He hesitated. 'If your husband claims on the insurance when it isn't lost, he would be committing a crime. You must bear that in mind. It makes no difference to me because I should be buying in good faith and the ring isn't stolen. But if your husband believes it to be lost then he could justifiably—'

'I don't care!' cried Agnes, her voice almost breaking. If she sat there any longer, humiliated and afraid, she might well burst into tears and that would be the last straw. All Agnes wanted to do now was to go home and crawl back into bed. She would suffer any problems later if she could only end the present nightmare on which she had embarked. She tugged at the ring and tossed it on to the desk. 'Take it, please. Take it all and give me fifty pounds.' She stood up, greatly agitated. The walls of the shop seemed to crowd in on her and she was desperate to get outside where she could breathe again. 'I have to go home now. Will you please make a decision.'

Eyeing her somewhat warily, he picked up the ring and examined it carefully. 'I can make you a total offer of fifty three pounds and I—'

'I accept!' She sat down again and her mind began to function once more. 'It will have to be in cash,' she told him. 'No cheques and – and you will have to collect the china Sunday morning while the family is at church. Ten o'clock to be exact.'

He opened his mouth to protest but seeing Agnes's expression, nodded instead and asked for her address. When she had given it, she said, 'You must ask for me and if for any reason whatsoever I am not there you must immediately go away again and I will be in touch to arrange another day. You must not discuss the purpose of your visit with any member of the household.'

After exacting a promise to that effect, Agnes ran down the road, back to the bus stop on the other side of the road. This time she had to wait for one to arrive but she breathed slowly in and out, regaining her composure. Only she knew how perilously close she had come to losing control. She had been on the point of collapse but now she was recovering. She was going to pay off her tormentor and save the family from ruin. In her hands she clutched her purse containing twenty-three pounds. The rest would come on Sunday when the rest of the china was collected.

Sitting on top of the bus on her way home, while her heart still battered against her ribs, Agnes smiled faintly. She had done it. Unaided, she had dealt with a major problem and no one need know anything about it. Closing her eyes, she made a conscious effort to relax and by the time she returned home she felt happier. She went straight upstairs, lay down on the bed and slept for three and a half hours.

Six

Three days later, Harriet announced that she was going to Havely House and would be back before midday. Both her parents appeared distracted and uneasy and neither bothered to ask any searching questions about her proposed visit and she, for one, was glad to be out of the house. The atmosphere was tense in a way that puzzled her but she had worries of her own.

Mrs Lester opened the door with her usual smile of welcome. 'What a lovely surprise, Miss Harriet!' she cried. 'Your great-uncle is a little more cheerful today. I think it's having my son around. He is not so determined to closet himself in the library. Go on into the big room and I'll tell him you're here. I just might persuade him to join you there.'

There was no sign of Godfrey, so Harriet opened the French windows and looked for him in the garden. She could hear the sound of sawing from the rear of the house but that was most likely the gardener. Her disappointment was extreme. All this way and she might not even see him!

Hurried footsteps on the stairs made her look round hopefully for they didn't sound like Mrs Lester's and were certainly not Great-Uncle Robert's.

'Godfrey!' Somehow Harriet resisted the urge to run to him. 'I'm sorry it's been so long since we met.' He hurried towards her, his expression as eager as she had hoped.

'Much too long!' he agreed.

'Mama has been a little strange lately and my father is anxious about her. And Wednesday I went on the train to Winchester with Papa to see Sam at his school.'

Mrs Lester appeared and smiled at Harriet. 'What's this I hear about wedding bells? The date is set, so I hear.'

There was a shocked silence. Godfrey's expression changed and Harriet felt her cheeks burn. 'News travels fast,' she stammered. 'I was going to tell you today.' She looked appealingly at Godfrey.

Sensing Harriet's dismay, Mrs Lester said, 'Oh dear. Have I spoiled your surprise, dear? Do forgive me. I'm a stupid woman at times.' Nobody denied this and she went on. 'Your great-uncle will be down directly – which means in twenty minutes if you're lucky. Why don't you take a walk in the garden while you're waiting? The rhododendrons are lovely.'

Harriet and Godfrey trailed obediently into the garden, neither breaking the subdued silence.

At last Godfrey said, 'Your *wedding*? I had no idea. I didn't know you were betrothed. Why didn't you tell me? Why let me think . . . let me hope that . . .' He looked at her reproachfully. 'That day on the seafront. You said we could go to the pier concert together. I've been imagining . . . Oh dammit! You must know what I mean, Harriet.'

'I do and I owe you an apology,' she said humbly. 'The truth is I didn't want you to know. I wanted us to have a little time together. I knew if I told you we never could. I did so much want to – to be with you.' They walked slowly across the lawn and Harriet wondered who, if anyone, was watching them. 'Do please say you forgive me – or at least say you understand.'

He stopped and turned to face her. 'I feel as though there has been a conspiracy,' he told her. 'My mother said nothing about your plans to marry. She must have known, surely.'

'Perhaps it slipped her mind.'

'I hardly think so. Who is this man? Do you love him?'

'A good question, Godfrey. Before I met you, I was quite prepared to marry him. It has always been understood by both our parents – and Marcus never gave me any reason to doubt that he wished it also. You know how parents are. They have always wanted a good match for me. Mama, in particular, is determined I should marry well. Papa . . . Well, I think he cares more about my brother's future. I don't know why. Mama says it is a normal bond between a man and his son.'

Godfrey regarded her earnestly. 'You haven't answered my question, Harriet. Do you love him?'

'How can I tell, Godfrey?' she cried desperately. 'I don't know what love is. Marcus doesn't excite me the way you do. There! I've said it! Very wrong of me but it's the truth. Is excitement the same as love? I hardly know you but I feel that I've been waiting for you all my life. Marcus proposed to me the other day and I didn't know what to say because I didn't know how you felt about me.'

He took her hand and pulled her gently towards him. '*You* excite *me*, Harriet!'

'Do I?' Her voice shook but she forced herself to continue. 'Then, while we were having supper at their house, he produced a ring and everyone was so happy. What could I say? It has happened too soon . . . or else too late! What are we to do?'

Instinctively, he pulled her closer but she resisted, glancing fearfully towards the house. 'Suppose someone sees us? Oh Godfrey! This is terrible. The longer I leave matters the more preparations they will make towards the wedding!' She felt trapped. 'Should I tell them? Suppose I do . . . I don't think my parents would agree to me marrying you. Not that you have asked me!' She blushed. 'Not that I expect anything of the kind but what reason can I give Marcus for my sudden change of heart?' Covered in confusion, Harriet stared at him helplessly.

'All I know,' he said carefully, 'is that I was falling in love with you. I've never felt this way about anyone else.'

'Not even about that woman in Italy?' The words came out in a rush and she immediately regretted them. Mrs Lester's careless confidence had been worrying her. 'Didn't you love *her*?'

Godfrey looked startled. 'Amelia? How on earth did you know about that?'

'Your mother mentioned her. How important was she to you?'

He avoided her eyes. 'For me it was serious but I was young and rather foolish. Amelia had a husband – a much older man. A music professor. They had no children and I thought she would run away with me but she couldn't face the scandal.'

Harriet watched his face and saw the anguish the memories revived and was aware of a fierce pang of jealousy. Godfrey had loved the woman. He didn't need to spell it out in words. It was painfully obvious and it pierced her like a knife. Her throat felt dry as she listened.

'It didn't last long, Harriet. A few months, that's all. One of those things.' He glanced up again. 'But if you are promised . . . Who is this man?'

Harriet forced herself to explain and his dismay deepened. 'A very good match, Harriet. Your parents have guided you well. How can I hope to compete when I have so little to offer.'

'For Papa it is a triumph of sorts. I think my betrothal to Marcus is the only thing I have ever done that has pleased him. If I refuse to marry Marcus Papa will be devastated and the Wellburys will be furious. Papa will lose face. It will be terrible for him and I doubt that he would ever forgive me!'

'That is a form of blackmail, Harriet. You mustn't think that way.'

'Blackmail? Don't say such a thing!' They reached a wooden seat and she sank down on to it. 'This is all my fault. I should have had more sense.'

'Don't blame yourself.' He sat beside her. 'If you had never met me, this would never have happened. Blame it on Fate.'

'But you thought me a free woman. I misled you.'

A squirrel ran down from the nearby chestnut tree and for a moment they watched its antics together.

Godfrey said, 'Does he love you, Harriet? Would it break his heart if you changed your mind?'

Harriet tried to imagine the scene where she told Marcus it was all over between them. Could she inflict such hurt upon him?

'I believe he does.' She turned from the squirrel to look at Godfrey. 'Do you, Godfrey? Do you love me?'

'Yes, I do.'

'On such a short acquaintance? Is it true love? Is it possible? You understand these matters more than I do.'

He thought for a moment, then sighed. 'I think about you all the time, Harriet, and every moment we aren't together is agony for me. I can't imagine how I could spend the rest of my life without you. I feel that if you won't be my wife I may never marry. Does that sound like love?'

She nodded.

He said, 'Haven't you ever heard of love at first sight?'

'Only in magazines.'

He shrugged. 'What about you, Harriet?'

She hesitated, choosing her words carefully. 'I know that never seeing you again would make me ill with misery . . . and that a future without you looks dark and dreary. I can no longer imagine being Marcus's wife and – and bearing his children.' She felt her lips tremble. 'It seems that in order to be together we have to make everyone else unhappy!'

The noise of sawing wood had stopped and they were startled by the appearance of a man pushing a wheelbarrow full of logs.

'Good day to you both!' he said.

Godfrey smiled. 'Good morning, Mr Cummings.'

They each murmured a reply and waited for him to pass by and be out of earshot.

An idea came to Harriet. 'Suppose you confide in your mother, Godfrey. Would she help us? Advise us, I mean.'

He brightened. 'Certainly I could talk to her. Yes, I will! I'll do it this evening. Mother is very sensible. Lots of common sense. Perhaps I should . . . Speak of the devil! Here she comes now.' He stood up and Harriet saw her crossing the lawn towards them.

'You can go in to him now, Miss Harriet,' she said. 'He has bravely agreed to meet you downstairs but he may not stay there long, so do hurry.'

Harriet gathered up her skirts and without a backward glance half ran back to the house. As she went in through the French windows she was conscious of a slight reprieve. Godfrey would speak to his mother, which meant that a little of the responsibility had been lifted from her shoulders.

*   *   *

The boy's funeral was to be held at one o'clock and Harriet, Agnes and James Wellbury arrived at Maybourne Workhouse as the church clock struck the quarter. When possible Agnes attended the funerals of workhouse inmates for the simple reason that they had so few friends and relatives. Harriet was also willing to attend out of curiosity and James Wellbury had presumably come out of loyalty to the Burnett family.

They found the coffin placed on a large trestle table in a corner of the infirmary enclosed by wooden screens. To their astonishment they saw a lighted candle at each end of the coffin which had obviously been burning for hours. Daisy Pritty was sitting at the head of the coffin, her hands clasped demurely round a borrowed bible. She wore a black armband over the sleeve of her workhouse gown, her expression was reverential and her eyes downcast. When she saw them, however, she jumped up. 'Doesn't he look a treat? A real sight for sore eyes!'

Harriet saw that the cheap coffin had been lined with pleated silk and that a matching cushion was beneath the boy's head. He was tied in a cheap-looking garment resembling a long nightshirt which was tied below his feet with a red ribbon. 'He looks wonderful,' she agreed although the young face was gaunt.

James Wellbury muttered, 'Good Lord! So young!' and shook his head.

Daisy said, 'The red ribbon was from Nursie. Off her best hat. I thought he needed something cheerful.'

Harriet looked at her. 'And the beautiful blue silk?'

Daisy hesitated, then shrugged. 'From one of those friends you can have. What's the word?' She screwed up her face in concentration. 'Nonnamous. A nonnamous friend. And look at the candles! They cost a lot of money, sixpence each, but I'm going to pay for them by doing some work for Mr Hawke. Sweeping up the sawdust, polishing his funeral carriage, things like that. He asked Mr Crane and he said I could.'

Agnes said, 'And you – you are guarding the body?'

Daisy nodded. 'I'm the vigil. They always have a vigil. Kings and queens and people. Even mayors. Mr Hawke told me. He's the undertaker.' She glanced proudly at the coffin

98

where the boy lay, his painfully thin hands clasped over his chest. 'The boy's name was Fred. Frederick Tutt. I mean his name *is* Frederick Tutt. Mr Hawke says that a dead person is still a person and deserves respect. The boy's name hasn't changed or gone away just because he's dead.'

For some reason there was a lump in Harriet's throat.

Daisy went on. 'He's loaned us the bier for nothing so the men can carry the coffin properly, and he's going to walk in front ringing a bell! There won't be much at the church – we can't have hymns or anything except a few prayers – but the boy would have enjoyed the procession.'

Agnes began to add her congratulations but at that moment a man drew back the curtains and they saw that four men in workhouse uniforms waited respectfully behind him. The man, wearing a black suit, introduced himself as Albert Hawke, the funeral director and Harriet saw him smile shyly at Daisy. He then produced a small screwdriver from one of his pockets and, after Daisy had taken a last look, fastened down the lid of the coffin. Harriet thought how little it would weigh.

Within minutes the little cortège was on its way – down the stairs, along the passage and out of the gloom and into the sunlight. The coffin rested on the bier and the four men, stationed one at each handle, supported it on its last journey. A few of the inmates followed and Herbert Crane walked with the members of the Board of Guardians. Harriet, unwisely wearing her best buttoned boots, clung to her mother's arm as they made their uneven way along the narrow and stony road which led to the Church of St John.

As promised, Albert Hawke rang the bell at intervals as they moved down the hill in the direction of the church, where a plot of overgrown land was reserved for the burial of paupers, criminals and those who had taken their own lives. Harriet, who had never attended such a funeral, was fascinated by it all and was glad to have something to take her mind off her own difficulties. Hearing the bell, people came out of their cottages to pay their last respects and whispered among themselves about the unusually elaborate workhouse funeral.

Here and there people joined the mourners and thus swelled

the group that eventually entered the church. The bier was set down and the coffin drew all eyes. The service was short and hurried and the coffin was then carried out to the graveside, where newly dug earth waited to be replaced and a gravedigger sat cross-legged beneath a nearby tree, smoking his pipe.

As they walked home, Harriet thought sadly of the young boy and his short and wretched life and told herself to be thankful for her own good fortune.

In spite of her dilemma she had her health and a loving family – and *two* men who loved her! Frederick Tutt had had nothing. It was a sobering thought.

That evening, while the family were at supper, there was a knock at the front door and Izzie went to answer it. A young man stood on the doorstep with a letter in his hand. Izzie had never seen him before but he was not unattractive and she returned his smile. Black hair curled from beneath a bowler hat and his eyes were friendly. He looked about twenty, she thought. As she opened her mouth to speak to him he put a warning finger to his lips. In a low voice he said, 'This letter is for your mistress, Mrs Agnes Burnett – and for her eyes only! You understand?'

Izzie looked at him doubtfully. 'For *Mrs* Burnett?'

'Yes. No one else must see it. No one.' He kept his voice to little more than a whisper. 'That is most important. Are you sure you understand?'

Izzie eyed the letter nervously. 'Who's it from then? The workhouse?'

That appeared to amuse him. 'The workhouse? Certainly not.' He grinned. 'It's from a certain gentleman – and your mistress will understand that.'

'You don't mean – it's from *you*!' Startled, she threw a quick look over her shoulder.

'No! It's from another gentleman who wishes to stay out of sight. I'm sure you know what I'm talking about – a pretty girl like you! Now, there's a sixpence for you if you promise to keep it safe until you can hand it to her personally. No one else must see it. What do you say?'

Izzie's mouth fell open. She had finally worked it out. Her mistress had taken a lover! Not that she could blame her, for Izzie had always found George Burnett a stern, coldhearted man. But suppose he found out about the letter – there would be fireworks then and she, Izzie, would be sent packing most likely. Shaken she considered what she should do about the letter. The sixpence would come in very handy.

She held out her hand. 'I promise.' She accepted the letter but her hand was shaking. Her mistress and a 'certain gentleman'? What was the world coming to? she wondered. And this young man thought *her* pretty! It was all very unexpected but rather thrilling. Whatever would Cook say if she knew?

As if reading her mind, the young man said, 'And you must tell no one. The gentleman insists. If you do . . .' His smile faded. 'You will be very, very sorry!' He held up his right hand and curled it into a fist. '*Very* sorry!'

Instinctively she took a small step back, but before she could recover from his threat he snatched at her right hand and thrust the sixpence into it. Then he turned and hurried away.

Izzie swallowed hard and pushed the letter into her apron pocket. As she went back towards the kitchen, George Burnett called out, 'Who was it?'

Fearfully she stopped in her tracks, thinking rapidly. 'No one, sir. Boys larking about the way they do. Bothering honest folk.'

He grunted something she couldn't catch and she fled into the kitchen. Later, she would find a suitable moment to hand over the letter.

Harriet woke in the middle of the night and lay gazing up at the ceiling, her senses alert. Something had woken her. For a moment she listened but heard nothing and her thoughts reverted to Godfrey. What had his mother said when he revealed their love for each other? He had promised to let her know somehow. Harriet knew that she could not keep visiting her great-uncle without arousing suspicion but if Godfrey came to the house that also would attract attention. Both her parents seemed strained since her father had returned but she had no idea what was troubling them. Her father's ship was being reloaded and reprovisioned for the next voyage and guiltily Harriet thought it couldn't be soon enough for her. If she had to confess her feelings for Godfrey and her doubts about the marriage, she would rather speak to her mother.

Suddenly she sat up, for her ears had caught an unfamiliar sound from downstairs. If it was her father, then she didn't want to intrude but it might be her mother. Sometimes Agnes slept badly and went downstairs to heat some milk. Cautiously, with as little noise as possible, she tiptoed to the door and stepped out on to the landing. She could hear her father's snores. So it was her mother – or else one of the servants. Moving to the top of the stairs, she peered over. Surprisingly, candlelight flickered in the dining room. Harriet went downstairs, keeping to the edge of each stair to prevent alerting whoever it was.

At the dining-room door she stopped and stared. Her mother had opened the window and was leaning out.

'Mama!'

Agnes gave a shocked gasp and withdrew her head. 'Oh Harriet!' Agnes put a hand to her chest. 'It's you! Thank Heavens! I thought it was . . .'

'What is happening?' Harriet made a move towards the window but her mother barred the way, her arm's outstretched.

'No, Harriet. You must go back to bed. I *beg* you, Harriet. Don't ask any questions but go! Now!'

When Harriet hesitated, Agnes took hold of her arm and tried to drag her back to the door. 'Go now, Harriet! Before . . . Before it's too late!'

Harriet retreated a few steps but then stopped. 'What do you mean, Mama? Too late for what?'

Panic filled her mother's eyes. 'Just go, Harriet. I have to . . . It's nothing to be alarmed about but I . . . I have to deal with someone.' Her voice rose shrilly. '*Go back to your bedroom, Harriet. Please!*'

Seeing that her mother was almost hysterical, Harriet nodded and reluctantly withdrew as far as the door and at that moment the church clock struck three and seconds later there was a noise from the window and they both turned to see a man peering into the room.

Agnes gasped and forcibly pushed Harriet back into the passage, but instead of retreating to her bedroom Harriet lingered, leaning forward to see round the door. Agnes rushed forward and drew something from the pocket of her night robe – it looked like a small bag and it sounded like money! There was a whispered conversation, the man's head vanished and there were hurried footsteps in the street. Shocked and confused, Harriet felt unable to face her mother and went quickly back upstairs. She sat up in bed, her heart pounding, and waited. What on earth was happening? she wondered dazedly, her thoughts chaotic, fear clutching at her heart.

'Harriet!' Her mother came into the room, candle in hand, her face pale with anxiety. Setting down the candle, she perched on the edge of Harriet's bed and regarded Harriet with something close to desperation. Pulling her robe closer to her neck, she shuddered and swallowed hard. 'You must forget what you have seen, Harriet. For my sake and your own. Pretend it never happened. Will you do that?'

Harriet wanted to say yes. She wanted to slip under the sheets and forget but she knew it was impossible. 'No, Mama, I won't do that because I *can't*! You were frightened, Mama. I could see it. Who was that man? Surely you can tell me. I won't tell Papa. I swear it.'

Agnes closed her eyes. 'There is nothing to tell.' She opened her eyes. 'Believe me, child, it is all over now. It was something . . .' She swallowed. 'It *was* a problem but now it's finished. But I cannot talk about it. There is no need now. It is settled.'

'But the bag. Was that *money* you gave him?'

'Money?'

Harriet saw a flash of panic in her mother's eyes.

'Money?' Agnes demanded. 'Why would I give anybody money? You must trust me on this, Harriet. It is for your own good.'

'But who was he? Was it to do with the workhouse?'

'No . . . that is "yes". In a way it was . . . but not exactly.' She drew several deep breaths and a little colour crept back into her face. 'Your father must never know, Harriet. Not a word or it will be terrible for all of us.'

Harriet felt a shiver of apprehension. 'Terrible? How do you mean, Mama? What will happen?'

Agnes covered her face with her hands. 'I cannot tell you anything but I am not exaggerating, Harriet. You have to trust me. George must never know.'

Harriet stared at her. This sounded truly serious though she could not begin to imagine the problem. Almost immediately, she realized that whatever the truth was, tomorrow would not be a good time to confront her mother with her own news about Godfrey. For a long moment they regarded each other breathlessly until Agnes have a little cry and threw her arms around her daughter.

'It's for you, Harriet. My darling girl, it's for *you*. For your sake. Just believe that. All I want is for your happiness. You deserved a happy life.'

'Mama . . . ?'

At that moment they were startled by the appearance of George. He stood in the doorway, his hair tousled, his expression irritable. 'What's the meaning of this? You woke me up.'

Agnes froze but Harriet said quickly, 'I'm sorry, Papa. I had a nightmare. Mama heard me cry out . . .'

Agnes looked at her gratefully. 'That's right, George. I'm sorry if we disturbed your sleep.'

Apparently satisfied, he shook his head and turned away. Agnes and Harriet looked at each other like two conspirators.

Harriet said, 'Won't you ever tell me, Mama? The truth?'

'There's nothing . . . something in my own past. Nothing to do with you. Now do try and go back to sleep.'

Agnes kissed her and returned to her own bed. Harriet tried, but sleep evaded her and the church clock rang the quarters through the next six hours. Tossing and turning, her mind teeming with a succession of dreadful possibilities, Harriet had no more sleep that night.

Seven

The quayside was busy as usual as George descended from the town and made his way past various bundles and bales, crates, boxes and assorted stores. Some had been brought down from newly arrived ships but others waited to be loaded to vessels preparing to set off again with their new cargoes to foreign parts. The *Saint Augustine* was one of these and as George Burnett stepped over coiled ropes and smelled the salt tang with its associated hints of tar and wood, his heart grew lighter at the prospect ahead. George hated to be surrounded by what he thought of privately as 'petticoats' and the thought of a long sea journey without fear of feminine interference always sent his spirits soaring. By the time he set foot on board he was actually smiling. The bo'sun, a thickset man by the name of Dick Maddocks, raised a hand in a salute and said, 'Morning to you, Skipper!'

George nodded and paused. 'How's it going?'

The bo'sun held up a calloused hand and began to tick off the fingers. 'Water aboard, likewise rum. Salt, flour, ship's biscuits, pickles, butter and lard, cheeses, salt pork, salt cod . . .'

'Fresh meat and fish?'

'Day after tomorrow, sir. Likewise vegetables and fruit. Not forgetting the lemons.'

'Good . . .' He gazed round thoughtfully. 'Cargo complete?'

'Yes, sir. Stowed away, sir, neat and tidy.'

'Any problems?' George asked.

'No sir . . . barring the crew. Three men signed off. Replaced two and looking for a third.'

'Get one!'

'Will do, Skipper!'

George went downstairs and looked with affection at the tiny room which was his domain. He drew in a long satisfied breath. His private space contained a large desk for sea charts, ledgers and the ship's log, a small shelf for books of reference, his bunk bed and a sea chest for his clothes. A lamp hung from the ceiling. Once they were under way, this would be his home and the worries about his wife would fade from his mind. He would have vagaries of the weather to contend with, the ups and downs of shipboard life and a stiff discipline to maintain.

This last reminded him of the pistol he kept in the top drawer of his desk and he drew it out lovingly and ran his fingers over it. It was not large and he rarely had to use it. In fact he had only once had occasion to fire it but it always gave him a sense of power. There would never be a mutiny aboard the *Saint Augustine*, he thought with a smile, nor any undue unruliness. The sight of this ultimate weapon was enough to subdue anyone who breached the ship's regulations and he had once shot a drunken seaman in the arm. Amazingly the sound of the discharging weapon had also sobered up three others who were hellbent on causing mischief.

Wrapping it up again in the chamois leather, George sat down at his desk and thought about the early morning when he had surprised his wife and daughter in Harriet's bedroom. He wasn't deceived. He recognized the guilty looks and stammering replies. They were hatching something but he had no idea what it was. If he had longer ashore he would pursue it but he was running out of time. He must be back in Maybourne for his daughter's wedding and if there was anything to know he would make it his business to find out then. He dared not confess even to himself that he was looking forward to Harriet's marriage. His duty to her would be done – she would be Marcus's wife. Marcus's responsibility.

For the present he had only two more days before embarkation. Once they had lost sight of England his other life would begin. George sighed deeply and switched his thoughts to his beloved son. He recalled the small face turned up to his – a face so similar to his own that no one could doubt the relationship. Unlike his daughter, who resembled neither himself nor Agnes and who caused him much disquiet. His wife insisted that she took after her grandmother in her youth but George had no way of knowing if that were true. The young Harriet had been a biddable child but his disappointment had been intense for, longing for a son, the girl was a poor substitute. His wife had miscarried two children before Harriet's birth and he had tried to be grateful for the child's survival but returning from sea to find a girl had been a crushing blow.

He had also come ashore to find his wife strangely changed – nervous and tearful – but the doctor had said that many women were depressed and anxious after the arrival of a first child. She would recover her spirits, he told George, but that had proved a hopeful forecast. The child had come between them as Agnes became overprotective and arguments began.

'Poor Agnes!' he murmured, reaching for the ship's manifest in the hope of distracting himself from unhappy thoughts. So much to do. He stared at the closely written details. So much to check and organize before they could put to sea. He wondered if the sail had been repaired . . . and if the pilfering would begin again. He had got rid of the man they suspected but he still had an occasional doubt.

'But Samuel! What a fine lad!' He smiled. Samuel was going to be a son to be proud of. Clasping his hands behind his head, George stretched out his legs and thought about his son and a little warmth touched his cold heart.

While her father was safely aboard his ship, Harriet was meeting Godfrey on the pier at Maybourne. Hand in hand they wandered along, lulled by the smell of sundrenched planks and the soft salt breeze that blew in from the sea. Around them early holidaymakers strolled languidly, the men sporting boaters, the women protected from the sun's rays by parasols. The children ran squealing among them, their faces alive with glee, ready for any chance of mischief that might come their way.

Godfrey, his arm round Harriet's waist, drew her towards the rail and they stared together at the waves breaking below them.

Harriet finally plucked up the courage to ask the important question. 'What did your mother say about us, Godfrey? Was she angry?'

'Angry? Of course not.' He gave her waist a little squeeze. 'But she was worried. For me, mostly, but also for you. She says Marcus is such a good catch you would be mad to turn him down for a wretch like me.'

'A wretch?'

'She was joking, naturally.' He sighed. 'Mother made several points and all valid. She said firstly that you have to think about your promise to Marcus. To jilt a man so close to the wedding is a dreadful thing.'

Harriet nodded.

'Secondly that if you *were* to give him up for me you would face an uncertain future for I have no money yet and I could offer you nothing concrete.'

'Oh Godfrey, I don't *care!*' Harriet cried. 'You know I don't.' She was trying not to hate Mrs Lester for being so discouraging.

'She said that if you are certain – about your feelings for me, that is – then you should talk to your mother and ask her advice. And the sooner the better.'

'I don't think I can do that,' Harriet told him. 'Mama is in some kind of trouble herself although I cannot begin to imagine what it might be.' She took a deep breath and began to tell him about her mother's assignation in the middle of the night.

He looked at her anxiously as the tale unfolded. 'And you think she was giving him money? Was it a blackmailer?'

'Godfrey!' she cried, then hastily lowered her voice. 'Don't even suggest such a thing! What would my mother have to hide? I can assure you she has done nothing wrong.'

'But if not a blackmailer, then who else?'

'Perhaps it was someone from the workhouse. Perhaps my father disapproves of the money she spends to help them. It is his money, when all's said and done.' Harriet clung to this possibility. It was easier to bear than the alternative. 'I could ask her,' she suggested. 'Papa will be leaving shortly and we will be alone again.'

'You're sure you didn't recognize the man?'

'I'm certain.'

They began to walk further along the pier – past the fortune-teller and the ice-cream seller and the man with the tarot cards.

She said suddenly, 'I shall be glad when Papa leaves. I don't think I love him the way I once did.'

He squeezed her arm. 'You do love him. You must do.'

'He doesn't love me – not the way he loves Sam!'

'I love you enough for ten fathers, Harriet!' He stopped and took her in his arms. 'I love you more than anyone else in the world – far more than anyone else could love you! Forget your father and think about us. If you cannot talk to your mother, you must talk to Marcus. See how he feels about delaying the wedding. That would be a start. At the moment I feel that a giant clock is ticking away our chances of ever being together.'

He held her tight and kissed her, and for a moment or two she felt an overpowering sense of joy. Then, as she withdrew reluctantly her eye caught two people standing hand in hand at the pier rail.

'Oh no!' she whispered. 'That's Daisy Pritty and the man she calls Digger. The ones that were fighting when she got herself stabbed!' Quickly she turned her face away, unwilling to be recognized.

Godfrey said, 'They look mighty pleased with themselves. Up to mischief, perhaps.'

'I hope not. Mama sets such store by the girl.'

As if to prove Godfrey right, there was a shout and a policeman began to run through the crowd, blowing his whistle.

Harriet and Godfrey watched in dismay as the constable pointed to Daisy and her escort and the pair took to their heels and fled back along the pier, scattering innocent bystanders in all directions and drawing down curses as they went.

Harriet groaned. 'I wonder what they've done now.'

'Nothing honest by the look of it!'

'Poor Mama had high hopes for Daisy. She is convinced that with the right help, a workhouse inmate can blend into the community and she wants to prove it. I sometimes feel it's that hope that keeps her involved.'

When the clamour had receded Harriet said, 'I wonder if anyone from the workhouse ever becomes a decent citizen. Or do they have too much going against them? Daisy Pritty isn't all bad, you know. She gave her best silk petticoat to be a lining in a young lad's coffin. It was so generous.'

'How on earth did she come by a silk petticoat?'

Harriet shrugged. 'Better not to ask, Godfrey! Whenever anyone tries to help her, she takes advantage. She was found a place as a maid but stole from them and ran away.'

'Ah!' He raised his eyebrows.

'Ah? . . . Oh! The silk petticoat!' She rolled her eyes despairingly. 'Possibly.'

Godfrey slipped his arm round her shoulders. 'I don't want to hear any more about her. I want us to decide what we are going to do next. Will you talk to either your mother or Marcus?'

She nodded. 'But what does *your* mother think of me as a possible wife for you? She may not approve. I suppose she will think it an . . . an uneven match. You can be honest with me.'

Smiling, he drew her closer. 'She says she is prepared to love anyone I love. That's good enough for me!'

Harriet moved closer to him. If only her own parents could be equally understanding, half her troubles would be over.

Half a mile away along the promenade, Daisy and Digger staggered to a halt, clutching their sides and grinning triumphantly at each other.

He panted, 'We've lost them, Dais!'

Nodding, she leaned against the rail to recover her breath. 'How did they know?' she demanded. 'Is it written on our foreheads or something? Do we look like felons?'

He hunkered down beside her. 'They didn't know anything for sure. It was just a guess. They've got it in for us, that's all. Anything goes missing, it has to be us! Bloomin' harrassment. That's what I call it'

'But it *was* us!' she protested.

'But can they *prove* it?' Getting no reply, he went on. 'They reckon that just because you worked there, it must be us that stole the stuff. They're not as daft as they look. They can put two and two together.'

Shrugging, Daisy glanced round to make sure they weren't being followed and saw a small boy licking a pink ice-cream. 'I could go one of those! Strawberry. My favourite.' She raised her voice. 'Oi! Give us a lick!' The boy gave her a frightened glance and ran past them to reach the safety of his mother, who was waiting further along by the news stand.

Digger hauled Daisy to her feet. 'Let's get away from here before they come looking for us again.'

'So what did you get?' Daisy asked. 'You didn't miss the copper kettle, I hope. And the jewels and the pewter . . . and the big glass bowl.'

'It was crystal and if you must know I dropped it getting out the window, so don't start moaning. I remembered the little bronze horse and the—'

'So where's it all stashed? 'Cos I've got somewhere in mind. That place I told you about. The undertaker. He's got sheds and a cellar. I could hide it there. I could even stuff it inside one of the old coffins. He'd never twig.'

'Why wouldn't he?'

''Cos he fancies me, that's why!' She grinned.

'What, a workhouse brat?'

'Brat? You mind what you're saying. I'm a young woman not a brat – and you should know better than most!'

'A man like that with his own business? He never would fancy you.'

'He does so! He's letting me do a bit of work there, on and off.'

Digger shrugged. 'Well, the stuff's not going to no under-taker's yard. It's safe where it is.'

She punched his arm. 'You mean *your* share is. Mine's going where I choose to put it. So *where* is it? I've a right to know. It was me that put you up to it and told you what to look for. Me that told you how to get in.' She glared at him. 'Fifty-fifty, we said. Now where's it hid?'

He wasn't listening. 'Anything worth anything in the undertaker's place? Apart from coffins!'

Daisy hesitated. Why should she tell him? He wasn't coming clean about the last lot and she wouldn't be surprised if he had already sold the glass dish and spent the money. That bit about dropping it had sounded a bit unlikely. 'A few tools, that's all. Nothing worth taking. So where's it all hid?'

He adopted an earnest expression. 'I'm not telling you, Dais, in case you're nicked and they beat it out of you, but I'll take you there tonight. I swear it on my grandmother's life.'

'She's already dead! Strewth, Digger, you're a devious sod!'

'I've told you, I'll take you there! We'll meet up at—' He broke off. 'Oh Gawd, Dais! Here comes another one.' He had spotted a dark uniform approaching from the opposite direction and, grabbing her by the hand, he pulled Daisy across the road and into a convenient alley.

'Follow me and run like hell!'

Later that same day Harriet and her parents sat at supper, all trying to make conversation and finding it difficult for their own reasons. Harriet was trying to decide whether or not to broach the subject of Godfrey before or after her father's departure. If she waited until he sailed she could more easily persuade her mother to her way of thinking about Godfrey but Agnes might well say they could make no decision without her father. That would mean she could not cancel the wedding for weeks, if not months, and that was hardly fair on the Wellburys or Marcus. There was no way she could pretend for much longer and Marcus had written again, hinting that she might need a passport in the not too distant future. She took this to be a reference to their honeymoon and she didn't want him to buy tickets for an expensive sailing trip they would never take.

Izzie came in to remove the soup bowls and Agnes smiled at her.

'I understand it's your birthday today, Izzie. I'm so sorry I forgot.'

'It's no matter, ma'am.' The little maid managed to make it sound as though it certainly did matter.

Harriet said, 'I have a pretty shawl, Izzie. The blue one you so admire. Would you like that?'

'Oh *yes*, please, Miss Harriet.' Izzie's eyes widened. 'Thank you.'

'I shall fetch it for you after supper.

George looked up. 'The soup was a little too salty, Izzie. Please remind Cook that I eat too much salted food when I'm at sea.'

'I'm sorry, sir. I'll tell her.' She balanced the soup bowls and the tureen and withdrew.

George said, 'You're not wearing your ring, Agnes. Please wear it at all times. I've told you before it is putting temptation in the way of—'

Harriet glanced in surprise at her mother's hand. She had not registered the fact that the ring was missing. 'I'll fetch it for you, Mama.'

She was already on her feet when she saw the expression on her mother's face. She had gone very pale.

'Mama? Are you feeling unwell?'

George looked at his wife. 'What is it, Agnes?'

Agnes swallowed hard, tried to speak and failed. Izzie reappeared with the plates and Cook carried in an earthenware dish containing stewed beef with oysters, George's favourite dish.

'There you are, sir.' She set it down on a trivet and stood back proudly. 'A treat, sir, because you'll soon be leaving us again. And I'm sorry about the soup. It won't happen again.'

George nodded, still watching his wife with a look of concern. She had put one hand to her throat and looked as though she might faint.

Harriet cried, 'Mama! What is it?'

Agnes waved a hand and looked pointedly towards the servants. Izzie brought in the vegetables and nobody spoke until the family was once more alone.

Agnes took a deep breath and turned to her husband. 'George, I'm sorry but . . . You must please, *please* forgive me . . . The ring . . .'

'Agnes!' George's face darkened. 'You're not telling me

you've lost your engagement because if you are I shall be—'

'George, I'm sorry. I don't know how it happened. I first realized when—'

'You have lost the ring I gave you when we were engaged? How could you, Agnes? *Lost* it! That implies great carelessness on your part.'

Harriet saw her mother's face crumple and said quickly, 'Please don't blame her, Papa! Think how upset she has been. Afraid to tell you. Oh, poor Mama!' She jumped up and hurried to her mother who was now unsuccessfully blinking back tears. 'Don't cry, Mama, please. It wasn't your fault. I know that.'

George was now glaring at his daughter. 'Sit down at once, Harriet. We are in the middle of a meal. And don't presume to know so much. Either your mother has been careless and lost the ring or one of the servants has stolen it. I see no alternative.' He looked at Agnes. 'Which is it?'

She produced a handkerchief and dabbed at her eyes. 'I . . . I lost it, George. I was shopping two days ago and when I returned I noticed it had gone and I went straight back to all the shops but no one had seen it.'

'And you thought I wouldn't notice? Hoped I wouldn't. You should know me better after all these years. I have never taken you for a fool, my dear.'

'I'm so sorry, George. You know how much store I set by your ring. It meant everything to me. I have treasured it all these years . . .'

'Not well enough, it would seem, for you have now lost it. That was an expensive ring, Agnes.'

'I know, George, but—'

'No, Agnes, you do *not* know. How could you possibly know its value? It was a gift. I have never told you the ring's value.'

'I mean . . . I assumed it was expensive. It's so – it was so beautiful. I could see it had cost a great deal of—'

He was struggling with his temper. 'They are – *were* very good diamonds. I shall have to notify the insurance company

114

if it does not reappear. Are you quite sure you haven't lost it around the house?'

'I'm certain, George. It is nowhere in the house.'

He stared at her, his eyes narrowed, and his voice rose. 'Certain? *How* can you be certain if you do not know where you lost it? Have you searched every corner? Every nook and cranny? Have you set the servants to search for it? If not, why not?'

'Because I . . . I was convinced I lost it while shopping and—'

'If you're lying to me, Agnes . . .' It was a veiled threat.

Harriet was becoming alarmed. Her mother looked close to hysteria and her father was becoming angrier by the minute. He had always been a stern man but now she sensed real anger. The food remained untouched. To distract her parents she began to serve the beef and oysters and handed the first portion to her mother, who stared at it blankly then slowly placed it on the table in front of her. Harriet set some before her father, who ignored it. She put some on her own plate and pushed the vegetables towards her mother and then her father but both refused. Harriet helped herself to leeks and potatoes and tried to eat but although she was hungry she was also nervous and the food seemed to stick in her throat.

She said, 'Do eat something, Mama.'

Agnes shook her head as fresh tears poured down her face. Harriet thought uneasily that her mother looked frightened. *Had* one of the servants stolen the ring? Was it possible and if so was her mother covering up the fact? No. Harriet was sure that neither Cook nor Izzie would do such a thing. Cook had been with them for more than five years and Izzie for just under three.

George said, 'So it is not the servants.'

'No, George.'

Harriet groaned inwardly. Her mother had fallen into another trap.

'You know that for a fact, do you?' George barked. 'You seem to know a lot about the whereabouts of the ring. You seem to know where it *isn't!*'

'I . . .' Too late she saw her mistake. 'Not for a fact but . . .

In my heart I know they are not thieves. You also know them, George. Do you believe it possible?'

Harriet said, 'Mama is right. They would never—'

'No one is addressing you, Harriet. Please don't interfere.' Her father regarded Agnes with an expression which Harriet found unreadable. 'Have you deceived me, Agnes? Have you *ever* deceived me? Think back, Agnes. Think back over the years. Over the many months I spent at sea.'

Harriet frowned. What on earth was this new line of questioning? Where was it leading? She was dismayed to notice that her mother did not appear to find it odd. Had something terrible happened before she was born – or before she was old enough to understand?

'Deceived you, George? What . . . How do you mean?' Agnes clutched the edge of the table.

He turned to Harriet and said, 'Take your food and eat it upstairs in your room. *Now!*'

Harriet stared at him. 'In my room? But why, Papa?'

Agnes said, 'The child is not to blame for anything. Please, George!'

Slowly Harriet stood up. Should she obey her father or stay to support her mother? Was she making things worse by staying? 'Mama?'

George slammed his fist on the table and shouted, 'Don't appeal to your mother! *I* am telling you to take your food upstairs. Do as I say immediately!'

Somehow Harriet resisted the urge to obey him. 'I'm no longer a child, Papa!' she protested.

'You are still my daughter and I am master in this house!'

'But I don't want to leave Mama. You're frightening her.'

'That may be but it is nothing to do with you. Nothing I can blame you for. But we have to speak alone.'

Harriet pushed back her chair and stood although her legs were trembling.

'All this over a lost ring?' she said shakily.

He stared at her for a long moment. 'You don't undertand, Harriet. Now take your meal and go! Or go without it. I don't care!'

116

He stood up suddenly, towering over her and Agnes said quickly, 'Do as you father says, Harriet. Don't worry about me.'

But upstairs, sitting at her dressing table, Harriet did worry. She also discovered that she had lost her appetite. From below she could hear raised voices and stood on the landing straining to hear anything recognizable. After a few minutes as her father's roars grew louder, Harriet ventured to the top of the stairs and looked down and was appalled to see Cook and Izzie listening outside the dining-room door. She began to creep down less from curiosity than from a need for company. Upstairs she felt alone and vulnerable.

Cook caught sight of her and straightened guiltily. Izzie also turned.

Cook whispered, 'We're afeard for your mother, Miss Harriet.'

Izzie said, 'Your pa's in a towering rage!'

Harriet nodded.

Cook couldn't resist the next question. 'Did he eat any of the beef?'

Harriet shook her head and Cook tutted her disappointment. There was a sudden crash from inside the dining room and they looked at each other in alarm.

'It's not my place,' Cook muttered.

Harriet said, 'I'll go in again. You keep out of sight.'

Inside she found her mother still seated, her head on her arms, which rested on the table. She was sobbing uncontrollably and didn't raise her head. Possibly she didn't hear Harriet come in. The dish of beef and oysters had been thrown at the wall. Gravy trickled down the wallpaper and soaked into the rug. The meat was scattered among the broken china.

Harriet rushed to her mother but her father stepped between them and caught her arm in a painful grip.

'Leave her alone, you . . . you . . .' His eyes were almost popping out of his head and for the first time since she was a child with nightmares, Harriet was terrified. He swore under his breath and then cried, 'Get out of here, damn you! Out! We have unfinished business here!'

Propelling her forcibly to the door, he pushed her out and slammed it behind her. Harriet crashed into the wall and fell to the floor and Cook and Izzie rushed up and helped her to her feet. They took her into the kitchen and sat her down. Izzie heated some milk while Cook coped with Harriet's tears.

'So what was that terrible crash?' Cook asked.

Harriet explained and Cook groaned. 'But at least he didn't hurt your poor mother. That's what I was afraid of. Should we call a policeman?'

Harriet stifled her tears. 'Oh no! He won't hurt her – at least I don't think he will. Do you?'

There was no answer but before they could make a decision the dining-room door opened and they heard Agnes running, sobbing, up the stairs. A moment later George stormed out, went up the passage and out of the front door.

'I'd better go up to Mama,' Harriet whispered but Cook laid a hand gently on her arm.

'Let her be for a moment or two,' she advised. 'She'll need to pull herself together, poor soul, before she faces any of us. Give her ten minutes and then take up some hot milk and honey.'

Harriet nodded.

Izzie said, 'D'you think he's coming back – the master I mean?'

Cook gave her a shake, 'Why, of course he is, you silly girl. Where else would he go?'

Izzie shrugged. 'My pa used to go and get drunk!'

'Well, the master is not your pa and he never gets drunk. In all the years I've worked here he's never had too much to drink. Thank the Lord for small mercies! With a drunken master the servants are never safe!'

Harriet wiped her eyes and accepted the milk Izzie had prepared. 'I'll drink it in my room,' she said. 'I have a letter to write but I'll be down to take Mama's milk up.'

Harriet learned no more that day for when she entered her parents' bedroom her mother, looking pale and exhausted, was fast asleep on the bed and muttering unhappily in her sleep.

*   *   *

The following morning Izzie and Cook sat in the kitchen sipping their first mug of tea, eating bread and dripping and whispering about the events of the previous day. Izzie shook salt and pepper on to hers and Cook said, 'I can never understand how you can taste the dripping with all that on it.'

'Makes it tastier.' To prove it, Izzie took a large bite and munched appreciatively.

'If you say so!'

'It's something to do with that letter,' Izzie insisted, returning to their conversation. 'I do wish I'd said No when he offered me that sixpence. If the master finds out he might blame me. He might think I'm in on it, so to speak. I might get the sack for passing on the letter!' She looked at Cook with fearful eyes.

'They won't know unless you tell them. They didn't *see* you take the sixpence or the letter. Tell me again what he was like, this man.'

Izzie brightened. 'Oh, the mistress knows how to pick a man—' she began.

Cook snorted. 'Then how come she chose the master? Smashing the china! Wasting that lovely beef I made specially for him! I've never seen such goings-on in my life. My own pa was no saint, but even he wouldn't waste good food and break good china! A wicked waste of money!' She shook her head.

'Well, this man was only about twenty, so much younger than Mr Burnett and much more handsome. Curly hair and a lovely smile. Nice teeth, too, and not fat nor anything horrible at all. I wonder why he likes older women?'

'Some men fancy them,' Cook told her. 'Sometimes it's because the men are poor and the women are rich. They see an easy way to get hold of money and go up in the world.'

'But the mistress is already married, so any money she had must have passed to the master.' She added another spoonful of sugar to her tea and glanced behind her at the range to make sure the fire was still going. 'Anyway the master comes from a wealthy family if you can go by Havely House.' A kettle stood heating for the washing water and a pan of water waited for the addition of porridge oats for the family breakfast.

Cook frowned. 'I just can't believe the mistress would do such a thing. A lover indeed. She's not the sort to go romancing. Not at her age. Not at *any* age. Think of what would happen if she did and she was found out. Ruination. That's what would happen. She'd be thrown out without a penny. Most likely end up in her own blooming workhouse up the road!'

Izzie's eyes widened at the vision this presented. 'Never! Oh, that would be too bad! Imagine us sneaking off to visit her . . . smuggling in an egg or a mutton pie!' For a moment this glittering vision of role reversal appealed to Izzie but, feeling disloyal, she pushed the idea resolutely aside. 'D'you think they meet up secretly? Her and him? D'you think he ever *kissed* her?'

Cook tutted. 'Kissing and cuddling! That's all you young ones think about. I don't think there's a love affair. The mistress would never take such a risk. Think what it would do to Miss Harriet and Master Samuel. She'd never risk losing them. No, it's more than that. Might be some member of her family that she's ashamed of coming secretly to visit her.'

'I wouldn't be ashamed of *that* young man!'

'You would if he'd been in prison.'

'He didn't look the prison type.'

Defeated by Izzie's logic, Cook shrugged. 'Might be money worries. She might have borrowed some money.'

'For what?' Izzie demanded crossly. Easy for Cook to mock kissing and cuddling but Izzie was still waiting for her share. So far, not even the butcher's boy had given her a second glance.

'I don't know – but there's going to be a wedding, remember.' She crossed to the porridge and gave it a stir. 'That's going to cost a lot of money. It wouldn't be the same here without the mistress. If Mr Burnett was to throw her out, I mean.'

Izzie frowned suddenly. 'I wonder if it's to do with that young man we met on the promenade? The one I told you about – when Miss Harriet sent me on ahead to do the shopping. Maybe it's Miss Harriet that's having a romance! I thought it a bit odd at the time. An *extra* romance – maybe the mistress found out about them from that letter you took in!'

'What? You mean someone was spying on Miss Harriet? Ooh!' Cook clapped a hand over her mouth.

'Who knows?'

'And had to tell the mistress about it, who then had to tell the master and he's gone berserk?'

For a moment they mulled over the idea in silence and it did seem a possibility.

Cook said slowly, 'But then they'd have had to speak to Miss Harriet and they didn't, did they?'

Izzie jumped up to stir the coals in the range and add a few more. Cook had removed the bread and the bowl of dripping, so breakfast was officially over.

Cook shrugged. 'We'll keep our eyes and ears open,' she advised. 'We'll find out somehow.'

At that moment they heard a door open above them and Cook said, 'That's Miss Harriet. She's up early.' She sighed. 'I have a feeling this is not going to be a very cheerful day, Izzie. Better get a move on with the porridge.'

Eight

A gnes and Harriet sat silently at the breakfast table while Izzie, smiling nervously, brought in the porridge, sugar and milk. The chair at the head of the table was empty and Harriet was longing to ask why. Her mother looked very pale and had obviously been crying and there was something lethargic in her manner that Harriet found odd. At breakfast her mother was normally wide awake and speaking eagerly of the day ahead – a day which was usually very full and interesting. Today she seemed uncharacteristically slow. Harriet, busy with her own worries, felt very alone. This was obviously the worst possible time to confide about Godfrey but she had promised the Lesters that she would speak to Agnes and she was determined to do so. In a way it would be easier while her father was absent but would her mother be able to concentrate on the problem while she was in a state of shock from yesterday's unhappy experience? Harriet's fear was that Marcus would call in on them again before Agnes could offer her advice. Harriet felt willing to confront Marcus herself but she could hardly do so if her parents were unaware of the problem.

As soon as the maid withdrew she turned to her mother. 'Is Papa unwell?'

Agnes shook her head. 'He isn't . . . He . . . didn't come home last night.' She spooned porridge into her bowl with a hand that shook slightly.

Harriet tried to hide her dismay. Her father had never slept anywhere but in his own bed when he was not at sea.

'Do we know where he was?' Her father had stayed away all night! It was unthinkable. Quickly, she reassessed the situation and decided that the previous day's quarrel was

122

more serious than she had thought, but if her mother thought she could keep her daughter in ignorance of the facts, she was wrong. She pressed on with her questions. 'Where do you think he is, Mama?'

'It's nothing to do with you, Harriet.' Agnes avoided looking at her.

'It *is* to do with me! He's my father!'

Agnes sighed but her lips remained firmly shut. She helped herself to porridge and added sugar and milk but she made no attempt to eat it.

'Mama!' Harriet laid down her own spoon. 'Papa has never done this before. Never walked out on us. Never been—'

'I expect he slept on board his ship.'

'And if he didn't? Mama, I'm not a child and I have a right to know what is going on.'

'I think you are better off if you don't know, dear. There are times when you must trust me and one of those times is now.'

Harriet felt a surge of resentment at being thus excluded and with it came a flash of anger. Her life was taking a disastrous turn and it was no time for family secrets. Taking a deep breath she said, 'Then, if we cannot talk about Papa I would like to talk about Marcus and the wedding.'

If Harriet expected a shocked reaction to this, she was disappointed. Her mother glanced up with dull eyes and said, 'Ah! The wedding.'

'I have to talk to you about me and Marcus.' She waited. Nothing. 'And Godfrey.'

Her mother's expression was distant.

'Mama? Are you listening? I said it's about—'

'You and Marcus. Yes . . . Look, Harriet, I'm afraid I have some rather disturbing—'

'Mama! I said it's about me and Marcus *and Godfrey*!'

Her mother drew a long shuddering breath. 'Your father has had some seriously bad news, Harriet, which has upset him very badly. He is going to need time to . . . to come to terms with something.'

Harriet stared at her. Wasn't her mother interested to know

about Godfrey Lester? Wasn't she the slightest bit curious to know what her daughter was trying to tell her?

Agnes busied herself with the teapot, pouring tea into Harriet's cup with shaking hands. 'There is just a chance, Harriet, that your wedding might have to be delayed. There. Now you know. I can't tell you more at present but it is a possibility. Your father is . . . He's badly shocked.'

'About what, Mama?'

'Something between us – him and me. We may have to speak with the Wellburys and apologize for a delay. I know this will hurt you, Harriet, and they won't be at all pleased but it really cannot be helped. The circumstances are such . . .' Her voice trailed away.

Harriet was stunned. For some reason her parents were considering delaying the wedding. Yet they had both been so delighted at the match which would mean that Harriet was secure for life and that she, Harriet, and her children would inherit the Wellburys' estate. Now, they were calmly preparing to put that in jeopardy. For a moment she forgot that this was exactly what she had wanted. 'But why?' she stammered.

Her mother shook her head. 'You may know in time,' she murmured. 'But for now . . .' She raised her slim shoulders in a weary shrug. 'So this Godfrey you speak of – is it Godfrey Lester?'

'Yes. I'm afraid that he and I . . .' She took a deep breath. 'Mama, were you and Papa in love when you married? Truly in love?'

Agnes looked surprised. 'I suppose we were. I don't remember, Harriet. It's a long time ago. Why do you ask?' She abandoned all pretence of eating the porridge and looked at the table. 'We don't seem to have any toast.'

Harriet wanted to scream. 'If you hadn't loved Papa would you still have married him? Did you have any choice?' She regarded her mother desperately. Why couldn't she find the right words, she asked herself, instead of going all round the houses. She should say, 'I want to marry Godfrey Lester,' but for some reason the words wouldn't come.

Agnes looked at her. 'Did I want to marry him? I don't

124

think my parents ever asked me. It was a very good match for me. Your grandfather was a very sweet man but hardly wealthy. He wanted my future to be secure.'

'How did he persuade Papa that he should marry you? Didn't Papa's father want his son to make a better match?'

Agnes fiddled with her wedding ring, deciding how to answer. 'Your father refused to marry the woman they chose for him. He could be very stubborn. The woman was from a wealthy family but Papa didn't care for her. She was a heavy, plain woman, poor soul. I was George's choice.'

'You mean you were prettier.'

'In a word – yes. We met through the church.' Her face softened. 'Your father wanted three sons. I don't know why. Of course it didn't happen. Childbearing isn't easy and I was delicate. But why is any of this so important, Harriet? It was years ago. History.'

Harriet seized her chance. 'Because I don't want to marry Marcus, Mama. I'm in love with Godfrey Lester.'

She frowned. 'The son of a housekeeper? Are you out of your mind, dear? It's out of the question.' She stood up distractedly. 'Now, I want you to walk down to the *Saint Augustine* and see if your father is there. On board, I mean. If not, you must enquire after him.'

'I will, Mama.' Harriet stood up quickly. 'But I won't marry Marcus. I don't love him any more. Maybe I never did. It was just accepted by all of us. I *love* Godfrey, Mama, with all my heart and—'

'Godfrey? How on earth can you say such a thing? You don't even know him. He's been abroad for years. You may not like him as much as you think. Sit down, Harriet, and eat your porridge.'

From habit, Harriet managed to swallow one spoonful while Agnes continued.

'I will not let you rush into something you may regret – and your father would be horrified. When you find him, you must promise me not to say a word about the wedding. Or Godfrey Lester.'

Agnes left the room, leaving Harriet thoroughly at a loss. The weird conversation had led nowhere useful. And what was she to say if she went to the quayside and found her father on his ship? Angry, confused and frustrated, Harriet covered her face with her hands.

The door opened and Izzie came in. 'Oh dear!' She stared at the untouched food.

Harriet said, 'We weren't hungry.'

Izzie stammered, 'I mean, it's not my business but . . . are we going to get the sack? Cook's that worried.'

'The sack? Of course not. Tell her not to worry. It's a . . . a family matter.' Harriet wondered whether the girl had been listening outside the door but on second thoughts that was unlikely or Agnes would have discovered her when she left the room.

Izzie began to pile the crockery on to the tray with deft movements and Harriet waited curiously to see if Izzie would ask a direct question about the previous night's events. Perhaps their future employment was all that interested them.

Suddenly Harriet said, 'Have you ever been in love, Izzie? Hopelessly, deliriously in love?'

Izzie glanced up. 'No, Miss Harriet, but I haven't given up hope.' She gave Harriet a shy smile.

Harriet looked into the hopeful face and thought suddenly of Daisy and it occurred to her that being poor might make being in love easier. There were no 'matches' to be made and no future to make secure because you had no prospects – nothing but each other. If you married a farmhand you would be a farmhand's wife for the rest of your life. Once again she felt a pang of envy.

'I'm sure your turn will come, Izzie. Somewhere out there –' Harriet waved a vague hand – 'is your future husband.'

'D'you really think so, Miss Harriet?'

'Certainly. And he'll be a very lucky man.'

To her surprise, Izzie blushed at this unexpected praise and said, 'Thank you again for the shawl. Cook says it suits me a treat.' She smiled. 'P'raps I'll catch the eye of some young man when I wear it to church on Sunday.'

Harriet nodded and then sighed. 'It's not at all what you expect, Izzie – true love – so be prepared when it happens.

You know what they say – "The course of true love never doth run smooth."''

'That's a shame then, Miss Harriet, 'cos it should!' She balanced the teapot precariously on top of the bowls and headed for the door. 'But I expect it's worth it in the end.'

'I hope so, Izzie.' Harriet's sigh was heartfelt. 'I certainly hope so.'

When Harriet eventually reached the quayside, she saw the *Saint Augustine* rocking gently at anchor but there was no sign of George Burnett. Men were busy carrying baskets up the gangway and Harriet spoke to one of them. 'Excuse me but I'm looking for my father. Captain Burnett. I'm his daughter and I—'

The man frowned. 'Skipper? Haven't seen him. You'd best speak with Mr Maddocks. He's bo'sun. Wait here and I'll tell him you've come.'

Dick Maddocks came down the gangway towards Harriet but gave her no answering smile. Instead there was a frown on his heavily bearded face.

'Good morning, Mr Maddocks,' Harriet began. 'I would like a few words with my—'

He was scratching his beard and now she imagined that he looked uneasy. 'Won't speak to nobody, miss. That's what he says. Not me, not anyone. Get the Hell out of it, Maddocks! Them's his exact words, miss. And me just trying to do my job, like.'

Harriet's stomach knotted uncomfortably. 'But – but why? I only want—'

His frown deepened. 'Don't ask me, lass. I'll likely be the last to know what's going on. Locked himself in his cabin, he has, and won't be disturbed. That's all I know, so don't press me.' He looked along the quayside, squinting against the sun, and shouted, 'Oi! Crump! You're late as usual! Get along here pronto, you sluggard!' He shook his head. 'They get worse! Every crew is worse than the last. Bone idle the lot of them.'

Harriet turned and saw a small man approaching with a sea bag on his shoulder. He broke into a stumbling run and arrived breathless and began to stammer excuses. He was unshaven and one eye was half closed. The bo'sun cuffed him round the ear and gave him a push so that the man almost fell.

'No idea of discipline!' Maddocks grumbled. 'Crews weren't like this when I signed on. Nowadays . . .' He rolled his eyes. 'Half don't speak the lingo, half don't want to and the other half—'

Harriet saw that he was enjoying his audience and interrupted the flow of his complaints. 'My father . . . did he sleep on board last night? He thought he might do so.'

'Slept like a babby I shouldn't wonder.' He mimed drinking. 'Bit too much of that, if you know what I mean, miss, no offence meant. Twenty-four hours before sailing and it's all up to me, like.'

Harriet stared at him in disbelief. 'Drunk? You mean Papa is . . . But he doesn't touch alcohol. He never even takes a glass of—'

'Well he does now, miss, so you'd best go home to your ma and tell her. Something's riled him proper and she might know about that. He came on board yesterday with a face like thunder, bawled out the second mate and went straight to his cabin. Not set eyes on him since. I know nothing 'cos he's clammed up.'

They moved aside as two men staggered up with a heavy crate which they manhandled up the gangway, cursing and muttering. Maddocks cried, 'Watch you tongues, you two. This here's the Skipper's daughter.'

One of them whispered something and they both laughed and Harriet felt her face flame with embarrassment. Did they all know the state her father was in? Whatever would her mother think?

She said desperately, 'Should I go down to him, Mr Maddocks? He might speak to me.'

'What? Let you go down there? More than my life's worth, miss! He gives the orders and I take 'em! Not that you'd get any sense out of him. He's ranting and grumbling and I don't know what else! You'd best try again later in the day. *Much* later.' He grinned showing two broken teeth. 'He may have sobered up by then but I give you fair warning – he'll have a very sore head and he'll be in a right pig of a mood! Rum does that to a man. I should know, I've downed enough and my missus has the bruises to prove it!'

He laughed raucously at this but Harriet did not find it at all funny. She hesitated then said stiffly, 'Then I'll say good day to you, Mr Maddocks,' and turned quickly on her heel and walked away.

On the way home Harriet tried to find a way to explain the situation without alarming her mother but then began to wonder if hiding the truth was the wisest thing to do. It might be possible for her mother to talk sense into her father – if she were able to get into the cabin. What was her father planning to do? she wondered. Surely he would not sail without saying his farewells. He always set great store by their partings since it was never guaranteed that he would return and her mother had a special prayer which he claimed had saved his life more than once in the past.

When she reached home, Izzie greeted her at the door. 'Mr Wellbury is here, Miss Harriet. That's *James* Wellbury. Come just a few moments ago but your ma went back to bed with a headache and is asleep, so I didn't know what to do. Should I wake her, poor soul? She looks so peaceful.'

Harriet unbuttoned her jacket. 'I'll see him,' she told her. 'He might want to leave a message for my mother.'

James Wellbury rose as Harriet entered the room and refused a tray of tea on the grounds that he had another call to make. When they were both seated he explained the problem, which, as Harriet expected, concerned Maybourne Workhouse. She would have to relay the information to her mother, so she listened attentively, glad that the subject of the wedding had not so far been raised and hoping to keep to matters connected with the workhouse.

James Wellbury explained that the casual ward, on the ground floor, provided basic sleeping accommodation for up to ten men, but frequently in the summer there were requests for up to twenty beds, which meant that many were turned away and must either walk on to the next town or sleep rough. Harriet had only had a glimpse of the casual ward and now asked her visitor about it.

'The so-called beds are nothing more than a row of separate

spaces which the men often refer to jokingly as "coffins",'
James Wellbury explained. 'Only they're rectangular. There's
no bedding provided – that is, no mattresses, because that
becomes a problem with – well, to put it bluntly, with fleas
and bugs . . .'

Harriet shuddered. 'So they sleep on bare boards?'

He shrugged. 'Most carry a blanket with them although
some don't and your mother feels that the *house* should
provide a few spare blankets. The Board provided some last
winter but by the spring they had disappeared – probably
smuggled out.'

A free blanket! Harriet nodded. All the men were really
being offered was space and a roof over their heads. In
summer it was enough but in winter it had occasionally been
so cold that a feeble traveller had died during the night.

'So is it only for men, Mr Wellbury?'

He nodded. 'They are mostly labourers who move through
the countryside looking for casual work. Mostly agricultural
labourers in fact. They're not destitute. Simply on the move.
The workhouses will give them overnight accommodation
and a simple breakfast and all for a penny or two. Not that
they all deserve it for there's some that always make trouble.
Turn up the worst for drink and pick a quarrel over nothing.
Fisticuffs, the lot! Mr Crane got a black eye once when he
tried to intervene.'

Breakfast, Harriet learned, would be a bowl of gruel and
a chunk of bread or porridge with salt. A mug of small beer
would go with it. No other meal was provided but many had
begged or 'borrowed' food along the way and would often sit
up in their beds and enjoy a simple meal of bread and cheese
or a slice of stale ham. If they had no money at all they could
work off the cost by a short session of stone-breaking.

'Sometimes they'll be asked to mop over a floor or clean
a few windows. It's all very easy.'

Harriet had stopped listening and was thinking what a
very decent man James Wellbury was and what a good
father-in-law he would make for someone. But not for her.

'The problem, Harriet, is that we, the Board, have suggested that the casual ward be rearranged to make space

for five more beds. The authorities have agreed to pay for the wood but not the blankets and the Board have to decide whether or not they will meet those costs again.'

'Mama will agree, I'm certain.'

He smiled. 'There is also the problem that Mr Crane has asked one of his friends to do the work at a rather exorbitant price and my feeling is that the funds should not be abused in that way and feel we should obtain two more estimates. I tried to speak with Miss Boothby this morning – Oh!'

Jasper had strolled in and leapt suddenly on to James Wellbury's lap. 'I'm not partial to cats,' he apologized, tipping the animal on to the floor and brushing the knees of his trousers. 'I went to Miss Boothby, first because I hate to disturb your mother when the Captain is ashore but Miss Boothby is away at her sister's in Ramsgate. I was hoping your mother would support me on this but I understand that today she is somewhat indisposed.'

'A little under the weather,' Harriet corrected him, wondering whether the servants had been indiscreet. 'Poor Mama had a sleepless night but no doubt she will awake soon, hopefully refreshed. Shall I ask her to contact you later today? I'm sure she will think the other estimates a good idea.'

'If you'd be so kind.'

As an afterthought, Harriet asked after his wife's health and that of Marcus, because not to do so would seem very odd if not downright discourteous.

'Both splendid!' he told her. 'And Marcus is being very secretive. He has plans for your honeymoon, he tells us, but further than that his lips are sealed!' He smiled at her fondly. 'Naturally we are both delighted and my wife is in such high spirits. The dressmaker practically *lives* at our house! But I do understand her excitement. We have never been blessed with a daughter and that was a disappointment to her. Two sons.'

'Two?' Harriet raised her eyebrows in surprise.

'One little boy died at the age of five months,' he told her. 'Such a terrible heartache. So my wife is looking forward to welcoming you into the family.'

Harriet glanced away, unable to confront his kindness.

'Marcus is a very lucky man,' he said.

'Oh! . . . Please . . .' she stammered.

James Wellbury stood up. 'You are too modest, Harriet. He *is* a most fortunate man. And when the grandchildren come along—' He stopped guiltily. 'I'm sorry. My wife has told me not to pressure you about a family and here I am doing just that! Trust me to do the wrong thing. I hope you'll forgive me, Harriet.'

'Indeed I will.' She was longing to get rid of him.

As soon as he had left the house, she hurried into the kitchen and made up a small basket of delicacies. A pot of honey, a bottle of wine and a newly baked milk loaf. Taking advantage of her mother's indisposition, Harriet had decided to visit Havely House on the pretence of taking a few delicacies to her great-uncle but in fact hoping to see Godfrey. She could also report to the Lesters on her unsuccessful attempt to ask her mother for advice.

Izzie said wistfully, 'Shall I come with you, Miss Harriet?' but was given a firm refusal.

When Harriet had left the house Cook and Izzie regarded each other soberly.

Cook said, 'I don't know whether I'm coming or going in this place! Is the master coming home for dinner and supper or for neither? What am I supposed to prepare with nobody telling me and the mistress still asleep?'

Izzie said, 'And the master not sleeping in his own bed!'

'And young Harriet off to Havely House to meet that young man of hers! Trying to fool us that it's her uncle she's concerned for. What is the matter with this family? Suddenly it's all at sixes and sevens!' Cook frowned. 'Maybe I'll do a pasty for supper then if no one eats it, it'll heat up midday tomorrow.' She shook her head despairingly. 'And while I think of it, nip up into the boxroom and see if you can find another big dish to replace the one the master smashed.'

'What – the good stuff in the tea chest?'

'Yes. And it *is* good, so don't go breaking any more of it!'

Five minutes later Izzie was down again, her eyes like saucers. 'They're all gone!' she cried.

Cook came out of the larder and stared at her. 'Gone? All of it?'

Izzie nodded. 'The tea chest is still there.'

'Well, who'd want an empty tea chest?' Cook sat down on the nearest stool, her face pale, her eyes dull. 'I knew it! I felt it coming – felt it in my bones but didn't like to say.' She turned slowly towards Izzie. 'There's a jinx got into this house!'

Izzie put a hand to her mouth. 'Don't talk like that!'

'We're in for it, now, you mark my words. Nothing but trouble for weeks to come. God help us all for nobody else will!'

Cook's doom-laden prophecy was proved to be horribly accurate later that same day. When Harriet returned from Havely House she was right outside her own home before she realized that something was different. A woman walking towards her glanced at the house then crossed herself. Slowly Harriet turned to look and saw that all the curtains were closed.

'Oh God!' she whispered as a cold fear clutched her. It could only mean one thing. For a moment she couldn't move and she found it hard to draw breath. A death! She uttered a small shrill cry and ran to batter her fists on the door and even as she did so, she tried to imagine what could have happened in her absence. Mama! Of course! She had been in some kind of trouble and that strange man had come to the window in the middle of the night. Had he returned and killed her? No . . . Fresh thoughts crowded in. Mama had been not tired but ill, she told herself, and no one had realized and she, Harriet, the neglectful daughter had sneaked off to Havely House.

The door opened and she almost fell inside. 'Who?' she gasped, clutching

Izzie's arms. 'Who's died? It's Mama, isn't it?' Tears burst from her eyes as she thought about her mother's last hours upstairs alone. 'It's my fault! I shouldn't have left her. Oh Mama!'

Izzie, red-eyed, shook her head. 'No, Miss Harriet. Not the mistress.'

'Not Mama? Then who? Not Sam?' Oh God, she thought.

133

Not little Sam with his cheeky face and endearing ways. 'What then, Izzie? Is it Sam?' She shook the distraught maid.

'No, Miss Harriet. It's your father.'

'*Papa?*'

Freeing herself from Harriet's grasp, Izzie fled back to the kitchen, leaving Harriet dumbstruck in the hall. Her father, was *dead*? That couldn't be right. Trust Izzie to muddle things. But if not her father then who? Her heart thumped painfully and she leaned against the wall for support. She could hear voices from the parlour and moved to the door. Turning the handle, she opened the door and drew in a sharp breath.

Her mother lay on the sofa with her feet on a cushion. Cook was on her knees beside her holding a bottle of sal volatile under her nose which was making her cough. A police sergeant sat in her father's favourite armchair but he rose to his feet as Harriet entered.

Agnes whispered, 'This is my daughter, Harriet.'

Cook glanced up. 'Your mother's had a bit of a turn. A terrible shock.'

Harriet looked at the policeman. 'My *father* . . . ?' she began.

'I'm sorry, Miss Burnett. There was a – an accident on board his ship. A shooting. The Captain is dead.'

Agnes waved away the sal volatile and pulled herself into a sitting position. Cook struggled to her feet and hovered anxiously. 'Maybe a drop of brandy, ma'am, for the shock?'

'No, thank you.' Agnes patted Cook's hand consolingly. 'You get back to the kitchen, Cook. I know you have work to do.' She looked at Harriet, her eyes dulled with incomprehension. 'They say George was shot.'

Harriet pulled up a chair and sat beside her mother, holding her hand tightly, trying to take in the extent of the disaster. 'Shot? By whom?'

Agnes turned to the sergeant. 'You tell her.'

He cleared his throat and consulted his notebook and Harriet could see he was trying to avoid looking at her.

'It seems from our enquiries that your father remained in his cabin for a very long period and refused to open the door or speak to anyone.' He spoke slowly and without a trace of emotion and Harriet presumed this was the way he'd been trained to deliver bad news. 'When the bo'sun – a Mr Maddocks – became worried they forced the door and found him already dead with a gunshot wound to the head.'

'Somebody killed him!'

'No, miss. The cabin door was locked on the *inside*. No one else could get in to kill him even if they'd wanted to – though that is unlikely. The bo'sun says that there was no trouble on board. Except the usual punishments for disorder: sloppy behaviour, late on watch . . .' He shrugged. 'No mutiny. Nothing of that nature. I'm afraid his death was self-inflicted.'

Harriet groaned and he glanced up. 'I'm sorry, miss. Shall I go on?'

She nodded but her mind was a teeming mass of impossible, incongruous thoughts. Someone had shot her father! He would *never* shoot himself.

The sergeant cleared his throat. 'The deceased had been dead for some hours and had written a last letter to your mother.'

Harriet frowned, still not quite understanding what the man was telling her. A letter to her mother . . . Did that mean he was leaving her? She looked at Agnes.

'Harriet, your father killed himself and I am to blame.'

'You've read the letter?'

'No, but I know why he . . . why he did it. I can't talk about it now but later perhaps.' She closed her eyes.

The policeman went on in the same monotone. 'The police were called to the scene and a doctor was consulted, who announced cause of death and signed the certificate. An inquest will be held but in the meantime . . .'

Harriet didn't hear the rest. She was too busy grappling with the unpleasant truth as she saw it. Her father hadn't loved them. He had left his wife and two children to an uncertain future. Why? Her mother seemed to think that she was to blame but her father adored Sam. *Had* adored him, she corrected herself. Why would he want to leave his beloved son? She thought of her brother and how upset he would be. How could her father have done such a terrible thing?

'Harriet!'

Her mother was speaking to her and she wrenched her thoughts back to the present.

'Harriet, I have to go to the hospital now, where they have taken your father's body. I have to identify him.'

Harriet stood up. 'No, Mama! You are in no fit state to go anywhere.' She looked at the sergeant. 'Can we do that later? An hour or so perhaps? When my mother is recovered?'

'Certainly.' He also stood, putting away his notebook. 'We shall be in touch again in due course but . . . My commiserations to you both. A suicide is a—'

'Don't!' cried Harriet. 'Don't use that dreadful word. He is dead and we have lost him. That's all that matters to us at the moment.'

He looked offended, drawing himself up stiffly and reaching for his helmet.

'We have a few more statements to take from the crew. We'll keep you informed of any new developments.'

Harriet swallowed hard, wishing she could cry but astonishingly her eyes were now painfully dry and tears seemed impossible. She walked the policeman to the door and then went back into the parlour, where her mother now sat, holding the letter George had written.

Harriet sat down opposite her mother. 'Did Papa really kill himself ? I can't quite believe it even now.'

Agnes nodded. 'You had better read the letter,' she said. 'You have to know or you will never understand.'

Harriet unfolded the sheet and read it with growing disbelief.

Agnes, You have just confirmed for me something that I have always suspected – that Harriet is not my daughter . . .

Harriet read the words again as the world seemed to shift a little. 'Mama? What is he saying? Not his daughter? But of course I am!'

Her mother sighed deeply and looked at her with deep compassion. 'No, Harriet. Your father was right. You are not his child. I have tried to keep the secret but somehow he has suspected the truth and recently I was forced to confess.'

'You mean . . . Does that mean you . . .' Her voice was hoarse. 'That I am . . . ?'

'Illegitimate? No, Harriet. You are not. You were born within wedlock. Have no fears on that score.'

For a moment Harriet allowed the words to sink in. Her mother sat twisting her handkerchief in her lap and suddenly Harriet snatched it away. 'How can that be? If Papa is not my father then you and another man . . .' She frowned and put a hand to her head, which was beginning to throb.

Agnes said, 'Read the letter, Harriet.'

It continued:

At least, not my daughter in the biological sense, but I have tried to be good to her, not wishing to know the truth and not daring to face the consequences. All I know is that you have been unfaithful to me and that cuts me to the heart after all the love I gave you. Sam is my own son – I feel that in my heart and I'm sorry for the hurt this will cause him. And you and Harriet. Poor girl, she is not to blame for what you did. I cannot face the shame of this scandal which will now break over your heads. Perhaps you will forgive me as I have tried unsuccessfully to forgive you. Take care of the children. I'm sorry our marriage has ended this way.

George.

Harriet could not speak. She could hardly think. A scandal about to break with herself as the central figure. Or was that Mama? The silence lengthened. Harriet was afraid to ask the crucial question but she had to know.

'Who, Mama? Whose daughter am I?'

'I cannot tell you that, Harriet, but he was a decent man.'

'Decent?' Harriet's voice rose. 'Does a decent man behave like – like that with a married woman? *Decent?*' She began to tremble and a terrible chill was spreading through her body but she felt she had to go on. 'How did Papa find out about this decent man? Did you tell him? Is that why you quarrelled and he walked out? Did you tell *him* who it was? Mama! I have to know!'

'I didn't choose to tell him. He found out because of the ring. I had to sell it to raise the money to stop him finding out the truth about you. I was being blackmailed, Harriet.' She lowered her voice. 'The man you saw at the window. I was handing over the money. Somehow he found out but I cannot imagine how.'

There was a long silence. Harriet was torn between pity for her mother and anger on her own behalf. She felt utterly betrayed. There was a knock on the door and Izzie came in with a tray of tea and cake. She set it down without a word and fled.

Harriet said, 'Am I like him?'

'Like who?'

'My *father*, of course!'

After a pause Agnes said, 'Yes. He was a fine-looking man.'

Harriet wanted to run away – anywhere. Instead she said, 'So this decent, fine-looking man did this to you . . . and then ran off. Disappeared. How could a fine, decent man do that? Leaving you to—'

'He died.' She stood up shakily. 'I'm deeply sorry for what has happened but I cannot tell you any more. You will have to trust me, Harriet. I must—'

'*Trust you?* Mama! Do please listen to yourself. I'm supposed to trust you after . . . after all this? How will I ever trust anyone again?'

Ignoring her mother's stricken face, Harriet finally felt the tears on her cheeks and stumbled towards the door and up the stairs. She heard Agnes call her from below but shut and locked her bedroom door. She threw herself on to the bed and began to cry – for herself, for her mother, her dead father and the real father she would never know.

Nine

It was nearly six o'clock before Agnes felt ready to attend the hospital mortuary for the identification. Then she and Harriet went by hansom cab and, arriving at the reception area, were asked to wait by a small harrassed man who seemed to have lost the necessary paperwork and somehow blamed them. He pointed to a row of stools and Harriet and her mother made themselves as comfortable as they could while he rummaged through drawers and riffled through ledgers, grumbling under his breath. Harriet had the thought that death seemed to inconvenience him. Agnes still looked very pale and Harriet slid an arm round her waist and drew her closer.

During the intervening hours Harriet had not spoken again with her mother but her mind was clearing and she was full of questions. She came to the conclusion that her mother had been in love with another man and this both shocked and excited her. She began to weave fantasies about her mysterious father and made up her mind that she would somehow visit his grave and lay flowers. If only she had known earlier! They could have met secretly. It was unlikely that her mother would fall in love with a labourer, so presumably he had been a wealthy man. How tragic that they had not been able to marry but possibly the man was also married. So did she, Harriet, have half-brothers or -sisters? That was an intriguing thought albeit a disloyal one and she was instantly ashamed of herself. There was no way George Burnett was responsible for the present catastrophe, she decided, even though he was the one who had pulled the trigger. Her mother was the guilty one – the one who had been unfaithful. Poor George had lived all these years with the terrible suspicion of her betrayal but had only now had these fears confirmed. He was to be pitied, Harriet reminded herself, not blamed.

'Burnett – George Henry?' The attendant was waving a handful of papers.

'Yes.' Agnes's voice was little more than a whisper.

'This way.'

They followed dutifully behind the attendant as he led them along a gloomy corridor and down four steps. They were soon in a cold, dimly lit room in which two shrouded figures waited on wooden trestles. One of these was covered in a white cotton cloth, the other was hidden beneath a grey blanket and instinctively Harriet knew that this was her father. He had committed a crime by shooting himself and would not be afforded the normal courtesies. She swallowed as she thought of his funeral, which would be the barest service and a hasty burial in an untended part of the churchyard. The Church did not condone the taking of life and even the deceased must be punished.

Without preamble, the man whipped back the blanket and Agnes swayed at the ghastly sight. Wearing a white hospital gown, George lay as though in rigid sleep but his face appeared to have collapsed in on itself. His eyes were sunk in their sockets and his cheeks were drawn in so that the bones were evident below the flesh. His hair was matted and there was a round hole in his right temple where the bullet had entered. His hands were folded across his chest and there was still blood on the pillow.

'Whoops!' The man put out a hand to steady Agnes and Harriet also supported her. 'Is that him?' he asked Agnes.

Agnes was staring at the man with whom she had shared so many years of her life.

'Is that your husband?' The attendant rolled impatient eyes.

Harriet nudged her mother who nodded reluctantly.

'Bit louder, please,' he insisted.

Harriet snapped, 'Don't bully her! There is no need.'

'I'm just doing my job!'

'You could be kinder.'

He glared at her, his face reddening. 'I'm not paid to be

kind! I'm paid to watch bodies.' He turned back to Agnes. 'Well?'

Agnes sighed deeply, her mouth trembling.

Harriet said, 'That is George Henry Burnett. Yes.'

Agnes looked as though she might faint and Harriet wanted to hurry her from the room but her mother seemed unwilling to go.

Agnes whispered, 'I'm sorry, George. You didn't deserve it.'

The man tutted impatiently as outside a church clock chimed. To Harriet's surprise her mother leaned forward and kissed her dead husband's forehead. Harriet, still mesmerized by the sight, stepped forward reluctantly and tried to follow suit but couldn't and instead kissed one of his hands. 'Goodbye, Papa. God bless you.'

Impossible to believe, she thought bitterly, that an all-seeing, all-loving God could turn away from George Burnett, who, in a moment of dark despair, had taken the final way out.

Daisy turned up for work on Thursday, eager for news. She regarded the coffin he was making with dismay and turned on Albert angrily.

'This is for the Captain? For Mr Burnett? This meagre old thing? That's disrespectful, that is. I know his wife and they're a good family.'

Albert spread his hands, palm upwards. 'Don't nag me. I don't make the rules. He killed himself and that's a crime. So he has to pay the penalty and that is a simple funeral. That's the law.'

She frowned. 'But our lot get better than that!'

'No, you don't – and that's the law. A suicide is not entitled to a proper burial with all the trimmings. He's like any other criminal.' He slapped a duster into her hand and said, 'You know where the polish is.'

'So we're giving it a bit of a polish, are we?'

'No, we're not. You're giving *Mrs Plaint's* coffin a bit of a polish. Nice bit of elm, that is. They're paying good money, so mind you do a good job.'

He watched her get started.

Daisy dabbed at the polish with the cloth. 'So what she die of, this Mrs Plaint? Too much food? These rich folk are all the same.' She thought of the family she had worked for so briefly and that led to thoughts about Digger and just how far he could be trusted. If she found out he was holding back on the money . . . Grimly she applied herself to the wood. There was the picture – the frame was worth a shilling but the picture was boring – bottle, some apples and a bunch of green grapes. Not much of a picture but she supposed some people liked that kind of thing and would be glad to part with their money.

She said, 'So why'd the Captain do it? Debts?'

'None of our business, Daisy.' Albert was sorting out a handful of brass tacks and then he sorted through the hinges, looking for something that looked good but wouldn't necessarily last. If it rusted a few months after internment who would know?

'I did hear,' she went on, 'that his wife cheated on him and the daughter wasn't his! Fine goings-on!' She laughed.

'Not up to me to criticize my clients,' he said, the reproof obvious by his tone. 'You shouldn't listen to idle gossip.'

She said slowly, 'What would you do if your partner – that is your partner in crime – was cheating on you? I mean, really, what would you do?'

He peered over half-moon spectacles. 'Something nasty! Very nasty!'

'Like a whack on the head? That's what I think. It's this ruddy Digger.' She straightened up to admire her work. She was working up a great shine and it was easier than picking oakum. 'I could swear he's conning me. Making out he broke something so he doesn't have to give me my fair share!'

She muttered something obscene and Albert stiffened, unused to hearing women use such language.

Abruptly changing the subject, Daisy asked, 'So what happened to Mrs Plaint? Might as well know what you can die of. Might come in handy.'

'If you must know, she died of a fall. Broke her leg, got pneumonia and then her lungs gave up the struggle. Mind you

142

she was sixty-five. A good age. Especially since she had nine children.'

'Nine? Lord love us! Me, I don't want any. I hate little'uns. Noisy, smelly little beasts. Always moaning. Always wanting something. You got any?'

'Haven't got a wife.'

'What – wouldn't nobody have you?' She laughed, but not unkindly.

'Never fancied it, if you must know.'

She paused to stare at him. 'What, don't fancy a bit of the other? Someone to warm your bed!'

'I'm happy as I am, thank you!'

'Don't thank me. I'm not offering.'

She resumed her work thoughtfully. Aware of her charms and the effect she had on the opposite sex, Daisy knew she could turn Albert Hawke around if she put her mind to it. The problem was she fancied Digger, but did she trust him? If he was playing fast and loose with her share of the profits . . . Her frown deepened and she sighed. Life was short. Perhaps she would give Digger one more chance.

Several hours passed and the clock had just struck three when Marcus Wellbury arrived at the Burnetts' house in a state of high anxiety. Izzie led him into the parlour and then Agnes, already in mourning black, was informed. She went immediately to her daughter's room, knocked and went straight in.

'Mama? You should be resting.' Harriet turned from writing in her diary.

Agnes went to the chest and drew out a black dress that was folded in tissue paper. She laid it on the bed and said, 'We have to be practical, Harriet. I cannot afford the luxury of rest and neither can you. Marcus is here, and you must come downstairs. But you must not talk to him alone, do you understand? I will be with you. This is going to be most unpleasant but whatever he says or does, you must not agree to break off your betrothal. It's most important that you remember that.'

Harriet closed the diary and slid it into the drawer. 'Will

he *want* to withdraw from the arrangement? Do you really think so?'

Agnes regarded her suspiciously. 'You don't seem worried by the idea and you should be. You have a lot to learn, Harriet.'

'Oh, I am worried but . . . if he doesn't want to go ahead . . .'

Agnes swallowed hard. 'I know what you're thinking, Harriet, but this is not an excuse for you to run off with the Lester boy. He is not at all suitable for you. In your position you must find a husband who will give you security . . . Now even more so!' She broke off, glancing round distractedly. 'But we're wasting time. Put on your black, tidy yourself and join me in the parlour as quickly as you can but remember – I am going to do most of the talking.'

Hurrying downstairs, Agnes drew several deep breaths and tried to calm herself. She must be prepared for the coming encounter. She must be strong for Harriet's sake. Marcus Wellbury must not now renounce his marriage to Harriet. That would be her undoing. Harriet was already the subject of gossip in the town since George's death had been reported. News that she had been jilted would put an end to any chance she had of a making a good match.

She went into the parlour. The closed curtains gave it a gloomy feel and the two tall candles flickered unhelpfully. Agnes smiled wanly as she held out her hand. 'Dearest Marcus, How kind of you to come. I knew you would. It's at times like these that one needs strong and loyal friends.'

'Well, I—' He shook her hand.

'I said to my daughter, Marcus will be the first to call to offer us support and to reassure you. Poor child, she is so afraid. This has been a terrible blow for her.' Agnes sat down and motioned for Marcus to do the same. She noted that he seemed ill at ease and her heart sank. 'Harriet will be down shortly. I told her you are made of sterner stuff and that the Wellburys do not break a promise lightly.'

He said, 'My parents are extremely disturbed by the rumours but felt unable to visit at such a time. I thought . . . I felt I should come and hear at first hand what has happened.

I cannot believe that your husband had acted in any way that was not entirely honourable. Talk of financial irregularities in the ship's affairs cannot be true.'

Agnes put a hand to her heart. So wicked rumours were already circulating. Appalled, she struggled to keep her composure. 'Irregularities? That is arrant nonsense, Marcus. I assure you the reason for my husband's distress was – was purely personal. A matter arose between us for which I am to blame, causing him such grief that he temporarily took leave of his senses. Poor George. It was a severe shock for him. Nothing at all to with my daughter, I hasten to add.' It was a lie but she hoped God would forgive her.

'That is a great relief, Mrs Burnett. We never, for one moment, believed ill of Harriet's father. We have always held all of you in the highest regard but naturally . . .' He stood up as Harriet entered.

Agnes tried to see her daughter through his eyes. The black dress suited her slim figure and the black lace she wore over her hair made her look foreign – Spanish perhaps – but did nothing to diminish her looks. In fact she looked quite beautiful. Surely Marcus would not change his feelings.

'Marcus!' she said and moved hesitantly towards him.

He muttered, 'I'm so sorry.'

He bent to kiss her but Agnes was disappointed. He should have swept Harriet into his arms with protestations of his devotion but instead he looked awkward and unsure. Harriet didn't sit beside him although there was plenty of room on the sofa. She chose to perch herself on a chair alone. Agnes sighed. Why hadn't she warned her daughter to be as affectionate as possible? Hadn't she any sense – or was this deliberate on her part?

Harriet said, 'And so am I. This is terrible.'

He said, 'This has nothing to do with you, Harriet. You have no reason to apologize.'

'What are they saying about us? Nothing good, I'm sure.' Harriet avoided Agnes's eyes.

'Nothing . . . that is, there are rumours but that's to be expected. But all our sympathies are with you both. It is a dreadful crime – No, I mean sin . . .' He faltered to a halt. 'My parents felt this was not the time to visit.'

'I'm sure they did!' Harriet's voice was sharp and Agnes gave her a warning look.

Why couldn't the silly child see that marriage to Marcus was her only chance? Quickly Agnes intervened. 'I have promised my daughter that as soon as George has been buried we shall carry on our lives as normally as possible.'

'But how will you manage?' he asked.

A good question and one Agnes had chosen not to consider. She had sold her few assets to pay the blackmailer and as far as she knew there were few savings. Captain of the the *Saint Augustine* had carried a certain amount of prestige but it was not so highly paid that George could have made much provision for the future. The unexpected, Agnes reflected unhappily. That is what doomed many people less well off than herself to a wretched struggle for existence. She thought fleetingly of the widowed Mrs Bly. Now she and Agnes were facing just such a problem.

She sighed. 'We'll cross that bridge later, Marcus.' She gave a little shrug. 'At present I am happy just to know that at least Harriet's future is secure with you. Poor child has—'

'Mama! I am not a child nor am I poor! You make me sound like a lost kitten!'

Marcus smiled uncertainly and Agnes sensed his dismay. He had never seen his betrothed at anything other than her best. Now Harriet seemed determined to disillusion him.

Agnes said, 'I think we should delay the wedding for a week or two until the fuss had died down but we can agree a new date and go ahead with the—'

Marcus interrupted her. 'We thought, that is my parents thought, we should do nothing further until—'

Harriet jumped to her feet. 'Until you can think of a way to get out of it! That's what you mean, isn't it?' Her face was reddening. 'Why not tell the truth, Marcus. You don't want to marry me now, do you? Damaged goods! That's how you see me. Oh, don't pretend. I'm not stupid.'

He also stood, his face pale. 'That's not it at all, Harriet. I still love you dearly. We simply think—'

'Well, when you've decided let me know!' Harriet turned sharply and without a further glance at either of them, swept out of the door and slammed it behind her.

Slowly Agnes rose to her feet. 'Please, Marcus! The poor child is distraught. I beg you to make allowances for her. She was relying on your devotion. The poor girl is not herself. Losing her father has been a terrible blow and she is understandably confused.'

He nodded. 'Grief takes people in different ways.'

'She cannot forgive her father for . . . for what she sees as a desertion. A dereliction of duty, if you like. She is a sweet-natured girl, as you well know. I shall speak to the doctor about her as soon as I am more composed.'

'You are bearing up bravely, Mrs Burnett. I am full of admiration.'

A few moments later she saw him to the door and they parted amicably enough with protestations of good faith, but Agnes knew in her heart that Harriet's behaviour had done considerable damage to her chances and that her marriage to Marcus was no longer a certainty. She stumbled back into the parlour and sank down on to the sofa, sick at heart and aware of a growing dread.

Phineas Chisom had finished his surgery for the day and was tidying his files at the cupboard below the window when his mother entered the room.

'I'm sorry, Phin, but there's a young woman to see you. I've told her she's too late and surgery's finished but she says it's urgent and won't give her name.'

He groaned. 'With child, perhaps?'

'Phin!' She tutted with mock exasperation. 'You are becoming very cynical. She doesn't look in the family way but she *is* very pretty.'

He grinned. 'Are you still trying to marry me off, Mother?'

'I shall never stop trying, Phin. So you will see her?'

'I suppose so. Tell her to come in.'

A moment later a young dark-haired woman entered the surgery. Her face was pale and her eyes showed strain. She was dressed in deep mourning and as he greeted her he felt an uncomfortable jolt of recognition and his heartbeat speeded up fractionally. It was the daughter of the dead sea captain. He remembered her from the brief meeting at the workhouse.

'Sit down, please,' he stammered and retreated from the window to the safety of his desk while guilt flared within him. 'It's Miss Burnett, isn't it.' He had already heard of the death of Captain Burnett and was horribly afraid that his blackmail of Mrs Burnett had somehow contributed to, if not actually brought about, the disaster.

She nodded.

'I was sorry to hear of your father's sad end.'

'Thank you.'

She seemed remarkably composed, he thought although appearances might be misleading. 'How can I help you?'

'I would like to take a look at the report about my birth,' she said, her tone level and unemotional. 'I think I am entitled to do that.'

'Your birth. Ah!' He frowned. Where was this leading? he wondered. Did she know about the blackmail? It was just possible that the mother had confided in her, in which case he must be very careful what he said and even more careful what he revealed. Blackmail was a criminal offence. 'It might be possible,' he hedged, 'but it was some years ago and I was not practising then. My stepfather—'

'They must still be in existence. A record of my birth should still be available.'

'The birth would have been registered elsewhere,' he said. 'What exactly are you looking for, Miss Burnett.'

She hesitated and her composure was beginning to break up. She fiddled with her gloves and avoided his eyes. 'I want to see the details. Name of father, mother, who was in attendance. Midwife. Doctor. Surely there can be no exception to such a request?'

'It is a question of confidentiality,' he began, seeing a way out of the difficulty. 'Between a doctor and a patient. The Hippocratic oath.'

'But I am not asking for another person's details, only my own!'

'The details of your birth belong to your mother, Miss Burnett. Why don't you ask her about the circumstances?'

'Because she is in a very delicate condition – from the shock of Papa's sui—' she bit back the ugly word, '– Papa's death. I want to spare her any more anguish.'

'Mmm . . .' He rested his elbows on the desk and steepled his hands thoughtfully. Would it do any harm to grant her request? Would it endanger himself in any way? He was actually rather attracted to the young woman and touched by the trust she placed in him. He was sorry for her and this made him even more ashamed of what he had done to her mother. He stood up. 'Let me see if I can find the notes,' he said. 'If I do, I could perhaps leave them lying on the desk unattended while I leave the room to speak to my mother. If you were to glance at them I wouldn't know, would I?' He gave her a conspiratorial smile.

She was working it out in her mind. 'Oh! I see.' She looked at him eagerly. 'Thank you, Dr Chisom.'

In fact he had no intention of showing her anything – it would be much too dangerous – but he would pretend they were not available and then she would be satisfied that he had tried to help her and convinced that he had nothing to hide.

He went to the cupboard where the old files were kept and made a show of finding the right one. 'Ah here we are,' he said. 'Details of . . . Oh! These are your brother's details. My father was in attendance, I see.' The mother's *first* child. He had looked in vain for an account of this young woman's birth but without result. The knowledge had made it possible for him to extract the money from Agnes Burnett. Not that it had done him much good, he reflected bitterly. The fifty guineas had repaid a few debts but the amount was too little, too late. He and his mother were still in a mess financially and he had made matters worse by committing a crime which he now deeply regretted. He had acted in a moment of panic.

'Let me see . . .' He gave Miss Burnett another smile. He frowned. 'I'm afraid only your brother's details are here. I'm afraid my stepfather must have mislaid them. Unless he was away or indisposed at the time and another doctor was called in as an emergency. In that case *he* would have the record.' He

149

smiled. 'My stepfather was an excellent doctor, Miss Burnett, but he hated paperwork. Inclined to muddle along, I'm afraid.' He prayed she would be satisfied by the explanation.

'Not there? Are you sure?'

'Quite sure, Miss Burnett.' He returned the file and pretended to search on. 'Ah! Here are some earlier notes.' He tutted. 'Oh dear. It seems she lost two babies earlier. How sad . . . But nothing here about you, Miss Burnett. It's all to do with the filing system, you see. In all probability, my father attempted to reorganize at some stage and files may have changed after a certain date. Or perhaps she was somewhere else at the time – out of Maybourne when you arrived. It was so long ago . . .' He shrugged as he returned the file to its place on the shelf. 'So I'm afraid our little plan will not work, Miss Burnett. There are no details of your birth readily available.'

She stood up, agitated. 'Why don't I believe you, Doctor? Why do I think you are hiding something?'

His mouth tightened and he regarded her warily. Her tone was hostile and she was making him nervous. Guilt made him suspicious. Was this really a ploy to discover more about the blackmail? Could she possibly have *guessed*? He felt himself beginning to sweat. His only chance was fight back. Closing the cupboard doors hastily, he said, 'Perhaps you don't want to believe them, Miss Burnett. Perhaps you suspect there is a reason for the missing details.'

She swallowed hard and said hoarsely 'Where is my file? My details! I have a right to see them.'

'It isn't here! You must ask your mother. Perhaps . . .' He changed his mind but too late.

'Perhaps what? *Tell me!*' She caught hold of his sleeve. 'Tell me what you were going to say. You know something. I know you do!'

He snatched his arm away and stepped back, fearful of losing control of the situation. There was a fierce look in her eyes and he was afraid she might become hysterical. If there was a scene, his mother would come in and there would be endless questions afterwards. He came to the conclusion that the truth might be the safest policy. If she *was* adopted,

150

her mother would have some explaining to do but at least he would not have added to his own mistakes.

He looked her squarely in the face. 'I was going to say you might have been adopted. Is that at all possible? That would account for the absence of details.'

She looked shocked but she was no longer threatening. Turning towards the window, she stared out, breathing fast. Perhaps he shouldn't have said that but at least it might throw her off the track.

'That's impossible,' she muttered, her voice unsteady. 'But it *is* possible that . . . Never mind. Thank you for your time. I can see myself out.'

He watched her go with a mixture of shock and relief. Please God let that be the end of it, he thought. Being adopted was hardly the end of the world. But what else had she thought of? She had said, 'But it *is* possible . . .' Perhaps she had thought of another explanation. Sighing, he went through into the kitchen.

His mother looked up from her sewing. 'So, Phin, *was* she expecting a child?'

'No, Mother. It was nothing important.'

'She made it sound important.'

'It was Miss Burnett in a bit of a state. She wanted a sleeping draught for her—'

'The captain's daughter? The one that—'

'The suicide. Yes.' He tried to think calmly about the meeting, trying to recall what had been said, desperately praying that he hadn't said anything that would arouse suspicion. He was beginning to feel that Maybourne was no longer a safe place for them to live. If Miss Burnett went to the police with her suspicions . . . If the finger once pointed in his direction . . . And there was the maid. He should never have trusted her. If pressed by the police, the sixpence he had given her would prove woefully inadequate and she would tell everything.

'Oh Phin! The poor soul. I hope you were able to help her.'

'I'm sure I did.' He took a deep breath. 'I was wondering – how would you like to leave here, Mother? A fresh start.' He

151

crossed his fingers behind his back. 'We could live nearer to your cousin, perhaps, in Sidmouth.'

She stared at him. 'What d'you mean, dear? Give up the practice?'

'Yes. I've told you how things are – that father left unpaid debts. I could start a new practice of my own or go into partnership. I'd like that.'

'Well, I don't rightly know. Leave Maybourne after all these years . . . What's got into you?'

He shrugged. He was almost as surprised as she was. The idea had sprung from somewhere deep inside him but he vaguely recognized it as a desire for flight. As an attempt at self-preservation.

Two days later Godfrey and his mother had just sat down with a pot of tea when they heard footsteps on the stairs and looked at each other in surprise.

Mrs Lester said, 'Don't tell me he's wandering around the house! Wonders will never cease.'

'If it is, it's a good sign, isn't it?'

'A very good sign.' She went to the door. 'Mr Burnett, is something wrong?'

He had reached the bottom of the stairs and now clutched the newel post anxiously. 'There's someone in the garden!'

'That's the gardener. Cummings. You know him, sir. Nothing to worry about.'

'Ah yes. Of course. I thought I heard carriage wheels on the gravel of—'

'That was the hansom cab, Mr Burnett, bringing my son from the station.'

To her surprise he ventured further along the passage, peering past her into the kitchen. 'Ah yes. Your son.'

To help jog the old man's memory Godfrey came out into the passage and held out his hand. 'Good morning, Mr Burnett. I hope I find you well.'

'Well? Yes, I'm well enough.'

Mrs Lester said, 'Godfrey's been away for a few days to visit a sick friend and now he's back. Arrived back ten minutes ago in fact.' The old man looked unconvinced, so she added, 'He plays chess with you sometimes.'

'Ah, chess!' He smiled. 'Well, any time you feel like a game, Godfrey . . .'

'Thank you, sir. I'll come up in half an hour if you like, when I've unpacked.'

'Fine . . . Fine.' He turned and made his way slowly upstairs.

Back in the kitchen Mrs Lester poured the tea thoughtfully. She was putting off the telling of the bad news. 'I sometimes wonder if he's as vague as he pretends to be. I had an aunt who used to pretend she was deaf but it turned out she wasn't and she'd heard a lot of things best unheard, if you know what I mean!'

Godfrey hid his impatience. 'Have you seen Harriet while I was away?'

She sighed. 'I've seen her. She came up one day with a few bits and bobs for her great-uncle – honey and home-made bread – and some wine which I hid from him. You know how it goes to his head and his brain is fuzzy enough already! But she really came in hopes of seeing you. She was most put out to know that you'd gone to London. So how was John?'

'Recovering, but they're still worried about the cause of the collapse, so he has to see a consultant in London. Is Harriet well?'

'I've seen her and she was fine but since then –' She glanced at him unhappily. 'To tell you the truth there's been things going on while you've been gone. Dreadful things.'

'Dreadful things?' His expression changed. 'Oh Lord! She's not hurt, is she?'

His mother took a deep breath. 'Not hurt exactly. Not physically, that is, but in a great state of shock, Godfrey, because . . . there's been a terrible accident. Her pa's dead!'

'George Burnett, *dead*?' His eyes widened. 'But he was as fit as a flea! My poor Harriet! What happened?'

She sipped her tea. 'He didn't just die. He killed himself. Shot himself in the head in his cabin on his ship. Nobody heard a sound.'

Now that the worst was over, she explained further and Godfrey listened with growing horror.

'Poor Harriet! How frightful for her – and for her mother. I must try to see them.'

'I don't know when would be a good time, dear. They'll all be in mourning.' Narrowing her eyes, she lowered her voice. 'But I did wonder, Godfrey, how the Wellburys will be taking the news. I mean, they're a well-established family and something like this – a *suicide*! They're not going to like it, are they?'

'Mother! What a thing to say! But . . . Oh! I see what you mean. You're absolutely right. They will *not* want their precious son mixed up with anything so unpalatable as a suspicious death.' He frowned. 'Why *did* he kill himself? Something must have provoked such a rash deed. You don't think he was sick and dying, do you? Some people, when they hear bad news—'

'Nothing like that apparently. I heard that his wife said it was a personal problem between her and him but what it was we may never know.'

Godfrey had brightened. 'Not that it would matter at all to me. Nor to you, Mother. Would it?'

'Of course it wouldn't matter, Godfrey. You love the girl and that's all that matters. If the Wellburys *do* oppose the wedding it will make things easier for you . . . But how could it be personal?' She hesitated. 'I did hear a whisper that the captain might have been involved in underhand deals connected with the ship but—'

'I can't believe that.' Emphatically Godfrey shook his head. 'I'd swear that any member of Harriet's family is as straight as a die. But even if he *had* done something wrong it would be unfair to blame the wife or daughter!'

'There'll have to be an inquest.'

'An inquest? Oh no!' The thought made him frown. 'Lordy! What a nightmare!'

His mother reached across and patted his hand. 'Fate is very strange, Godfrey. It may be a terrible thing that has happened – and it *is* – but you know what they say: "*It's an ill wind . . .*" If the Wellburys decide that Harriet is no longer a suitable daughter-in-law it would make matters much easier for you!'

Ten

H arriet rose next morning and, pulling on her dressing robe, went to tap on her mother's door.

'Come in.'

Her mother was sitting up in bed reading her bible. Her hair was dishevelled, her face was a dull white and her eyes seemed to have sunk into their sockets. Harriet, shocked by her mother's appearance, tried to hide her distress as she approached the bed.

'Can we talk, Mama. There are things I must know.'

Agnes sighed and laid down the bible. 'I've been expecting you, Harriet. Pull the chair up.' She waited while Harriet obeyed. 'I tried to compose a letter to Sam but I could think of no way to soften the blow, so instead I have written to the Head Master, asking him to break the news gently. Poor Sam has to know his father is dead but how much can I hide from him? He will soon hear the gossip for himself. And should he come to the funeral, I wonder? If he does, he will see George buried in a cheap coffin without even a headstone! What will he think, poor child?' Tears filled her eyes. 'I don't want to lie to him.'

'You have lied to me, Mama'

Agnes nodded miserably. 'And what good has it done? You have had to learn the truth and now you are hurt and angry.'

'I went to see Doctor Chisom, Mama, to ask to see the details of my birth. He couldn't find them. Why was that?'

'The old doctor was out of town. There was a locum. Perhaps he didn't fill in all the required forms – or filed it in the wrong place.'

Harriet fought back her growing anger. 'Doctor Chisom

155

was lying to me and so are you! I can tell! He suggested that I am adopted. Is that true, Mama?' Harriet could hardly bear to look at her mother's face but forced herself to continue. She had promised herself she would stay until she heard the truth no matter how terrible it might be. 'Because if so that would mean that you are not my mother.'

'I've told you it is better you don't know! Oh Harriet, my dearest girl, *please* believe me. I know what's best.'

'You had a lover. You told me that much.'

'I didn't say that. I said your father was a decent man.'

Harriet stared at her furiously. They were going round in circles. 'A decent man. So why can't you tell me who he is? Is he still alive? You said he was dead but that could be another lie.'

'It's the truth, Harriet. And I didn't take a lover.' Her shoulders drooped. In a low voice she said, 'The truth is you are adopted. Now does that satisfy you?'

'Go on, Mama!'

'I lost two children and your father was beside himself with grief. He longed for a child. He wanted a boy but a girl would be better than no child.' Agnes drew the bedclothes closer.

Harriet closed her eyes briefly and counted to ten. 'I'm not leaving this room until I know the truth, Mama. I have to know.'

Wearily Agnes shook her head. 'He was away at sea when I lost a third child but I couldn't face him. I knew how it would hurt him so I – I decided . . .'

'To adopt a child and pretend it was yours. Yours and his.' Harriet sat back in her chair. At last the awful truth. 'So who is my real mother? You might as well tell me that. You've come this far.'

'She died.'

'That sounds like another lie. A very convenient lie.' Harriet leaped to her feet. 'Who is she, Mama? *Where* is she?'

'I'm not lying, Harriet.' Agnes began to cry but Harriet hardened her heart. Quivering with anger, she waited and at last Agnes wiped her tears and faced her daughter.

156

'I'll tell you, Harriet, but you'll be sorry.' She patted the bed and Harriet sat down.

There was a long silence.

'A few days after I lost my child, a little girl, a woman, was admitted to the workhouse.' Agnes avoided Harriet's eyes. 'She was in labour and—'

Harriet cried, 'The *workhouse*? Wait! *Wait*, Mama!' Suddenly alarmed, Harriet wondered for the first time if her mother was right. Suppose the truth was unbearable . . .

But Agnes went on, appearing not to hear. 'I was called in to help as the nurse was very inexperienced and the doctor wasn't available. I knew little about childbirth but the nurse said there were problems. The mother was very weak.'

'This woman?' Harriet's voice was little more than a whisper.

Agnes nodded. 'Her husband was a thatcher but he'd fallen and died. The woman was walking home the twenty or so miles to her parents' home when the labour pains started.'

Harriet felt the colour drain from her face as the truth began to sink in. 'No! *No!*' she whispered.

Agnes had closed her eyes. 'The birth was going to be very difficult and I was desperately afraid. I sent the nurse out again to look for a midwife. While she was gone the child was born and I wrapped her up. The mother kissed her. But she, the mother, was in a terribly weakened state. There was so much blood. I could see she was dying. I . . . I tried to stop the bleeding but it was hopeless. Then she died.'

Now Harriet wanted to stop the story but words failed her.

Opening her eyes, Agnes said, 'I'm sorry, dear, but you insisted.'

Hardly able to breathe, Harriet remained frozen with horror.

'I stole the child, Harriet.'

Dimly Harriet heard her mother's voice.

'I stole *you*, Harriet. I knew the motherless child would be brought up in the workhouse and I knew we wanted a child. I knew George would never agree so I stole you. I ran home with you and left you whimpering in the middle of our bed. When I got back to the workhouse the nurse was still not there. The poor mother – *your* mother, Harriet, was dead but at least I had saved her child from a terrible fate.' Agnes stopped, exhausted.

'How . . . How did you explain it?'

'I told the nurse that mother and child were both dead and I would deal with it. I sent her straightway to the undertaker's with a message and while she was gone I cleaned up the mother and wrapped her in a sheet.'

Harriet said, 'Did you say she kissed me?' She closed her eyes, picturing the scene. 'When I was born?'

'Yes, she kissed you. And she smiled. She was so happy you were alive. I ran home to spoon a little milk into your mouth. When the undertaker came with a coffin I didn't mention the child . . .' Agnes sighed. 'Nobody cared. Nobody asked awkward questions. The poor soul was just another destitute woman fallen on hard times.'

'So that's it?' Harriet whispered. 'That's the truth. The whole truth.'

Her mother nodded. 'I went away for a few days, taking you with me, and stayed in a hotel. When I came back I pretended you were born very early and that your birth had taken me by surprise. When George next came ashore you were seven weeks old. I didn't expect to have another child. Sam, when he came along so many years later, was a great shock.'

Harriet struggled for breath as she listened to the rest of the story. At last she knew everything. Totally shattered, her whole world crumbling, she tried to look at Agnes but her eyes were full of tears and her mother was nothing but a blur. Crushed by the terrible truth she whispered, 'Workhouse brat!' and then, swaying, she slipped into a merciful darkness.

She roused again to find three anxious faces looming over her and for a few seconds she forgot what had happened. Then she gave a small cry of distress as thoughts whirled in a great confusion, so that she found it difficult to separate them. She struggled to a sitting position to find herself in her own bedroom with Izzie holding a bottle of sal volatile, Cook nearby and her mother – but no. Anguished, Harriet told herself that Agnes was not her mother. Memories rushed into the void that was her mind. She didn't know her mother or her father – but she *had* been saved from a dreary existence in the workhouse.

'You fainted, Harriet.' Her mother – Agnes – leaned forward to kiss the top of her head.

Cook said, 'Good thing you didn't hurt yourself when you went down.'

Not to be outdone, Izzie smiled at her. '*I'd* have fainted if my Pa had—' Then stopped suddenly as Cook's elbow connected with her arm. 'I mean, with a shock like that . . .' Realizing that she was making things worse, Izzie reddened and, handing the sal volatile to Cook, fled from the room.

Harriet looked at Agnes and saw the deep concern etched into her face and knew how much it had cost her to tell the story. Harriet shook her head. Agnes was the only mother she would ever know and nothing could change that. Reaching out, she took hold of Agnes's hand but her mother immediately began to sob, her whole body shaking with the ferocity of her emotions. Cook tiptoed from the room and for a long time Harriet's tears mingled with her mother's as they clung together, adrift in a changing sea that might well drown them both.

Harriet was the first to recover. She drew back, wiped her eyes and took a deep breath. 'No one will ever hear the truth from me,' she said. 'Except Godfrey. I shall marry him, Mama, if he will still have me. Your secret is safe with me.'

Agnes, stemming the flow of her own tears, gave Harriet a watery smile. 'I daresay I could be sent to prison because I think it was kidnapping. It was certainly illegal concealment or intent to procure a child! I truly don't know. I've never dared to find out my position. It all happened so quickly. A life or death decision when I first saw you. You were undernourished and almost too weak to cry. My instinct was to give you a chance. If your mother had survived I would have handed you back to her.'

Harriet tried to imagine the grim scene and shuddered. 'Weren't you frightened by what you had done?' She went to the small set of drawers and found two clean handkerchiefs and gave one to Agnes.

'Most certainly I was.' Agnes dabbed at her eyes. 'I was terrified. After your mother died I had a chance to confess and hand you back but I couldn't do it. Afterwards, as the weeks passed I thought at any moment I would be discovered and arrested and that your father would disown me. It was a terrible gamble.'

'But he didn't.'

'He was delighted that we had a child at last although he wished you had been a boy. He never knew the truth but I was in a very nervous state and he began to suspect something was wrong. He began to ask a few questions and I thought he had worked it out that you couldn't be his child but if he suspected he never put it into words. Then of course you didn't take after either of us and I think he wondered if there was another man in my life.'

'So the quarrel over the ring just before he shot – before he died? Did he learn the truth? Was that why he . . .'

She couldn't go on.

Agnes nodded. 'He was so angry about the ring that I had to tell him I'd sold it and bit by bit he forced the whole story from me. About the blackmailer and the money – and about you, of course.' She looked earnestly at Harriet. 'We mustn't blame George for what he did. Twenty years of lies from a wife he loved and trusted and then to find out that he had brought up a child from the workhouse.'

Harriet flinched at the word. Daisy Pritty's image floated into her mind. Workhouse brat. That would have been her life. Instead . . .

Agnes had picked up the bible and now pressed it to her heart. Harriet saw that her mother's eyes were closed and she was praying silently. After a moment Agnes resumed.

'George couldn't accept it and who can blame him? It's no reflection on you, Harriet, but it *is* a reflection on me and on our marriage. I did what I did for all of us but no amount of longing can make it the right thing to do.'

Harriet leaned forward. 'But if you hadn't done it you would have watched me grow up and seen my wretched existence . . .'

Agnes smiled faintly. 'If I had the chance again – if I could turn back the clock – I would do the same again.' She picked up her daughter's hand and kissed it.

Harriet, choked, was near to tears again but forced herself to think practically. 'So you have no idea who the black-mailer is.'

'No, I don't. Nor do I know whether he will demand more from me.'

Harriet saw her tremble and gave her a ressuring hug. 'But now that Papa is dead – how *can* this wretch black-mail you?'

'He could threaten to tell everyone! He could go to the police! It's still not too late.' She shrugged helplessly. 'I suspect it is someone connected with the workhouse.'

'But who has been there long enough? Herbert Crane has only been there about eight years and Mrs Fenner—'

'It might be one of the old inmates who remember – or who were told about it. People in a closed community like that gossip and love to tell stories.'

For a few moments they were both silent then Harriet said, 'It must have been awful for Papa all these years, wondering about me. I never felt that his love was as strong for me as for Sam and now I understand.' She frowned. 'We don't have to tell Sam anything, do we? Except that Papa is dead. Nothing about me.'

'I think not. If you wish, when he is older – it will be up to you.'

'What was her name, Mama? My real mother.'

'I knew you would ask that but I don't know. I don't think I ever took note of it. While the emergency was happening I was too busy and afterwards, after I had snatched you – I was in such a panic. I hardly knew what I was about. Is it important that you know?'

Harriet shook her head although in fact she was already determined to find out more about her birth parents if she could do so without alerting anybody to her mother's plight.

The thought that Agnes might still face the shame and misery of a prison sentence sent shivers down her spine.

Albert Hawke was planing wood and he did this with a smile on his face because he loved the work. He watched the curls of wood ease from beneath the blade of the plane and fall to the ground. Sometimes on a blowy day when the door was open, a draught would stir the shavings on the floor, so that they seemed to have a life of their own, but today there was no wind. At other times Snapper would decide to play with them, rootling through them like a boar after acorns, but now the dog slept noisily on a pile of sacks in the corner, whimpering now and then in his sleep. Albert hummed tunelessly as he moved the plane with easy, practised strokes – and he thought about Daisy Pritty and wondered whether or not she would be allowed time out from the workhouse today to work an hour or two with him.

When he heard the gate open his smile deepened. Snapper leaped to his feet and raced out into the yard, barking furiously, and Albert glanced outside but it was not Daisy and he tried to ignore his disappointment. It was, however, a woman in full mourning black, wearing a fine veil over her head and face, and for a moment he watched her. She stood her ground as Snapper approached and said, 'Stop that noise!'

To Albert's surprise, Snapper obeyed and moved quietly forward to lie at her feet. The woman threw back her veil, glanced around the yard, then called, 'Hello? Anybody here?' She looked younger than he expected, so perhaps she was a Miss and not a Mrs. Receiving no reply, she shaded her eyes from the sun and stared straight into the room where Albert was standing. He laid down the plane and went outside.

'Albert Hawke, Funeral Director and Coffin Maker at your service. I'm sorry to see you've suffered the loss of a loved one.' It was his usual approach, blending courtesy with friendliness. Or so he hoped. Subservience had never been his forte.

She stared at him and he could not read her expression.

'Mr Hawke, I need some information and . . .' She fumbled within her purse and produced a shilling, which she held out to him.

162

He didn't take it. 'You don't want to order a coffin?'

'No, I don't. Can you help me?'

'That depends.' Albert was intrigued. 'Should I know your name first?'

'There's no need. I would like you to search your records for—'

'We'd best go inside to the shop, ma'am. This way.' He led her through the workshop, past the woodshavings and the piled-up coffin shells and stacks of wood. 'Mind you don't get sawdust on the hem of your skirt.'

'Oh . . . Thank you.'

Albert led the way through the workshop, along the passage and into his shop, which also served as an office, and here he dusted the chair so that the young woman could sit down. He hoped she would comment on the photograph of the mayor's funeral cortège or the sample headstone but instead she handed him a small piece of paper on which she had written a date in August 1847.

'I am interested in the person who died on this day in eighteen forty-seven. I believe you made her coffin and—'

'That would be my father, miss, but I'd have been helping him. Learning the trade. I was a very quick learner and a hardworker. So . . . you want to know something about this man – or is it a woman?'

'A woman. I want to know her name and if possible where I can find her grave.'

'That shouldn't be too difficult.'

'She was a – I *believe* she was an inmate of the Maybourne Workhouse.'

'Ah.' He screwed up his face. 'Not quite so easy then. Not much of a headstone for a start and maybe no more than a small wooden cross and they do rot after a time – but I'll try.'

He was intrigued. What would this handsome young woman want with a dead woman from the workhouse? He found the ledger for the correct year and began to turn the pages. Snapper was now resting his front paws on the hem of her skirt and he coughed apologetically.

'Dog might have the odd flea, miss.'

'Oh!' She tugged her skirt free and Snapper took the hint, retreating reproachfully to his pile of sacks.

Albert said, 'He usually goes mad. Barking like a lunatic! You must have a way with dogs.'

'I prefer cats. We have one called Jasper.' She smiled faintly as she thought of the animal.

He found the right page and said, 'Well then, here we are. Two deaths that day. A Mrs Hannah Wenright and a Master Cecil Flyte. The latter aged—'

'It must be the former. Hannah Wenright? What age was she?'

'None given, miss. Often they don't know, you see. The kind of people they get in that place – they don't sometimes read or write and many don't even know how old they are or their date of birth. All it says here is "Died in childbirth". Not much to go on, is it.'

She sighed and bent her head.

'Servant or something, was she? We do get the odd runaway servant in here. They run off with a military man mostly and then he abandons her.'

'Not this woman. She had a husband, but he died. She was a respectable widow woman who died in childbirth. So what happened to the child, do you think?'

He shook his head. 'Must have survived. We didn't bury a baby. I'd remember, you see. I was young and impressionable. The sight of a dead woman with a dead baby in her arms was so sad . . .' He sighed. 'You'll most likely find a note of his or her birth in the register at the Workhouse.'

She stood up abruptly and held out the shilling. As Albert slipped it into his pocket there was a commotion in the yard and Snapper once more rocketed out of his bed and into the yard. Albert and his client followed him outside.

This time it *was* Daisy Pritty but a very dishevelled, panic-stricken Daisy, pursued by the sound of police whistles. She slammed the wooden gate shut behind her, tried to lock it but it proved too stiff for her and, cursing roundly, she pushed a sack of firewood against it and ran into the workshop.

Ignoring Harriet, she hurled herself at Albert and cried,

164

'Hide me, quick, for pity's sake! In your loft! The ruddy Law's after me!'

Harriet cried, 'Daisy! What's happening?'

There was a hammering on the wooden gates. While Albert hovered uncertainly Daisy scrambled past him and climbed up into the space above them. At the same moment the gate burst open and a young policeman ran in, breathless and clutching his side.

'Where did she go?'

Albert glanced at Harriet, who looked shaken but made no reply.

'Now then! One of you must have seen her.'

Albert nodded. 'Through the workshop – but what's she done?'

Ignoring the question, the constable ran into the workshop and looked around and Albert and Harriet followed him. 'Little hussy!' he grumbled, gulping for air. 'I had her once but she bit me. Little wildcat! Wait till I get my hands on—' He stopped as from somewhere overhead someone sneezed.

Albert caught Harriet's eyes apologetically and muttered, 'It's the sawdust.'

The policeman stared up at the figure clamped to a broad rafter. 'Get down here or I'll fetch a stick and *poke* you down!'

She dropped down almost on top of him, knocking him off balance and he ended up on the floor with her, but he retained enough sense to reach out and catch her by the ankle. Snapper was leaping about, barking shrilly, half mad with excitement. Thoroughly confused, he bit the nearest limb, which happened to be Daisy's left arm. She let out a shriek and Albert dragged the dog off but the damage was done. Her wrist was bleeding, Daisy was howling with pain and cursing dramatically but somehow the constable managed to put the handcuffs on her.

Albert and Harriet watched in dismay as Daisy was led out of the yard. The constable blew his whistle for assistance and while Harriet began to argue with the constable another uniformed figure appeared at a run. He was older, heavier and less fit than his colleague and for a moment or

165

two he rested his hands on his knees while he recovered his breath.

Albert stood in the gateway. 'What's she done, constable?'

'She half murdered her gentleman friend, that's what!'

Daisy twisted and turned in a frantic effort to escape but found enough energy to shout, 'He's no friend of mine, the conniving, thieving little rat!'

The older policeman said, 'Shut your mouth or I'll shut it for you!'

Undeterred, she aimed a kick at his leg and missed.

He said, 'Oh no you don't!' and grabbed her arm.

Daisy stamped on his foot and he let out a yell.

Daisy caught Harriet's eye and her rage suddenly vanished. Her expression changed and tears filled her eyes. 'Digger cheated me,' she cried, half sobbing. '*Cheated* me! Took my share and was going to run with it. But I found him. I'm glad I hit him.' Her voice broke. 'After all I done for him, and there was me thinking he loved me! Stupid fool that I was! I wish I'd done for him! Ruddy Digger! I'd like to see the wretch rot in hell!' She jerked again at her restraints.

Harriet cried, 'Daisy! Don't go on so. You'll only make things worse for yourself.'

The constable, struggling to hold on to her, turned breathlessly to Harriet and Albert. 'Now you two are witnesses. You heard her confess. She wishes she'd "done for him". Those were her exact words.' He shook her. 'Keep still, damn you! She was trying to kill him and nearly succeeded.'

Albert laid a hand on the policeman's arm. 'She's an acquaintance – that is a friend of mine. She works for me sometimes. I can vouch for—'

'A friend? Well you've got some funny friends, sir, that's all I can say. This one's known to us already. Workhouse. What can you expect?'

Harriet felt a rush of emotions – shame, anger, doubts. There but for the grace of God, she thought. But then Daisy *had* behaved badly. Or so it seemed. She tried to imagine a slight figure like Daisy getting the better of Digger. 'What did she do . . . ?' she asked. 'That is, how did she . . . ?' She stopped as Daisy glared at her.

'She tripped him and kicked him in the head. When he got to his feet she punched him in the face. Bloody nose, the lot! Then he went down again and didn't get up. Out cold.' It was his turn to glare at Harriet. 'Satisfied now, are you?'

Daisy shouted, 'Course he wasn't out cold! He was play-acting, cunning little runt! Shamming! He's more cunning than a cartload of monkeys, that one! I hardly touched him and that's the truth.'

The younger man took names and addresses from Harriet and Albert. 'We'll need statements later, so we'll be in touch. But for now we'll get this crazy wench round to the station and into a cell, where she belongs. She won't be biting any more policemen for a very long time!'

The inquest on George Henry Burnett was held on the following Friday at ten in the morning. The heavily panelled room was very full and Harriet and her mother sat together, hand in hand. Although their faces were hidden by black veils everyone appeared to know who they were and curious eyes watched their every move.

The proceedings got off to a late start but by twenty past ten the post-mortem result had been read out by the physician who had investigated the death and the unpleasant catalogue of gruesome medical details made Harriet shudder. One by one they made vivid the last terrible moments of George's life and she was grateful when the account came to an end and the coroner was answering questions.

'Doctor Carteris, you are in no doubt that the deceased died by his own hand, are you not?'

The doctor was a tall man with greying side whiskers and a permanent frown.

'I am, sir.'

'No doubts in your mind?'

'None at all.'

'A single gunshot to the head?'

'Exactly, sir.'

'Thank you, Doctor Carteris. You may step down.'

The bo'sun was then called and Harriet saw that he was wearing his best clothes for the occasion and looked very different from when she had last seen him on the quayside.

'Mr Richard Maddocks, bo'sun of the *Saint Augustine*?'

'At your service, sir!' He stood stiffly to attention and stared straight ahead.

'Will you please give your account of the last hours of your captain to the police sergeant exactly as you remember it.'

Agnes drew in a sharp breath and Harriet squeezed her hand and whispered, 'Not much more, Mama.'

Maddocks scowled at a point just above the coroner's head. 'The Captain, he come back to the ship and went straight below. Not so much as a word to any of us, what we all thought was a bad sign 'cos the skipper, he was always civil to the crew.' He put a hand to his mouth and coughed.

Outside the church clock struck three.

'Go on, man!'

'Bit later he come up again, took a turn around the deck, thoughtful like. Still no word. Then he went down again and that was the last anyone saw of him alive. We got worried and the lad took down some food 'n' drink and knocked but got no answer, so he left it outside the door.'

Harriet could see that he was sweating. Probably nerves, she thought, as he took out a crumpled neckerchief from his pocket and wiped his face.

'And?' The sergeant glared.

'Later I went down myself. 'Ad to tell him that we were still one crew man short and what should I do? Still no answer, so I wondered should we bust in, like . . .' He glanced to a man sitting to his left and Harriet assumed this was another crewman. 'Spinks and me argued the toss and Spinks reckoned Skipper must be drinking heavy and we'd cop it if we did but we did anyway. Bust the door and there he was! Fully dressed but on the bed. He was very still. Very quiet.'

Harriet shuddered. She wanted to cover her ears but some part of her needed to know. Glancing at her mother, she saw that Agnes was wide-eyed, listening intently.

The bo'sun crossed himself hurriedly. 'Skipper was lying

on his side with his face to the wall and when we got closer we saw the pistol and smelled – well, sir, you can guess. There was blood 'n' guts – Well, hardly guts, but brains and stuff on the pillow.'

Harriet felt bile rise in her throat and closed her eyes. She felt her mother's hand tighten on hers.

'Mr Maddocks, did you think he had been shot?'

'At first, but then we knew no one else could have got in because the key was on the inside.'

'And nobody heard the shot?'

'No, sir – but a ship's a noisy place best of times – timbers creaking, waves slapping, like, and wind in the rigging. 'Specially noisy when she's loading.'

'Hmm . . . Did anyone to your knowledge have a grudge against the Captain?'

'No more'n usual, sir. Most men have a gripe against the skipper now 'n' then. Only natural. It's the discipline.'

'Had you seen the pistol before?'

'Yes. It was his pistol which he often wore in his belt.'

The courtroom had fallen silent.

The sergeant leaned forward. 'Did you deduce it was suicide, Mr Maddocks?'

'Ad to be, sir.'

Harriet was thankful when the verdict was reached and they could leave. Nothing had changed. George Burnett had taken his own life while the balance of his mind was disturbed. Suicide.

As they left, reporters appeared waving notebooks and pencils and shouting questions at them but Agnes hailed a hansom cab and she and Harriet were quickly carried away from the milling crowd and back to the curtained confines of their stricken home.

Eleven

A letter arrived for Harriet by hand the next day, which was a Saturday. It was from James Wellbury and Harriet took it into her bedroom. For a long time, she stared at the unopened envelope, recognizing the handwriting and unwilling to read the contents. Intuitively she knew that they would make unhappy reading – and they did. The letter was dated Friday morning.

> *Dear Harriet, I'm sure this letter will come as no surprise and it grieves me to write as I must. I refer to the sudden tragic death of your father in what we may call unsavoury circumstances. We are all shocked and outraged by his unhappy passing and are unable to understand what prompted him to commit such a sin against his religion. No doubt you and your mother will be asking yourselves the same questions – unless you have a clearer grasp of what was in his mind at the time . . .*

Harriet's heart beat a little faster. Such a hypocrite, she thought. Where was the compassion they might have expected? Not one word of consolation. She would have expected a glimmer of regret after all the families had been to each other over so many years.

> *. . . We read the account in the newspaper with growing dismay and note that the date of the inquest is later today. I may decide to attend but shall prevent my wife from accompanying me. Such unpalatable events are not for womanly sensitivities and I hope that you and*

your mother have the wisdom to stay away. Marcus is
distraught and wants to see you . . .

Do you, Marcus?' she whispered. 'Or are you, too, reluctant
to risk your reputation by associating with the likes of us?'
Was he happy to let his father write for him? She would
have expected better from him. Even a few lines couched
in sorrowful terms would have lessened the blow.

. . . but I have forbidden it for the near future. I regret
to say that in the circumstances his mother and I are
no longer agreeable to a match between you and our
son and I am sure that you will see this as entirely
reasonable. That said, if we are able to help you in
any way, you can call on us and we will all remember
you in our prayers. Ask the good Lord to forgive your
father and pray that He will be merciful. Please give our
regards to your mother.
Your friend James Wellbury.

So that is how it ends, Harriet thought, dazed by the sudden
withdrawal of support and the veiled criticism of her father.
Her first instinct was to reply in anger, her second to ignore
the letter. Perhaps already James Wellbury's conscience was
pricking him. They had certainly been genuinely eager for the
marriage but maybe she should not judge them too harshly.
They were acting to prevent harm to their son. That, for them,
was paramount. If Marcus was indeed distraught and still
wished to go ahead with the marriage, they would have to
act swiftly to prevent it. She thought back to her last meeting
with Marcus when she had been less than courteous. In the
circumstances she had been unnecessarily touchy if not
downright rude and she now regretted it.

'Shrewish is the word!' she muttered. She had thrown a
most unladylike tantrum but at the time she had no longer
been trying to impress him as a suitable wife. If he *was*
grateful for the chance to end the betrothal she could hardly
blame him. Was it possible they might remain friends? From
the tone of James Wellbury's letter it seemed unlikely.

171

Thoughtfully, she went downstairs and found her mother in the kitchen.

Agnes at once left the servants to their own devices and followed her into the parlour. Harriet handed her the letter and sat quietly while her mother read it.

Agnes looked up. 'I know you no longer want to marry Marcus but I do feel they are being less than generous. I'm disappointed in him, Harriet. James, I mean. So quick to blame . . . Was he at the inquest? I didn't see him.'

'Neither did I. I think he stayed away. Fearful of the publicity.'

Agnes returned the letter. 'I'm so sorry all this has happened. It has ruined your life and mine. I shall have to resign from the Board of Guardians – partly because of the scandal but also because that wretch, whoever he is, has robbed me of what little money I had left to donate. And even if I still had it, we would need every penny of it to survive.'

'Didn't Papa ever wonder how you managed to give them money?'

'He wasn't here that much and I made sure I gave when he was at sea. I don't think he ever realized that I did anything other than take an interest in their welfare. He felt it was a charitable thing to do and probably he felt it reflected well on himself. Poor George. I never shall be able to forgive myself.'

'But you gave him Sam. That was a great gift.' Harriet felt a slight sense of the old resentment but it was weaker than before.

Agnes clasped her hand. 'I gave him *you*, also, Harriet and that was a great gift and it cost me more than he will ever know. More than anyone will ever realize. He walked out before I could give him my reasons or ask for his understanding.' She sighed. 'But you know how much giving up the workhouse will hurt me. I have always felt it my duty to help the inmates in any way I could because . . .' She smiled faintly. 'Because in a way I owe them a deep debt of gratitude. Because of the workhouse I have a beautiful daughter! They don't know that, but I do.'

Harriet hesitated. She had not told her mother of her visit to the doctor nor of her enquiries at the coffin makers. Suddenly she thought the time had come to reveal a little of what she had learned and told her quickly about the discovery of Hannah Wenright. 'I think she must be my real mother—'

'Hannah Wenright? Yes! You're right, Harriet! I remember the Wenright but not the Christian name.'

'—and I want to find her grave, which will be in the same sad corner as Papa's when he is buried. I won't go looking until after his funeral for both our sakes. I mustn't draw attention to the fact that I am curious.'

Agnes looked at her in alarm. 'Most certainly not! You must be very careful, Harriet. Whoever blackmailed me might be watching us, waiting for another chance.'

'Or perhaps he will give up.' Harriet looked at her mother hopefully. 'It must surely dawn on him that without Papa's income we have no money. Nothing.' For the first time since the tragedy Harriet wondered what they would do and how they would live but forced the problem from her mind. 'I also have some bad news about Daisy Pritty,' she said. 'She has been arrested.'

'Oh no! That poor unfortunate girl!'

'Not quite *unfortunate*, Mama, if the police are to be believed. They say she attacked that man she calls Digger. *She* says it was justified because he was cheating her of some money.' She explained briefly about the scene in Albert Hawke's yard.

Agnes clutched her head in despair. 'I ought to speak with them but – Oh Harriet! I hardly have the strength or the will at the moment. I am so exhausted . . .'

'I have already decided that *I* will follow it up, Mama,' Harriet told her firmly. 'You must stay in the house and rest. I shall go to the police station and ask to speak with her or at least find out what charges they are bringing against her. The police may have been exaggerating. Then I'll go the hospital and find out how Digger is. The police think he is half dead but Daisy says he was shamming.'

'And you will write to Marcus, won't you, Harriet? If it is all over you must at least end it on a pleasant note. Life's too short to make enemies.'

Harriet promised and went back upstairs to fetch a shawl.

* * *

173

The hospital staff were unwilling to talk to her and wouldn't tell her which ward Digger was in.

'It is not visiting hours and you're not next of kin,' the nurse told her. She was heavily built with a swarthy skin and wide-set eyes. Harriet thought she looked rather foreign but she spoke without an accent. 'You have no right to be here. Are you a reporter?'

'I'm a friend,' Harriet told her, repeating the lie. 'His own mother is unable to come and I said I would—'

'I'm sorry. I can't discuss the case. It's a matter for the police. It was a very serious assault and the young man's life is in danger.'

Harriet felt a shiver of apprehension. 'In danger?'

'He tells us he was kicked in the head and the kidneys and—' She broke off abruptly. She had almost given the information that Harriet was demanding.

Harriet held up a small cloth bundle. 'I've brought him some food. He has such an appetite and hospitals never feed—'

The nurse bridled at the implication. 'We're feeding him well enough, *thank* you!'

'So he can eat! Then he's not unconscious.'

'Did I say he was?' She crossed her large arms and glared at Harriet. 'What did you say your name was?'

'I didn't say. It doesn't matter.' Harriet thought rapidly. Assuming a sorrowful expression. 'When's his operation?'

'He doesn't *need*—'

She stopped again and Harriet could see she was annoyed with herself for falling into so many traps.

The nurse's expression became grim. 'I've had enough of you! I'll have to ask you to leave. Right now!' With a meaty finger she pointed towards the door.

Harriet said meekly, 'I was just leaving!'

Outside in the sunshine, she was aware of a feeling of power. Being protected from birth from the rigours of a harsh world, she had never had to behave this way before and the knowledge that she could do so was new to her and went to her head like wine. She set off for the police station with her head held high and a new-found confidence. On the way she thought of Hannah Wenright and wanted her to be proud of the daughter she had never known. She thought also of Godfrey and longed to see him again. She had to talk to him. To confide in him and to discover what difference, if any, her loss of status would mean to him. Would he still want to marry her? She would have no money spent on her by her father because he had died in miserable circumstances. Nothing was ever going to be the way she had expected it, thought Harriet, but she must face that fact and get on with the rest of her life. Buried somewhere in this frightening prospect Harriet was aware of a small but growing excitement.

At the police station she met a similar response to the one she had received at the hospital. Who was she? What relation was she to the accused? Who had given her permission to make these enquiries?

'The Board of Guardians at Maybourne Workhouse,' she replied to the last question. Who would know that she lied? Would anyone at the workhouse care what happened to Daisy Pritty?

The man looked at her under beetled brows. He was small and dark with eyes like currants. 'The board of what?'

She repeated it. 'I need to speak to her.'

'Well, you can't.'

'Then I must speak to someone about her case. We believe it to be mistaken. I have just come from the hospital and they say—'

'What's your name?'

She hesitated. 'Harriet Burnett.'

His eyes widened. 'Burnett? You connected with that fellow what topped himself down at the harbour?'

'I'm his daughter – and proud of it!' She looked him straight in the eye.

He flinched. 'I was only asking! Bit of a bummer for you, wasn't it?'

'None of your business. Now about Daisy Pritty . . .'

He considered for a moment. 'You can't see no one, that's an order, see. No one can. But I might have some information . . . ?' He raised his eyebrows in an unmistakable message.

Harriet fished in her purse. 'There's a shilling for you.'

She had intended to keep it until she had the required information but he snatched it from her and stuffed it into his pocket. 'Shilling? What shilling?' He grinned at her and leaned forward. 'Being charged with affray and serious assault upon the person of one Digby Wise and resisting arrest and assault on a constable, to wit biting a policeman. She'll go down for months if not years, she will, and serve her right, little wild cat. Folk like her must make you ashamed to be a woman.'

'Well, it doesn't!' Harriet glared at him. 'But it makes me sorry that folk like her lead such sad and sordid lives!'

He pulled a face. 'Oh, hoity-toity!' he mocked. 'Listen to you!'

Harriet knew when she was beaten. With her face burning she turned away with her hopes shattered. Even she could see that there was no way Daisy was going to escape custody.

The man leaned forward and grabbed her arm. 'Why'd he do it?' he asked in a hoarse whisper. 'Your pa, I mean. Why'd he shoot himself, eh?'

Harriet was so angry she almost struck him but remembered just in time that brute force was no way to settle a dispute. She had only to think of Daisy to learn that. She said, 'First you tell me something. Where exactly did this happen? The – the affray?'

With an exaggerated sigh he consulted his notes. 'Middle of Market Street.'

'Thank you!' she said and walked quickly away.

'Oi! You!'

In spite of herself she turned back, waiting.

'Your Daisy Pritty! In a right pickle, she is.'

Harriet stared at him.

He grinned, revealing missing teeth. 'I mean a *right* pickle!' Reluctantly she returned to the desk. He said, 'Another shilling for a tasty titbit!'

'Sixpence or nothing!'

He accepted it. Leaning forward, he breathed onions over her. 'Up the spout, isn't she! Laugh that off, *Miss Burnett!*'

*   *   *

176

On the other side of town at Havely House, Godfrey was writing a letter while a small black and white kitten played with his shoe laces. He was sitting in the library at the desk Robert Burnett had allotted him for his work but he was not working. The truth was he was finding it hard to know where to start for the old man's papers were in a hopeless muddle. Every shelf bore loose papers, mostly faded to a pale brown, some brittle with age. There were papers in folders, sundry notebooks and countless letters. More bundles were tied with string and a few were stuffed into brown envelopes that bore cryptic references in a spidery hand. Every drawer held more of the same and there were sheets of notes stuffed into many of the books which Robert referred to as his reference library.

It was also difficult to pin Robert down to exactly what he wished Godfrey to do with the material when he finally managed to put it in some sort of order. It seemed the old man wanted some kind of permanent record of his life or his travels or both. He had told Godfrey that within the papers he would find a philosophy of life that had stood him in good stead. A *raison d'être* for living.

'You'd do well to read and inwardly digest!' he told Godfrey with a rare smile.

The book was also going to be an account of Robert's travels as a young man – before the malady claimed him and turned him into a virtual hermit. He had been in Borneo for nearly four years and had sketched extensively with a light but sure hand. There were also hundreds of letters in a variety of languages. Godfrey was optimistic, however, and was determined firstly to create order from chaos and secondly to put forward a feasible form the book could take.

Today the old man had retired for an afternoon nap and Godfrey was allowing himself an extended lunch break so that he could write to Harriet.

. . . My dearest girl, I am counting the hours (and the minutes!) until I can see you again. If you do not come to Havely House soon I shall have to come to you. The news of your father's death has left us all horrified and dismayed. I wanted to be with you at the inquest but

*Mother thought my presence there might embarrass you
and I didn't wish to cause you further distress. But I
was with you in spirit. Knowing you as I do, albeit on
short acquaintance, I am sure you are feeling somehow
responsible for your father's death. That is not the case
and you must put such thoughts from you . . .*

Godfrey glanced up as footsteps signalled the old man's
return.

'I couldn't sleep.' Robert shuffled into the room. He was
wearing his slippers and his clothes were rumpled. 'I have
to talk to you. About my family. My nephew's wife and my
great-niece Harriet.' He lowered himself into a chair, fished
in his pocket for his spectacles and put them on.

Godfrey slid a sheet of paper over his letter and turned
from the desk.

'I found the local paper this morning. Not very pleasant
reading. All about my nephew, poor fellow.' He peered at
Godfrey through narrowed eyes. 'Did you think I didn't
know?'

'About . . . ?' Godfrey tried to look innocent. His mother
had insisted they keep the news from the old man in order
to spare him any anguish.

'About George. Did you think I can't read? Of course I
was going to find out. I'm not quite senile!'

'Senile? Nobody is suggesting—'

'Aren't they? I think they are. Your mother, I don't doubt.
Well-meaning but a fussbody!'

Quickly recovering from his surprise, Godfrey now felt
irritated. 'I'm sure my mother—'

'Shooting himself!' He frowned. 'Dreadful thing to do and
a dreadful way to go! No philosophy of life, poor devil. Poor
George. I had no idea he was so weak but it shouldn't surprise
me.' He shook his head.

Taken by surprise, Godfrey wondered how much he should
say. 'It's all very sad,' he ventured and knew at once that it
was a mistake.

'That's an understatement!' Robert shot him a scornful
glance. 'It's quite appalling. The question is: why did he

178

do it? You know, do you? There was nothing in the article about why he did it.'

'I – I think it was a . . . personal problem between himself and his wife. A disagreement.'

'Disagreement? What nonsense!' He glared at Godfrey. 'If every disagreement led to a shooting, there'd be very few of us left!'

Godfrey felt himself being dragged into deep water and wondered how to extricate himself. 'Perhaps you should speak to Mrs Burnett. I'm not the one to help you.'

'Obviously! Is Agnes here?'

'No but—'

'Then send your mother up. Somebody has to know something.'

Minutes later, Mrs Lester hurried into the room, drying her hands on her apron. 'Now you mustn't go upsetting yourself,' she began. 'What's done is done and there's an end to it. No cause to worry yourself, Mr Burnett. I'm sure the poor widow will come to see you when she feels fit enough.' She glanced at the window. 'Are you in a draught there?'

'I want to know why he did it!'

She stopped halfway to the window and turned. 'We don't know, Mr Burnett, and maybe we never will. Something between husband and wife. That's what they're saying. Nothing illegal. Nothing ungodly. Just something between the two of them.'

'Ah! Family secrets. They're the very devil, Mrs Lester. Very dangerous. The very devil and I speak from bitter experience. They fester away and then suddenly . . .' He sighed. 'Tell your son I shan't need him again today. I've a letter to write. Please close the door as you go out.'

Monday morning dawned with a clear sky but there was surprisingly little heat in the sun. Agnes however was in no mood to enjoy or appreciate the weather for she was on her way to the bank to speak to Mr Wylie, the manager, a man she had never met before. Previously her husband had dealt exclusively with the family finances and Agnes had been

179

discouraged from asking even the most basic questions about them and indeed had never wanted to do so.

She was shown into his office by a young woman whose curious glances revealed that she was aware of the name of the client and the scandalous circumstances surrounding the Burnett family. Agnes tried to ignore the hurt this provoked. She would have to get used to it. She might never again be shown the deference that she had always taken for granted.

A thin, tall man rose to his feet, shook her hand and indicated a chair. Agnes thanked him and sat down. He had a beaky nose and a sallow complexion but Agnes was not interested in his looks. It was his attitude that offended her. She sensed quite clearly from his manner that he felt judgemental towards George's behaviour. He offered her no refreshment and after a few insincere condolences, she could bear it no longer and came straight to the point.

'I need to know exactly how we are placed financially,' she told him. 'I have no idea whether or not we have savings or whether or not my husband's life was insured.'

He leaned forward. 'I will deal with the former presently, Mrs Burnett, but I'm afraid I have to advise you that your husband *did* in fact take out insurance but that his – er – untimely death . . . *by his own hand* – ' he peered at her over his glasses – 'renders the insurance null and void. I'm sorry but that is the law. Suicide is a crime, Mrs Burnett. A sin against the Lord. Nothing I can do will alter that.'

He sat back, watching her as the implications dawned on her. Without insurance money there was only one alternative – savings.

'We have savings, I believe,' she suggested, trying to hide her fear.

'Some but they are not readily available. I'm sorry to be the bearer of bad news, Mrs Burnett, but –' he spread his hands helplessly – 'the money is tied up very firmly in a trust for your son's education.'

Agnes closed her eyes to hide her desperation. 'And no way at all—'

'No way it can be used for any other purpose. The school he attends is very expensive. You may not have been aware of that.'

Agnes nodded. She had realized that there were sacrifices to be made for Sam's education but a situation like the present one had never, she was sure, occurred to her husband.

'So there are no other savings? None at all?'

'Not as such, but there is money in the current account. A small sum of . . . let me see now.' He reached for a sheet of paper and studied it thoughtfully and Agnes got the distinct impression that he was enjoying himself and didn't care if she knew it. Perhaps he was a strong churchman and full of righteous disapproval for what George had done. Perhaps he felt she must bear some of the blame and was punishing her in his own way.

He glanced up. 'Five hundred pounds, thirteen shillings and sixpence.'

'I see.'

'A not inconsiderable sum but . . .'

'But it won't last long.' Overwhelmed by the disappointment and the realization of the trouble they were in, Agnes could not bear to face Mr Wylie a moment longer than was necessary. She felt a wave of nausea as a cold fear settled within her. Surely there was something he could do to help. A loan, perhaps? Why did he offer no sympathy, help or reassurance? Wasn't that part of his job? Close to tears, she could not bear to break down in front of him.

'I have to go home!' she stammered and stood up on trembling legs.

He began to offer her a cup of tea but she refused. Too late, she thought angrily. A more sensitive man would have thought of that much earlier. She experienced a fierce hatred for his lack of caring and, had she felt stronger, might well have told him so to his face. But she was now aware of a growing frailty and sat down heavily in the chair. 'Please be kind enough to call a hansom cab,' she whispered and was pleased to see that he now looked contrite if not actually guilty.

The cab arrived promptly and he offered to help her out to it but she declined. He followed her to the door and held it open for her.

She heard herself say, 'I shall be writing to your superior.' It was spoken with what little dignity she could muster.

Sinking back in the cab as it carried her home, she was

astonished by her threat but it had made her feel less of a victim. Agnes made up her mind to carry out her threat. Perhaps a reprimand from Head Office would teach him to treat the bank's clients with a little more consideration.

Sam put the last of the chocolate into his mouth and chewed contentedly. He was sitting in a corner seat on a train which was taking him back to Maybourne and Mama and Harriet and maybe Papa. Sam stared out of the window. The scenery always interested him – cows, sheep, little villages, people working in the fields – but his mind was busy with the main question. Why was Mr Bragg taking him home when the term wasn't over? Surely he should be taking games on the field. They should be playing cricket. And why was he being so nice to him? The Headmaster had sent for him and talked a lot about God and his father and life and things like that and Sam hadn't understood any of it. Then Matron had come into his history class and called him out and he'd been glad because he didn't like history.

The history teacher had said, 'Don't worry, Burnett. There'll be better times ahead.' Ahead of what?

He glanced across at Mr Bragg, who was reading a copy of *The Times* – a paper his father liked to read when he was ashore. Mr Bragg had ginger hair and a pink face and a funny voice but he was nice. He never twisted Sam's ear or hit his knuckles with a ruler but he did roar at him on the field. 'Run, for Pete's sake, Burnett!' or 'Take a swipe at it, boy!'

Sam looked round the carriage and saw that the fat lady had gone and so had the old man with the chicken under his arm.

Sam said, 'Please, sir, why have I got to go home?' He hoped he wasn't being expelled. Cheetham Major had been expelled for something and had been disgraced in front of the whole school.

Mr Briggs lowered his paper and looked at him in surprise. 'Don't you know? Didn't the Headmaster tell you?'

'I don't think so, sir.'

The teacher folded the newspaper.

'Am I being expelled?'

'Good Lord no!' He sighed. 'The sad truth is, young

Burnett, that . . . that your papa's died. Something happened that . . . upset him and he was so upset . . .'

'Whose Papa? Mine?' Sam was puzzled. He'd seen Papa recently in the cake shop with Harriet and he hadn't seemed at all upset then.

'That's why you're going home. You have to go to the funeral with your mother and sister. You know what a funeral is, don't you?'

Sam nodded. 'But it can't be Papa's funeral.'

'I'm afraid it is, old son!' He leaned across and patted Sam's knee.

Sam frowned. 'Is he in hospital then?'

'No. He's in his coffin, Burnett. Waiting for the funeral so he can . . . so he can be sent up to Heaven. You all say prayers, you see, and that helps him to go up to Heaven.'

'Will he have to be buried? We had a puppy once – a black puppy – and it ran under the wheels of a cart and got dead and we had to go into the woods – me and Harriet – and dig a hole and Harriet said a prayer and we sang a hymn.'

Mr Bragg was giving him a funny look. 'Yes. That's about it, Burnett. Well done! So you see everything will be fine. You still have your Mama and your sister. They'll look after you.'

'And Great-Uncle Robert.'

'Really? A great-uncle? That's splendid.'

'So will I come back to school?'

'Of course you will.'

'Oh, I see.'

He sat for the rest of the journey in silence, mulling over what he had been told. Was his father dead? Was that what the Headmaster had been telling him. He tried to imagine Papa lying in a wooden coffin and just before they drew into the station two fat tears trickled down his cheeks.

Twelve

'Phineas, there's a young woman to see you. The one that came before. The one that doesn't care to give her name.'
He jumped to his feet. 'Not Miss Burnett?'
She looked at him in surprise. 'Is that who it is? I didn't recognize her. She's in mourning and the veil. How on earth did you know that?' Her eyes widened. 'She's the one whose father . . .'
'Thank you, Mother.' He tossed the paper into the armchair he had just vacated. 'I'll deal with it.' He pulled down his waistcoat and smoothed his hair.
Moments later he was in his surgery, greeting her somewhat nervously. 'I don't usually see patients after my rounds,' he began, 'but do sit down.'
'I'd rather not.' Carefully she lifted the veil away from her face. 'I won't keep you long.' She drew an envelope from her purse. 'I expect you can guess what I have here. Something you wrote to my mother a few weeks ago.'
Suddenly Phineas began to shake. 'I-I don't know . . .'
'You *do* know, Mr Burnett!'
Her voice was also unsteady and he realized that she, too, was in a state of great agitation.
'It's a letter that frightened her terribly and led to her selling some of her most precious possessions.'
He was shaking his head. 'No, no! Not me! I know nothing about it!' He prayed his mother wouldn't come in. 'I must ask you to go. These unfounded accusations . . .' His voice had risen.
Her mouth tightened and his hopes faded. She knew. But how? Unless the mother had told her . . . But then the mother didn't know the identity of the man who had blackmailed her.

184

'There's no point in denying it. This is your handwriting.'

'No! That's impossible! I have never written to your mother—'

'I checked it with a letter you wrote to my father some years ago about a petition you wanted him to sign. It's identical. The police would find no problem with that.'

Stricken with fear he gave up his denials and began to stammer. 'T-the police? Oh no! Oh God!'

She went on inexorably. 'The same slanting hand. The same loops under the "y", and the "g" and the same misplaced dot over the "i"! Do you still deny that you wrote it?' She put the letter away. 'Blackmail is a serious crime, Doctor Chisom. And whatever would your mother say if she knew? Your letter had repercussions, Mr Chisom. It led directly to my father's suicide. Think about that!'

He sank down on to a chair, his face ashen, his body trembling. Full of shame and fear, he knew what an abject figure he must present, but he was past caring about appearances. He had no thought except to appeal to this young woman's pity.

'I had no idea it would lead to this,' he told her. 'Please believe me! No idea that anything else . . . that anyone . . .'

'My mother might have died from the shock of it! How could you do such a thing. Why?'

'We're in desperate straits, Miss Burnett. My father left us penniless. I panicked. I swear I didn't mean to harm anyone. It just seemed—' He choked back the words. How could he ever make this young woman understand? 'My father left debts. Terrible, ruinous debts. We can't begin to pay them!'

'I understand your problem but now my poor mother has lost her husband and we have no support – because of your wickedness.'

Mesmerized by her pale face framed by the black veil, he managed a question. 'How did you find out?'

'I just worked it out. My mother told me everything except that it was you that sent the letter. She doesn't know that yet.' Her voice was weary as she went on, her eyes never leaving his face. 'You must have been looking through old files and you saw that my brother was my mother's first live child after several miscarriages. You wondered where I had come from!'

She took a deep breath and asked the vital question. 'Have you worked it out yet?'

'No. I . . . And I won't because . . .' He bent his head.

'I don't think prayers will help you, Doctor Chisom.'

Then he looked straight up into her eyes. 'In the name of God, Miss Burnett, I meant you and your family no real harm. It was just for the money. I had no intention of sharing what I knew. Even my mother doesn't know – and never will. I swear it! Please, Miss Burnett. I *beg* you to try to forgive me. I shall have your father's death on my conscience for the rest of my life!'

'And we must live the with scandal of a suicide!'

'If you have come for the money I no longer have it. It has—'

He stopped in confusion as his mother popped her head round the door and asked if the visitor would like some refreshment.

Miss Burnett shook her head and Phineas prayed for his mother to leave them without any argument. To his relief she did.

In a low voice he asked, 'So are you going to the police?' He felt faint, cold and sweaty and was glad he was sitting down. 'They'll send me to prison.'

She stared at him. 'What I want is for you and your mother to leave Maybourne before the end of the week. If you are still here I shall take this letter to the police and tell all. I may also inform the Medical Authorities of your conduct and if that happens I think—'

'Oh God, no!' he covered his face with his hands to blot out the sight of her.

'Take your chance, Mr Chisom. A chance which you don't deserve! Go a long way away and don't come back!'

He felt faint with relief. He had wanted to leave Maybourne and now he would have to convince his mother that they had no alternative. He began to splutter his thanks but without another word she left the room. He heard his mother in the hall telling Miss Burnett how sorry she was about the Captain.

Let her go, Mother! he begged silently. If I never see her again it will be too soon! Phineas sat for a long time feeling too ill to move or even think. When he started to recover, he went into the parlour and poured himself a whisky. With no room to manoeuvre it was time to move on.

By the time Harriet returned home it was nearly six o'clock and Sam rushed to greet her.

'Oh Sam! My pet!' she cried, hugging him.

'Papa is gone to heaven! I wanted to say Goodbye but he didn't wait!'

His voice quivered and she wondered who had told him. Before she could ask, he said, 'Mr Bragg told me on the train when he should have been taking cricket. I thought I was being expelled but I'm not. Why is Mama in bed? Is she ill? Cook is making me some gingerbread and Izzie gave me a handful of nuts and she was crying.'

'We're all very sad, Sam, and you will be sad also but eventually we will be happy again because that is what Papa would want.' She blinked back her own tears. 'But Mama is in bed? Let's go into the kitchen and I'll talk to Cook.'

Cook glanced up as she entered the kitchen.

'Ah, Miss Harriet. You just missed that nice Mr Bragg. So charming and so kind to poor Sammy. Brought him all the way, had a bite to eat and is now on his way back. I gave him an apple turnover to take back for his supper. But as for your poor ma –' she shook her head – 'I'd call it a collapse. She came back from the bank and sat down, pale as death. I said, "What on earth is it now?" and she just stared at me.'

Izzie nodded. 'She stared at me, too. Just staring like she couldn't speak. Then she said, ' "Things are very bad, I'm afraid," and—'

Cook gave her a look and she subsided. 'And I said, "Worse than before, you mean, ma'am?" and she nodded. Then she just crumpled up in a dead faint. Lucky Miss Boothby called in just then and she helped to get your ma up to bed. I sent Izzie round to Doctor Chisom but his mother said he was with another patient and couldn't come.'

Sam said, 'When I came home with Mr Bragg Mama was asleep. Is she awake now? Can I see her?'

Harriet said, 'When she wakes up, Sam. There's no hurry.'

'She's not dead too, is she?'

'No, my pet. Mama is fine.' Harriet spoke reassuringly but she was feeling full of renewed anxiety. It seemed that she had just dealt with one problem and another had taken its place. Bad news from the bank could only mean one thing and now her mother had collapsed. Presumably she, Harriet, was the 'patient' the doctor's mother had referred to.

She said, 'Izzie must go round to Doctor Fletcher and ask him to call. I heard recently that Doctor Chisom and his mother are leaving Maybourne so we must change our doctor.'

'Leaving Maybourne?' Cook looked affronted by this disloyalty. 'What are they thinking of?'

Harriet shrugged. 'It *is* rather sudden, I agree, but it's none of our business.' She looked at Izzie. 'Off you go, please, Izzie. Mama needs attention. It may simply be the strain she's under but it may be something else.' She turned to the cook. 'What did Miss Boothby have to say?'

She braced herself for the reply. Miss Boothby, a middle-aged spinster, lived alone with her several cats and was known for her outspoken comments. Harriet always found her intimidating and, whenever she saw the sticklike figure approaching in the street, would cross hurriedly to the other side in order to avoid a conversation.

Cook frowned, trying to recall the conversation. 'She said to tell you all how sorry she was and how she always admired your pa and if there was anything she could do to help, you was to ask. She brought your ma an embroidered handkerchief and some lavender water.'

'Good gracious!' Harriet's conscience pricked her.

Sam said, 'Miss Boothby looks like a witch.'

Harriet frowned at him although she had to agree. Miss Boothby was dark featured with a large chin and small dark eyes. 'If she does, then she's a very nice witch. A white witch. Only black witches are horrible. White witches help people. They make crops grow and they – they cure warts and sometimes they tell people nice secrets. That sort of thing.'

He looked unconvinced. 'Could she cure Papa?'

'No, Sam. Nobody can cure dead people.' She thought about Godfrey and how much she had to tell him and longed to see him.

Sam asked, 'Can I go down to the harbour?'

'I think not, Sam. It won't look right with your Papa lying in his coffin.'

'Then what *can* I do?'

Harriet sighed. Intuitively she understood that Sam needed to fill the hours in order to keep the twin spectres of death and loss at bay. The full intensity of the disaster had not yet touched him and she hoped it would be a gradual process.

'Don't you want to see Mama?' she suggested gently. 'We'll go upstairs together.'

It proved a waste of time as Agnes was still in a deep sleep and there was no point in waking her. Sam was reassured to see her and together he and Harriet crept downstairs again. Glancing at the boy she would always think of as her brother, Harriet had a brainwave.

'As soon as the doctor's been, you and I will go to Havely House.' He looked horrified but she went on quickly. 'Last time I was there Mrs Lester was waiting for a new kitten from her neighbour. Her old cat has disappeared and the mice are getting cheeky. I'm sure you'd like to see—'

'A kitten! Oh yes, Harriet. Please!' The idea chased the shadows from his face and Harriet smiled faintly. He had a hard row to hoe, she thought, and it would be difficult for him – but one step at a time. A kitten would keep the immediate heartache at bay – and *she* would be able to be with Godfrey for an hour or so.

Doctor Angus Fletcher arrived within the hour – a comfortable man in his late thirties with a mass of springy brown curls and bright blue eyes that belied his age. When he finally came downstairs from visiting Agnes, he expressed concern at her condition. 'It has all been too much for such a delicate soul,' he told Harriet.

She thought of her mother's dramatic past and the years of self-imposed silence and fear of discovery. How right he was, she reflected. Not such a delicate soul but a very courageous one. Abruptly Harriet realized that she was very proud of Agnes – but sadly no one must ever know why.

The doctor smiled cheerfully. 'Loss, the shock and grief

and the money worries. She has been quite frank with me, you understand.' Humming to himself, he fumbled within his black bag. 'These pills will help her to sleep at night – one only, mind. During the day she should have complete bed rest. She needs to build up her energies – so light food, nourishing food and drink. When is your father's funeral? I shall try to attend.'

'Oh but . . . You do understand—'

'About the suicide? Certainly but no man should go to his grave without a few well-wishers. There but for the grace of God! Barring accidents I shall be there, Miss Burnett.' The blue eyes twinkled briefly. 'Don't thank me. It will be a pleasure. So, when will it be?'

'We don't know yet. The police will notify us – but it should be soon. The inquest is over.'

He nodded. 'Hurry them up. Give them a nudge! They do sometimes forget that the relatives have feelings and the long delays aren't helpful. I always think that the funeral helps the healing process to begin. Let your mother get up for the funeral but then back to bed for another day or two. Call me if there is a deterioration in her condition.'

'A deterioration?' Harriet was immediately anxious.

'I'm not expecting one but it's early days. Just be alert to a change for the worse.' He snapped shut the fastener on the bag and turned towards the door. 'So the young Doctor Chisom is leaving Maybourne after all these years. We shall miss the family in the town. I can just remember his grandfather. A very eminent man in London. Specialized in tropical diseases.' He shrugged. 'So the Chisoms are moving away. Well, makes way for new blood, I suppose. I know of a young doctor – newly qualified and looking for an opening who might be interested to step into the gap. I'll write to him.' He gave Harriet a friendly nod. 'Sweet lady, your mother. You look after her!'

Half an hour later Harriet and Sam arrived at Havely House and Sam was sent off into the backyard in search of the kitten while Mrs Lester ran upstairs to fetch her son. As soon as he came down she went out into the backyard after Sam to give

Harriet and Godfrey a few minutes together. Immediately Godfrey crossed the room and took Harriet in his arms.

'Dearest Harriet! I began to think I would never see you again. The hours went so slowly!' He kissed her and briefly Harriet forgot all her sorrows and allowed herself to be happy. Just to be close to him was a joy and for a long minute she clung to him, grateful for the warmth and strength of his body. At last, however, the need to talk overcame everything else and they walked together across the front lawn hand in hand while Harriet told him everything that had happened. Everything.

'I don't know how to think,' she confessed. 'I don't even know how to *feel*. It's so confused. I seem to have lost my family – Mama and Papa are not my true parents and even Sam is no relation – except by love and familiarity. I have parents I have never met – and never will meet. The truth is I don't know who I *am*! My identity seems to have disappeared.' She shook her head despairingly. 'I'm a workhouse brat. A *stolen* workhouse brat. It sounds terrible.'

'Not to me, Harriet. To me and everyone else you are still Harriet Burnett.'

'Promise me it doesn't make any difference to you,' she begged. 'At present the fact that you love me is all I have to cling to in a sea of troubles. And tell me that we will all find a way through these terrible times and will be happy again.'

Godfrey told her all that she wished to hear, and then he kissed her and told her again and she burst into tears. Clinging to him, Harriet cried helplessly and he wiped her eyes and told her a third time that he loved her until at last she believed him and could smile again.

Eventually a tapping noise from an upstairs window alerted them to a face at the library window.

'It's Great-Uncle Robert!' cried Harriet. 'He's beckoning to you.'

Godfrey pointed to himself but the old man shook his head.

'It's you he wants to see,' Godfrey told Harriet. 'You'd better go up to him. He'll never venture out here.'

'Perhaps we should go together,' said Harriet, reluctant to leave him.

He grinned. 'I'll be superfluous! You go alone. I'll still be here when you come down again.'

As Harriet hurried back across the garden she caught sight of Mrs Lester and Sam. They had tied a bunch of leaves with a piece of string and Sam was towing the leaves across the grass while a small black and white kitten pursued them in a comical series of leaps and bounds which had Sam in hysterics. He stopped long enough to tell Harriet that they were to choose a name for the kitten.

'I'm to think of ten names before I come here again and bring the list with me.' His eyes shone in anticipation. 'Then we'll put all the names in a hat and Great-Uncle Robert can pick a name and that will be the one!'

'It sounds fun, Sam. What about Sooty? That could be one of the names.'

He thought about it. 'Ye-es . . . but what about Mouser because he will catch mice?'

'That's good too, Sam. So now you've got two names for your list.'

'Shall I ask Godfrey for a name?'

'That's a good idea.'

Upstairs in the library Great-Uncle Robert waited for Harriet beside his desk. To her surprise, one of the windows had been opened and the musty smell was less evident than it had been before. She wondered if Godfrey had brought about the change. The old man seemed brighter also and Harriet guessed that was probably because he now spent less time in solitary pursuits and was able to converse without leaving the library.

'Come in, child. Sit down.'

She obeyed, amused at his choice of words. When you had reached the eighties, she thought, twenty must seem awfully young.

When they were both seated, one on either side of his desk, he began to speak in a nervous way. 'This is about your mother, Harriet. I know what has happened to George and I suspect that your mother is blaming herself and the guilt won't be good for her. It will prey on her mind. No. I have something to tell her which will help her come to terms with the tragedy.'

He frowned and she saw that a response was expected. 'Are you going to write to her?' she asked.

'No, I'm not. I want her to come to Havely House so that we can talk.'

'I'm afraid that won't be possible just yet. She has recently had some more bad news and the burden has affected her very badly. A collapse, in fact. Mama has been—'

'Oh drat!' Great-Uncle Robert slapped himself on the head. 'Then I'm too late! This is what I wanted to prevent. A husband and wife quarrel, one takes his life and the other accepts the blame. It is so unjust! So . . . so *pitiable!*'

He leaned back in his chair and stared at the ceiling. 'So unnecessary! Poor Agnes.' He drew his gaze back to Harriet. 'All the cares of the world on those slim shoulders. I always did wonder, you know, if she was the right woman for George. I mean a sea captain's wife has a lonely time of it. Such responsibilities . . . and she was so young and innocent of all that would – or might – come her way. My brother Edwin – your grandfather, that is – shared my doubts but chose not to interfere, because his son was so madly in love.'

Harriet tried to imagine George Burnett as a young and passionate man but failed. She had never seen any sign of real affection between him and Agnes but with hindsight she could understand what had soured the relationship.

Robert said, 'My brother feared that if George were not allowed to marry Agnes – he called her "his heart's desire"! – he would never marry. In the end he gave in and you and Sam came along.'

Thank goodness he has no idea what really happened, thought Harriet. But why exactly was he telling her all this and how would it help her mother?

As if he had read her mind he said, 'If she cannot come to me then I will write to her. She needs to understand that there is a certain inevitability to all that has happened.' He stood up awkwardly. 'I'll pen the letter now so that you can take it with you when you go. When is the funeral? I'm sorry I shan't be there, but you know my problem.'

'Indeed. I believe it has been planned for Wednesday but it will be a sad affair. Myself, Sam and the servants.' She shrugged. 'Poor Papa. He deserved better but people often shun the burial of a suicide as a mark of their disapproval.' She brightened a little. 'Oh yes! I forgot Godfrey and Mrs Lester! They will attend. That's two more. And Doctor Fletcher might be there. He seems a very caring man.'

He was staring at her. 'No man of the family? Good Lord! That's terrible. If Edwin were alive he would be there. A rock in time of trouble.' Shaking his head, he led Harriet to the door and opened it. 'Time presses, my dear, and I must put pen to paper. I hope Mrs Lester has refilled the inkwell . . .'

That evening after supper Harriet told her mother that she was going for a walk, but when Sam asked to join her she dissuaded him with the suggestion that he use his paintbox to paint a picture of the new kitten for Mama to see in the morning. 'Round the edge of the picture you could write all the names you have thought of for the kitten. Maybe Cook and Lizzie could think of a few more.'

Leaving him happily installed at the kitchen table under Cook's watchful eye, Harriet slipped from the house and made her way to Market Street. It was narrow and roughly cobbled and the houses were old and mean, jammed together in a higgledy-piggledy line on both sides of the street with no front gardens or area steps to hold them back from the road itself. One or two were shops – a small bakery and an ironmonger's caught her eye – but the rest were tenements and her courage almost failed her. Several people made their way past her, going up or down the hill and all stared at her in her expensive black clothes.

An old woman touched her arm and Harriet jumped.

'You shouldn't wander about round 'ere, love,' the old woman advised. 'A lady like you – they'll pick your pocket as soon as look at you! Where you going?'

A young man pushing a barrow full of coal lingered nearby to hear Harriet's answer. He wore a pair of trousers that revealed bony ankles and a threadbare waistcoat over a grubby shirt that had seen better days. A sooty cap was set on his head at a racy angle; he was good-looking in a

194

raffish way and Harriet imagined that he would appeal to Daisy. The 'Digger type' perhaps.

'I'm . . .' Nervousness made her voice hoarse and she swallowed. 'I'm trying to find out what happened to a friend of mine. A young woman called Daisy Pritty.'

The old woman shook her head. 'Daisy Pretty? Never 'eard of her – 'ave you, Tom?' She appealed to the man with the coal.

'Daisy Pretty? No-o. Who wants her?'

'She was involved in a fi—a bit of a scuffle,' Harriet corrected herself. Then she hesitated. 'Well, it was a fight, actually. In this street.'

A young woman staggered up the hill, pushing a very battered perambulator with twins in it. One wheel squeaked at intervals and as they drew nearer, Harriet could see that the handle was beginning to rust. From the pram two pairs of identical blue eyes looked up at her while identical mouths sucked on large dummies. 'Here, what's going on?' the woman asked, staring curiously at Harriet. 'Have I missed summat?'

The old woman repeated Harriet's question.

'You mean *our* Dais?' She jerked a thumb to indicate the next street. 'Our Dais is in clink and not before time if you ask me! Done some chap in, she did.'

'Oh no! He's not done in – I mean he's not dead,' Harriet told them. If these people thought he *was* they'd be less likely to talk to her for fear of the law. 'He's certainly in hospital but he's still very much alive. I'm a . . . a friend of hers. I don't think she meant to hurt him and I want to find someone who saw what happened. Who actually *saw* it.'

One of the twins spat his dummy on to the cobbles and the woman picked it up and shoved it back into the child's mouth. 'You want to ask old Mother Hatton in number twenty-five. Right outside her window it was. Scared her out of her wits! Run upstairs and hid in her bedroom!'

The old woman rolled her eyes. 'Never did! Mother Hatton don't scare that easy. Went upstairs, is what I 'eard, to get a better view!' She found this hilarious and Tom joined her.

Harriet thanked her and as an afterthought turned to the young mother, 'Are you a friend of hers? Of Daisy?'

The young mother tossed her head. 'Friend of Dais'?'

195

She considered this for a moment then tossed her head contemptuously. '*Friend* of Dais'? Not really! I mean, she's nice enough in a way – Never done me no 'arm – but she's a workhouse brat! Came from nowhere and going nowhere! That's what they say, isn't it?'

Harriet felt her insides twist in panic at this cruel observation but she tried not to let it show in her face. This was something she must get used to. She must learn to rise above it if she was to have any peace of mind in the future. She said, 'Is it?'

'Now me, I'm a *respectable* woman!' She thrust out her hand and Harriet saw the slim wedding ring.

The old woman cackled. 'Shotgun wedding tho', wasn't it, Annie!'

Annie made a rude gesture with her finger and to Harriet's relief went on up the hill.

Number twenty-five Market Street was no worse than any of the others. In one way it was better for the knocker had been polished and the step recently whitened. Mother Hatton came to the door with her grey hair in curling rags and a sacking apron round her broad waist. 'What?' she demanded suspiciously, looking Harriet up and down. A young lad raced towards them, bowling an iron hoop and she shouted, 'You! Watch it with that ruddy hoop!' but instead he pretended to run into Harriet, who jumped back in alarm and the woman shook a fist after him. Shouting after him had brought on a coughing fit and Harriet waited until she had recovered.

'Mad as a hatter!' gasped Mother Hatton. 'One of the Trew boys. Mad, the lot of them! Father's done a runner and their poor ma can't cope.'

Harriet explained why she had come.

'The fight? Oh yes, I seen it all,' the woman told her, eyes gleaming at the memory. 'She went for him good and proper. Said he owed her money. Shouting at him that he had to pay up. He just laughed and kept saying "You'll get your share when I'm good and ready and not before!" Cheeky little tyke. She was nearly in tears.'

She stopped to take a deep breath, wheezing horribly. Harriet wondered if she had consumption and had to steel herself not to step back.

Mother Hatton went on. 'She's tough, that one, but kind-hearted with it, so they say. Know what I mean? People look down their noses when you're from the workhouse, but we might all end up there if we run out of luck.' She paused again for breath, her chest heaving convulsively.

Harriet seized her chance. 'Did you see Daisy kick him in the head because that's what the police are saying. They're going to charge her with trying to *kill* him.'

'Kill him? Never!' She glared indignantly. 'She kicked him, yes, but not in the head. And I'd have done the same. If I was skint and he owed me money and thought it a great joke, *I'd* give him a kicking!'

'How did he come to be on the ground?'

Mother Hatton pursed her lips thoughtfully. 'Let's see now. She slapped him round the face and he slapped her back and she punched him and he laughed and punched her back and she nearly fell and then she gave a sort of roar and rushed him with her head down . . .'

She was stopped by another burst of heavy coughing and this time Harriet did move back slightly. Oh Daisy! she thought. The things I do for you!

Exhausted, the woman leaned against the door jamb, determined to finish her story. 'She butted him in the chest with her head – like a goat. Know what I mean? That took him by surprise and he tripped and fell. Bashed the back of his head on the corner of my windowsill and went out like a light. I shut the window quick and went upstairs to watch it from there. I seen it all. Daisy didn't realize he was out cold and she give him a couple of kicks but not in the head! Tried to murder him? Rubbish!' She began to gasp, one hand on her chest.

Harriet hesitated. 'Would you be prepared to tell the police that – if one of them came to ask?'

'What?' Mother Hatton looked horrified. 'Don't you go sending no policeman to *my* door, thank you very much.'

'But if one did come . . . And if you did tell them the whole truth and they told me you had helped their enquiries – I'd be very grateful. I'd give you half a crown.'

Mother Hatton stared at her. 'Half a crown? You never would!'

197

Five minutes later, having finally convinced her with the first shilling in advance, Harriet left Market Street and made her way home. She was feeling rather pleased with her progress on Daisy's behalf but the next step was going to be very embarrassing. She was going to ask her mother about Daisy and the meaning of 'up the spout'!

Alfred Cummings started work the following morning at seven thirty-five. He usually arrived at Havely House at that time, satisfied that he had cheated his employer out of exactly five minutes labour. He did this from Monday to Friday, amassing the satisfying sum of twenty-five stolen minutes. Nearly half an hour for which he was paid but did no work. Nobody knew of this small deceit because Mrs Lester was preparing breakfast and the old man was never around anyway. Like most labourers Alfred thought, with some justification, that he was underpaid and this made him feel that he had tipped the scales a little in his favour.

He unlocked the shed and went inside to the familiar smell of oil, sacking, bonemeal, cold metal, sawdust and earth. He sat down on an empty container that had once held weedkiller and changed from his everyday boots to his working boots. Today he was going to water the three new hibiscus plants, run the roller over the lawn and do some weeding. Outside, the sun was still lacking warmth and he nodded, pleased, as the day stretched before him. He'd eat his cold bacon and bread under the shade of the sycamore, he promised himself, and the housekeeper would bring him a jug of small beer to go with it.

He left the shed and had taken no more than a dozen paces across the lawn when a small movement caught his eye and he stared. Someone was standing at the front door of the main house, beckoning to him. Alfred changed direction and hurried across to the house. To his astonishment he saw that it was his employer, Robert Burnett. The old man was fully dressed, which was unusual at this time of day. Normally he could be glimpsed at the windows still in his dressing gown until maybe ten or later. Wonders will never cease, thought Alfred.

'Morning, sir!' He hoped his late arrival had not been noticed. Best to put a good face on it. He would pretend it was the first time ever. Better think of an excuse, quick!

'Are you the fellow who does the garden?'

'Yes, sir, I am. Cummings, sir. You do know me.'

'Do I?'

'Alfred Cummings, the gardener. Can I help you in some way, sir?'

'Yes, you can. I've been waiting for you. You were five minutes late.'

'Was I sir?' Alfred injected a note of astonishment into the words. 'I'm very sorry sir. Not like me to be late, sir, but I daresay the old timepiece isn't as accurate as it—'

'But you're here now. Take my arm.'

Alfred hesitated. 'Your arm?'

'Yes, dammit. I want to go outside into the garden. I want to walk outside and I want you with me. In case I . . . In case I don't manage it alone.' He swallowed. 'In case anything goes wrong.'

'I see, sir.' Alfred was baffled but decided to play along. Was his employer supposed to come outside the building? He had never done so until now and in fact it had once occurred to Alfred that Mr Burnett might be being held prisoner in his own house. 'I'll hold your arm, then,' Alfred suggested, realizing suddenly that this little escapade meant *more* time-wasting. He smiled. 'What about a walking stick, sir? There's usually one or two in the hall stand if you'll excuse the liberty.' He stepped past him into the hall and reappeared with a carved stick. It had a handle shaped like a duck's head. 'Lovely bit of ash, that!' Alfred told him, wiping the stick with a rag he produced from his back pocket. 'You lean on that and hold on to me and you'll be right as rain!'

Setting words to action, he placed the stick in the old man's right hand and grasped his left arm. 'Ready now?'

'I think so.' Mr Burnett closed his eyes.

'There's a bit of a step, then it's level and then down two more and we're on the flat. On the drive. You'll hear the crunch of the gravel.'

Slowly the old man allowed himself to be edged forward

199

and when urged, he cautiously took a step into the unknown. Another two steps and they came to a halt.

Alfred watched him closely. 'You can open your eyes now.'

Seconds elapsed and the old man opened his eyes, squinting nervously around him. Alfred could feel him trembling.

'Going to be a nice day,' he said soothingly. 'Now, here we are, Mr Burnett, sir. On the gravel drive like I promised. No problem, was it? Where shall we go next? We could walk round the house or we could go across the grass towards the rhododendrons.'

Mr Burnett scraped at the gravel with his stick then raised his head slowly and snatched another look around while Alfred resisted the urge to hurry him. He was by now feeling quite excited by the adventure and wondered whether a coin or two might later on be his reward. He could imagine Mrs Lester's surprise when she knew that their employer had ventured outside for the first time in many years.

His employer took a deep breath. 'I . . . I think we'll go across the grass.'

'Good idea, sir.' Alfred tightened the grip on his arm. 'Feeling steady, are you? Don't want you to stumble, do we?'

They went forward slowly.

The old man said, 'It's a bigger garden than I remember.'

'Oh, it's big all right! Big lawn, too. Proper devil this lawn to keep neat. We could do with a bigger mower except that I'd never be able to push it.'

Step by step they inched their way forward until they were in the middle of the lawn.

Alfred said, 'I keep it nice and short, the grass. Looks so much better.' He pointed ahead to the confusion of pinks and purples which was the rhododendrons. 'Lovely splash of colour, aren't they, sir, even though they're past their best.'

Mr Burnett stopped walking and said, 'Let go of my arm. I want to stand alone.'

Alfred obliged and the old man raised his head and smiled. 'The sky hasn't fallen!'

'Sir?'

'Chicken-licken! The old folk tale.'

'Ah!' Now the old man had lost him but at least he was smiling and hadn't had a fit or died of fright. 'Shall we walk on, sir? There's a blackbird's nest in one of the bushes. Lovely it is. Hatched three young'uns last year. You might like to take a look at it.'

But at that moment Mrs Lester appeared from the side of the house and gave a scream of excitement as she saw them. The old man clutched Alfred's arm in alarm, but the gardener explained and they both turned to greet her. She came running towards them, her apron flapping, her face pink with the effort.

'Oh Mr Burnett! You're out here!' She fanned herself with her hand as she stood in awe of the sight. 'This is the last place – I wondered where you were, Mr Burnett, I was searching the house . . .' She gulped for breath. 'And here you are – *outside*! Heaven be praised! It's a miracle!'

Mr Burnett continued to smile, but Alfred positively beamed. 'The master and I just fancied a little walk,' he explained airily. 'Such a nice day. Mr Burnett thought he'd take a look at the garden.'

She was still staring at her employer with a rapt expression. 'How do you feel, sir, in yourself? The fresh air must be doing you good. Airs your lungs. That's what they say.'

He spoke at last. 'It's not as bad as I expected. Not bad at all. Alfred, here, has been a great help . . . The rhododendrons make a lovely splash of colour, don't they, Mrs Lester?'

Still dazed, she gave them a quick glance. 'Yes, they do, sir.' She glanced at Alfred, who winked at her. 'Suppose I bring out a deckchair, Mr Burnett, and a small table and a pot of tea. Would you enjoy that?'

The old man hesitated. 'If Alfred could spare another quarter of an hour . . . ?'

'I certainly could, sir.' He began to see that this might prove very interesting in the future. Better than digging.

'Then a pot of tea for two, please, Mrs Lester.'

They strolled on to admire the now empty blackbird's nest and then they settled in two chairs while Mrs Lester produced a small table and then brought out a tray of tea and cinnamon biscuits.

*　　*　　*

When Robert returned to the house he went straight into the library, where Godfrey, busy with the papers, congratulated him on his expedition.

'I had to do it,' Robert told him, sinking thankfully into a chair. 'I have to attend my nephew's funeral. I cannot allow the womenfolk to suffer such an ordeal unsupported. Now I must finish my letter to the Pope and then I shall lie down for an hour or so.' He put a finger to his lips and smiled. 'And not a word to Agnes or Harriet. I want to surprise them!'

Thirteen

While Robert Burnett was still relishing celebrating his first steps back to the outside world, Agnes was re-reading the letter he had sent with Harriet the previous night. She was sitting up in bed feeling fragile, her eyes large in her face, her skin pale and almost transparent. Her hair had been brushed and lay in two braids, her nightdress was buttoned to the chin and her fingers moved restlessly. Thanks to the doctor's pills she had slept long and late but the hours had been filled with nightmares from which she awoke dazed, frightened and exhausted. Now she had eaten a few spoonfuls of Cook's lightest egg custard and had drunk a few mouthfuls of China tea. Tired and wan, she tried to come to terms with yet another family secret.

My dear Agnes, I hoped never to have to write this letter but George's death by his own hand has forced me to reveal a long kept secret . . .

'Another one!' Agnes murmured.

The male side of the Burnetts has been plagued for many generations by the spectre of a deep depression border-ing on melancholy and leading on occasions to suicide (which I believe to be a morbid disease). This is the reason why I vowed never to marry. Living alone, I sus-pect I have become eccentric over the years but I thank God that at least I have never harmed either myself or distressed anyone else by choosing such a lonely road. George's father (my brother Edwin) was a sickly child prone to melancholy, which the doctor assumed was

*brought on by the death of our father when Edwin
was only five. I say 'assumed' because we had moved
recently into the Maybourne area to escape the scandal
of our father's death in frightful circumstances. Father
had jumped from London Bridge and drowned after
discovering that he was being sacked from his law firm
for an improper liaison with a female client. At first he
denied it but shortly before the case was due to be heard
in court Father confessed to his wife that it was true . . .*

Agnes turned the letter face down on the bed and tried to
calm herself. Her heartbeat was beginning to frighten her and
she felt dizzy. She drew some deep breaths, took a quick whiff
of sal volatile to clear her head and reached once more for the
offending letter.

*He had made advances to a newly widowed woman who
reported him to the senior partner. Although my mother
promised to try to forgive him and agreed not to leave
him, Father travelled up to London a few days later
and made his way to the bridge . . .*

*So that you may properly understand your late hus-
band, George, it is necessary to know that something of
this nature had happened before he was married to you.
When George was only twenty-one he became friendly
with a man named Roger Champney, who interested him
in a tract of land for sale in Southern Spain. George
rashly speculated to the tune of three hundred guineas
(he borrowed the money) but Champney was a fraud
and the land did not exist. Champney went to prison
and the young George was left with a large debt. He
tried to take his life then with an overdose of laudanum
but was saved by his mother's prompt actions.*

Agnes was stunned by the revelation. She had never had
the slightest suspicion that George was prey to this 'morbid
disease' and she now shook her head at the twists and turns of
Fate. All these years she had kept a secret from George only to
discover that he had kept one from her. Should she feel

marginally less guilty? she wondered with a frisson of hope.

So whatever happened between you and George that spurred him to shoot himself, only a part of it was your responsibility. Cling to that thought, Agnes. The rest of the responsibility lies with the emotional weakness he inherited . . .

'Oh George! My poor dear husband!' For a moment Agnes tried to hold back the tears, but it was impossible and she quickly gave in to a torrent of grief. Was she never going to reach a time, she wondered, when she could start to recover from all the spectres that haunted her? Would any of the family ever be able to rebuild their shattered lives or would they all be dragged down because of her action that day at the workhouse when she stole a child from a dying mother? In spite of what her Uncle Robert said – and she knew he meant well – she knew she had done wrong but could never, *never* regret it. Without her theft of Hannah Wenright's baby, Harriet might well be another Daisy Pritty, with a life that staggered from bad to worse and threatened to end in disaster one way or the other.

You may well feel that our parents owed it to you to tell you of George's problems but the fact is they knew how deeply he loved you and hoped you would be his salvation. I think they believed that to separate the two of you might put George at further risk and they took a gamble. You have to believe that without your love George may well have killed himself for one reason or another. Don't think that you killed him, Agnes. Think that your love kept him alive for many years.

My last paragraph has to be a warning but I am sure you are already ahead of me in this – the need to watch young Sam for any sign of the disease. The death of his father may trigger something. I will pray to God that he will escape, but please rely on me to help in any way I can.

Your affectionate Uncle Robert

* * *

That evening, when Agnes was sleeping and Harriet was thinking about retiring, there was a frantic knocking on the front door and Izzie rushed to answer it, followed closely by Harriet.

It was Miss Boothby. 'It's the workhouse!' she told them, her voice high with agitation. 'The casual ward! There's trouble developing and Mrs Fenner's there alone.'

Harriet grabbed her coat and sent Izzie back to the kitchen with orders that, if Agnes should awake, she should not be told of the disturbance. As Harriet and Miss Boothby hurried through the darkening streets, Harriet heard the rest of the story. Herbert Crane had taken two days off to attend a wedding but three days later had still not returned. A couple of men had turned up asking for a night in the casual ward, but they were abusive and smelled of alcohol and Mrs Fenner had refused their application. To avoid annoying them she had pretended the ward was full but they loitered outside, hurling insults until a group of genuine labourers arrived seeking a night's accommodation and Mrs Fenner was forced to accept them all.

Miss Boothby finished her account as they hurried up the steps. 'They forced their way in and began to threaten Mrs Fenner, who sent one of the inmates to Mr Wellbury but he was sick in bed, so he was sent on to me and I came to ask your mother's advice.'

As they entered the building the noise led them to the source of the trouble. Miss Boothby and Harriet paused in the doorway and surveyed the casual ward with dismay. Mrs Fenner had been forced into a corner of the room by two obviously drunken men who were holding the rest of the men at bay with lengths of wood which they had torn from the 'beds'.

Miss Boothby crossed herself and Harriet uttered a quick prayer. She could see that Mrs Fenner, utterly defenceless, was terrified, as well she might be. One of the labourers turned to see who had arrived.

Harriet called to them. 'You two! You'd better get out of here! The police are on their way!'

Miss Boothby whispered, 'Has anyone sent for them?'

Harriet kept her gaze on the troublemakers. Lowering her voice, she said, 'I don't know. We'll ask one of the men.'

She beckoned to a thin man with ginger hair and asked him if anyone had sent for the police. On hearing that it seemed unlikely, she asked him to run for help and he disappeared without a second glance at the fracas. No doubt glad to be out of danger, thought Harriet.

Taking her cue from Harriet, Miss Boothby now stepped forward and called loudly to Mrs Fenner.

'Do you have the names of these two troublemakers?'

Mrs Fenner nodded but one of them turned, grabbed her arm and slammed her back against the wall shouting, 'You hold your tongue, missus, or I'll hold it for you!'

Mrs Fenner looked as though she might faint at any moment but one of the other men betrayed them. Pointing he shouted, 'That's Sam Harker from the bakery and that's Daniel Stick.'

At that moment three of the labourers made a run for the malcontents but they were too slow and one of them received a blow on the right shoulder which sent him reeling back in pain and the others retreated in disarray. A frightened old man at the back of the room began to pray aloud in a trembling voice which set Stick and Harker laughing derisively.

'Pray all you like . . .' Harker growled, his words slurred. 'We're no' . . . We're no' leaving. We've a righ' to bed and . . .' He blinked, trying to clear his head. '. . . to bed and . . . a bite of breakfast and – Ow! God's trewth!' He suddenly clamped a hand to his face.

One of the men had thrown a raw turnip at him with unerring aim and it struck him in the mouth. Blood oozed and Harker spat out a tooth. Then with a shout of rage he dropped his makeshift weapon and ran towards the owner of the turnip. He hurled himself at him but the man was tall and burly and the fight that followed quickly became one-sided and others rushed in to pinion Harker's arms behind his back while someone produced a piece of cord to bind his wrists.

To Harriet's surprise Miss Boothby rubbed her hands together and muttered 'One down! One to go!' Her face was now flushed and she seemed to be enjoying the challenge.

That left Daniel Stick. Without his companion, he looked lost and he glanced round fearfully for an escape route. While he was distracted, Mrs Fenner snatched the makeshift weapon from the floor and swung it against the back of his legs so that he lost his balance and fell.

Miss Boothby cried, 'Well done!' and pushed her way through the crowd.

Harriet followed as they forced Daniel Stick face down on the floor. Overcome, now that the worst was over, Mrs Fenner burst into tears and Miss Boothby put an arm round her and led her out of the room. The men jostled round Harriet, each telling his own version of the story, but then two constables arrived and ten minutes later order was finally restored.

As Harriet and Miss Boothby walked home, the latter said, 'I have to tell you, Harriet, that Crane is going to ask your mother to resign from the Board – because of what has happened to your father. James Wellbury agreed – weak man that he is. I'm so sorry. I argued against it but—'

'Mother would have had to resign anyway,' Harriet told her. 'Her health has suffered these last weeks and the doctor says she is in no fit state to do anything but rest. I shall be glad for her, but her going will leave a gap.'

Miss Boothby glanced at her. 'I suggested you might take her place. I know you are young, but you can lean on your mother's experience. Of course James Wellbury might not be too happy about the idea . . .' She shrugged. 'Your marriage to his son . . . ?'

Harriet lowered her head briefly. 'The marriage is no longer possible.' With an effort she faced Miss Boothby. 'I shan't lose any sleep over it. Times change. People change.' Harriet said nothing about Godfrey Lester.

They walked on in silence for a while until Harriet said, 'Where was Mr Crane? He should never have left Mrs Fenner to cope without a man on the staff. She might have been injured. It was fortunate the trouble ended the way it did and no worse.'

Miss Boothby nodded. 'He was given leave for two days

and a man was hired to support Mrs Fenner in case of trouble. He left this morning assuming that Crane would be back.' She sighed. 'The casual wards are often a breeding ground for quarrels and they can lead to serious disturbances. I did hear, a year or so back, that in one of the London workhouses one man actually set fire to the ward! A man was trying to steal from one of the others and objected to being turned out in the early hours of the morning. He sneaked back and set the fire. One man died and another was badly injured. Men and alcohol don't mix! I should know – my father was a drunkard and a bully!'

'How awful for you!' Shocked, Harriet turned to her. 'I'm so sorry, Miss Boothby!'

'Call me Eveline, for Heaven's sake!'

'Thank you, Eveline.' Harriet hid her surprise.

In bed later that night, Harriet found herself wondering about Eveline's childhood. A drunken bully for a father was Harriet's idea of a nightmare. Was it the reason Eveline had never risked marriage? Sleepily she turned over the events of the evening and wondered about Daniel Stick and Sam Harker. What kind of childhoods had *they* had? And at what stage should an unhappy past be cast off? *Could* an unhappy past be rejected or was it just wishful thinking? As her eyelids fluttered and sleep descended, she thought of Godfrey and wondered if it were ever possible to know and truly understand anyone else.

'Or even understand ourselves!' she whispered as the long day came to an end.

Harriet, Sam and Izzie walked slowly along the pathway towards the church, where Miss Boothby waited in the porch. It had been decided that Agnes should not be left alone at home and Cook had reluctantly agreed to stay behind. She would also prepare a plate of cold meats and pickles for the few people that would come back to the house.

They greeted Miss Boothby and were about to enter the church when Sam cried, 'Look! It's Great-Uncle Robert!'

Harriet swung round and was astonished to see three people

descending from a hansom cab – Doris and Godfrey Lester and Robert Burnett. Sam dashed back along the path, deaf to appeals to 'Walk, Sam!' and Harriet followed. First she was hugged by Doris, and then Godfrey took her hand and squeezed it and Harriet understood that the churchyard was too public for a display of affection.

Great-Uncle Robert said gruffly, 'I had to come. One of the family had to be with you and there was only me.'

'Thank you!' she cried. 'This is so wonderful! You don't know how much this means – and Papa would have been so pleased.'

Sam shook the old man's proffered hand and said, 'Is it a miracle, Great-Uncle Robert?'

Robert smiled. 'I think it is, you know, young Sam. What do you think of my walking stick? Cummings found it for me in the hall stand. See the duck's head?'

Sam examined it solemnly.' I think it's very nice. I think when I am as old as you I might have one just like it!'

At that moment the vicar appeared, looking remote and unapproachable, and they all fell silent as they followed him into the church. George's coffin stood on two trestles before the altar but to Harriet's surprise she saw that it was covered by a handsome black and gold sheet.

Seeing Harriet's puzzled expression the vicar whispered, 'It was lent by Mr Hawke, the coffin maker, who claims to be a friend of yours.'

He nodded towards the rear of the church, where Albert Hawke sat in his full mourning wear, flanked by four similarly dressed men. Harriet smiled at him and mouthed the words, 'Thank you!' and he nodded and smiled in return. Harriet was also touched and surprised to see Mr Maddocks from the *Saint Augustine*. She hadn't realized that the ship's sailing date had been delayed by the events but, on reflection, they would have needed a new skipper.

Mrs Fenner was last to arrive, the clock struck the hour and the brief service began. There was no organist or choir, so there were no hymns or psalms, but the vicar read several prayers and they all recited the Lord's Prayer. Officially the service was over but before the vicar could say so, Robert

Burnett stood up and walked carefully towards the front. He nodded politely to the surprised vicar and then turned to face the small congregation.

'I want to say that I am George Burnett's uncle and very proud to acknowledge the relationship. George was a fine man – a decent Godfearing man who did his best for those he loved. George was a good husband to his wife, Agnes, and a loving father to his children, Harriet and Samuel. He worked hard in his chosen career and reached the position of Captain, where he was, I'm sure, respected by his crew. The manner of his passing is irrelevant to those of us who knew and appreciated him and we shall all miss him. May God take him into his blessed care. Amen.'

The vicar walked past the congregation and he led the way outside. Albert Hawke ushered the four men forward and they carried the coffin into the churchyard, to the quiet corner reserved for the poor and unworthy. There, the coffin was lowered into the grave already prepared for it and Harriet, with a lump in her throat, found Albert Hawke at her side. He presented her with a small but beautifully carved wooden cross. George's name was on it and so were his dates. Overcome at last, Harriet thanked him tearfully and he patted her arm and stepped away and it was Doris Lester who comforted her while Sam watched anxiously. Harriet pressed the little cross into the grass at the head of the grave and whispered a final 'goodbye'. It would be George's only epitaph. When tears appeared in Sam's eyes, it was Izzie who produced a handkerchief and wiped his eyes.

'Be a brave little man,' she whispered and gave him a quick hug.

Back home once more, the sad group began to recover and a sporadic conversation broke out. Neither Albert nor Mrs Fenner had come back to the house but Cook plied those remaining with food and cups of tea or glasses of sherry. Robert took Harriet on one side and spoke to her in a low voice.

'I've been thinking over your problems, Harriet, and have decided to ask you to share Havely House with me. There is—'

Shaken, she stared at him. 'Share your home? Good

heavens! That is so generous. I hardly know what to say.'

'I wanted to talk to your mother but I know she is hardly in a fit state to make any decisions, so if you would pass on this offer she may talk to me at a later stage. No, my dear!' He held up a hand. 'You don't have to say anything. I'm not doing this entirely for your sakes, you see. I realize how isolated I have become – my own fault entirely – and I would enjoy being part of the family again. And there's plenty of room. Havely is a big warren of a house.' He gave her a sly smile. 'Sam could have a pony when he is older – to help keep down the grass in the paddock and to pull the new mower which Cummings is hinting at! What do you think of my little scheme?'

Harriet shook her head, lost for words. Instead she reached up, put her arms gently round his neck and kissed him.

His smile was shaky. 'I realize I was never close enough to my nephew,' he told her. 'This is my chance. By helping his family I can perhaps atone somewhat for my neglect.' He glanced over her shoulder. 'Ah, here comes young Godfrey. I'll leave you in his safe hands.'

A week later Harriet attended the court where Daisy Pritty's case was being heard and was delighted to discover that Digger was recovering and there was no longer a threat to Daisy of a charge of attempted murder. Harriet's letter, quoting Mother Hatton's evidence, was read out and taken into consideration but nothing could excuse Daisy from the charge of affray or that of resisting arrest and assaulting the police constable. For these crimes she was sentenced to eighteen months in prison and she was led away from the court looking unusually subdued. Harriet left the court wondering if the punishment might do something to curb Daisy's wild streak. Hopefully when she came out she would be a little wiser.

'But perhaps not!' she muttered with a wry smile.

Earlier in the week she had talked with her mother about Robert Burnett's offer of a home and Agnes had accepted immediately. She explained to Harriet that without an income they could no longer afford to rent their present home and the move to Havely House could be accomplished without too much disturbance.

They had also discussed the possibility that Daisy Pritty was expecting a child, but Agnes thought it had probably been a ploy to enable Daisy to escape the wrath of the law if Digger *had* died as a result of the fight.

'We shall know before too long,' she told Harriet. 'She will be allowed visitors, no doubt, and you can ask her yourself. Even if she doesn't choose to tell you, it will become obvious as time goes by.'

Sam was returned to his school, accompanied by Harriet and Godfrey, and he went off as cheerfully as could be expected with the promise of a new life at Havely House, the kitten and a pony. On the way back to Maybourne, Harriet and Godfrey had time to talk.

Godfrey sat beside her, her hand in his. Opposite, an elderly man sat ensconced behind his copy of *The Times* and beside him a middle-aged woman was knitting a white shawl, frowning in concentration at the intricate pattern

Godfrey spoke in a low voice. 'My mother is eager to return home to *her* mother, now that she has the chance. Grandmother's sight is failing rapidly and Mother has been torn between the old man and Grandmother. Now she could go home if your mother would take over the running of the house instead of simply moving in as family. What do you think? At the moment your mother is not fit enough but what of the future?'

Harriet thought about it. 'I think it would work out in a month or more perhaps, but in the meantime I could take over. If I had married Marcus I would be running a home so I—'

Godfrey cast an anxious glance towards the people opposite and saw that they were paying them no attention. He went on. 'I'm very glad you're not! Marrying Marcus, I mean!' He turned to her. 'I'm secretly hoping that you'll marry me instead.'

Harriet smiled. 'Whatever gave you that idea? Do you think I love you? Is that it?'

He grinned. 'I certainly hope so – although Mother thinks it too early to be sure. We haven't known each long but . . .' His voice had become a loud whisper. 'Dearest Harriet, I am sure that *I* love *you*.'

'And I know that I adore you, but we shouldn't rush into

anything. We'll see so much of each other when we move into Havely and the parents will have time to get used to the idea. At a time like this we shouldn't rush into anything . . . Should we?'

'So you *will* marry me?'

'Of course I will! Is this a proposal?'

He looked at her in surprise. 'I suppose it is!'

They both grinned broadly and the woman lowered her knitting.

'Thank goodness that's settled,' she told them with a smile. 'I get off at the next stop. I was beginning to think I'd never know!'

The man lowered the newspaper a fraction and glared at them. He said gruffly, 'Congratulations are in order, I suppose – but don't think being married is going to be easy! It isn't. I should know!'

He raised the paper once more and Harriet was forced to press her face against Godfrey's shoulder to muffle her laughter.

Epilogue

T he last meeting of the year at the Maybourne Workhouse started at ten o'clock two weeks before Christmas. Those present were Eveline Boothby, Harriet, a Mr Edgar Laycock who replaced James Wellbury, Mrs Fenner and the new Workhouse Master, Charles Swift, an enthusiastic man in his thirties who had been forced to give up his theological studies when his father died and a new income was desperately needed.

Harriet found him pleasant enough and he had agreed to Eveline's suggestion that they spend a little more on the Christmas festivities than they had done in other years. Swift had contacted the local churches and persuaded them to give a small proportion of their Christmas collection to the workhouse, describing it as 'a thoroughly deserving cause'. Because of the churches' generosity the Board had been able to spend an extra three pounds and two shillings on making Christ's birthday a happy one for the inmates.

Edgar Laycock was hardly to Harriet's liking, being a rather bumptious man, but he had money and was not mean with it and the workhouse benefited by his presence on the Board.

Now he said, 'I understand the children from the local school want to sing a few carols here on Christmas morning. A nice idea.'

Miss Boothby nodded. 'They do so every year and the inmates love it. We usually have them early – around ten thirty – so the parents can take them home and still have time to cook the goose!'

Harriet made a note in her book. 'What about mulled wine?

215

One glass per adult only – and last thing, so that they all go to bed happy and sleepy.'

'And drunk!' Laycock, who was strictly teetotal, raised his eyebrows.

'On one glass?'

He shrugged.

Charles Swift, the new Workhouse Master, interrupted. 'I nearly forgot. Some less than pleasant news. I visited Daisy Pritty today and was told she is definitely with child. The baby is due in January.'

There were groans from everyone except Harriet, who was doing some arithmetic. 'That means it isn't Digger's child. Oh dear! Is that good or bad, I wonder.'

Miss Boothby tutted. 'It depends whose child it is – if she even *knows*!'

There was a gloomy silence and then Harriet asked, 'Will they allow her out for a few hours on Christmas Day?'

He shook his head. 'Sorry. The request was denied. They think she'd make a run for it.'

Mrs Fenner shrugged. 'I think she probably would. I did think Miss – I mean Mrs Lester's, idea was rather ambitious – not to say risky!'

Harriet blushed. She and Godfrey had been married exactly ten days and it still thrilled her to hear her married name. 'On to our alternative plan then. One of us should take Daisy a few sweetmeats.'

To her surprise Laycock said he would go. 'Get me away from all the relatives,' he explained. 'The wife's three sisters are coming. Heaven preserve me from so many women!'

Miss Boothby gave him an icy look but no one commented and the visit to Daisy was agreed.

As the meeting proceeded, Harriet's thoughts wandered a little. The family's first Christmas at Havely House promised to be a wonderful affair. She and Agnes would prepare the food while Godfrey chopped logs for the fire and Sam would share his presents with Great-Uncle Robert. They had bought Sam a toboggan and were hoping for a little more snow. It was already four or five inches deep, much to Mouser's disgust, but Sam and Godfrey had made a large cheerful snowman and had been having snowball fights for days . . .

Ten minutes later, the menu for the workhouse had been settled. Goose (donated by the Board of Guardians) with stuffing, potatoes, cabbage and gravy, followed by mince pies. There would be no work that day and in the evening there would be oranges for the children and a glass of mulled wine for the adults. All in all it was very modest but for the unfortunates in the workhouse it would be what the Workhouse Master called 'a veritable feast!' When the meeting finally came to an end the participants went home feeling well satisfied with their efforts.

A twenty-minute diversion on the way home brought Harriet to the churchyard. She went to her father's grave and knelt to pray that he would be forgiven – if forgiveness was necessary. She laid a red silk rosebud close to the wooden cross and said, 'We haven't forgotten you, Papa. We still love you dearly.' But, of course, he wasn't her real father and she would probably never know where *he* was buried. With a sigh she moved slowly on to Hannah Wenright's grave.

She whispered, 'You see, Mama, I am happy and well loved. Agnes and George have cared for me well all these years. God willing, we will all be reunited one day. Be at peace.' She kissed her fingers and laid them on the grass above her mother's coffin. She wished she could commission a wooden cross from Albert Hawke for her grave but knew that was impossible. Taking an interest in Hannah's grave would always be dangerous for Agnes. That particular secret was shared by so few – herself, Agnes and Godfrey – and must remain locked away in their hearts for ever.